MOORLAND MIST

Emma Greig has seen little of the world when she leaves school at fourteen to become a maid at Bonnybrae Farm, a life far removed from her carefree schooldays. The Sinclair family both welcomes and rejects her: Maggie is kind and warm; her brothers, Jim and William, playful. But the haughty Mrs Sinclair, disturbed by her children's friendship with a maid, resolves to remind Emma of her place in the world. When Emma and William defy her and strike up a closer bond, Emma is sent away — and William banished from the farm he loves . . .

Books by Gwen Kirkwood
Published by Ulverscroft:

ANOTHER HOME, ANOTHER LOVE
DARKEST BEFORE THE DAWN
BEYOND REASON

GWEN KIRKWOOD

MOORLAND MIST

Complete and Unabridged

ULVERSCROFT
Leicester

First published in Great Britain in 2015 by
Robert Hale Limited
London

First Large Print Edition
published 2016
by arrangement with
Robert Hale
an imprint of The Crowood Press
Wiltshire

*A catalogue record for this book is available
from the British Library.*

ISBN 978–1–4448–3081–1

Published by

1

'I don't want to live anywhere else. I dinna want to leave you and Mother, and everybody.' Emmie Greig stared at her father in dismay. She loved their cottage in Locheagle, the village where she had been born and gone to school and where everybody knew everybody else.

'We all need to earn a living, lassie. You'll be fourteen in a couple of weeks.' Bert Greig loved his only daughter dearly but they were not a wealthy family and he believed honest toil never hurt anybody. His tone softened. 'Ye're a wee tot of a thing but ye canna stay at school for ever. Your brothers were all working before they were fourteen.'

'But they still bide here with you and Ma. Why can't I do the same?'

'I'm not having you work in the mills, nor anywhere near yon coal mine. Anyway, I've spoken to Mr Sinclair and got you a place up at Bonnybrae. The farm is on the edge o' the moors and the fresh air will help ye get rid o' that cough. There should be plenty good food. Maybe you will grow a bit more. I've heard Mistress Sinclair is strict, and a bit too fond of her Bible, but her family were better class than most of the farmers round here. She's known for training her maids well. You'll be fit for a job in one of the big houses after a few years at Bonnybrae,' he added in the nearest Bert Greig ever got to coaxing.

'But Dad, I dinna want to live away from home . . . ' Emmie strove to blink back her tears but drops sparkled on her thick dark lashes. Bert had to turn away from the sight of them and harden his heart. He was sure he was doing what was best for his lassie.

'You're to be paid twenty pounds a year as well as your board and lodging and two dresses, caps and pinafores for working. If you drink plenty of milk and eat up your bacon, you'll make a fine healthy woman.'

Emma turned to her mother, her green-blue eyes luminous with unshed tears. Her chin wobbled with the effort of holding her emotions in check. She knew tears irritated her father, and her brothers would tease her.

'Do I have to go away, Mother?' she pleaded. Eliza Greig lowered her eyes. She didn't want Emmie to leave home but she knew Bert was right. Emmie would be safer in the country, away from temptations. She had to earn her living and she might be healthier if she was out in the country instead of working in one of the factories as so many of the women were doing these days. The new railways were spreading up and down the country and bringing more industry and more people every week. The boundaries of Glasgow and Paisley were expanding out into the countryside.

In five more years they would be into a new century. She sighed, wondering what changes it would bring to the vast British Empire which Queen Victoria continued to rule, even without her beloved Prince Albert. The gossip forecast wild times ahead when the Prince of Wales became King.

Eliza raised her eyes and looked at her daughter.

'None of us want to see you leave home, lassie, but you're lucky to get taken on at Bonnybrae. Mr Sinclair is giving you a job because he and your father were at the village school together and they were friends in those days. It will be a lot healthier on the farm than working in a bleaching mill or in the print works, or the tannery.' She shuddered. 'The smell would turn my stomach.'

'Ma's right, Emmie,' Richard, her eldest brother, said gently. 'There's some would be grateful for the chance to earn their daily bread at all. You'll get a day off once a month and we'll walk over the hill to meet you. Won't we, lads?'

'Aye, we'll meet ye, Emmie, if only to tug your braids.' Joe grinned, eyeing his sister's thick brown hair. It was one of her best features, curling at her temples and falling in glossy waves almost to her waist when it was not plaited to go to school.

Although he could tease her unmercifully himself, he was always ready to protect her. He had a fiery temper if it was roused.

'I'll lend you my book of poems, Emmie,' Davy offered. 'I think you'll enjoy looking after the animals.'

At sixteen he was nearest in age to Emmie and they had always been close. Like her, he was finely built and small for his age. He was more studious than his brothers and the school master had tried to persuade his father to let him stay on at school. His treasured book of poetry had been a school prize.

Bonnybrae Farm was four miles from Locheagle, high up the glen. James Sinclair was known as a hard man but a fair one, and he ruled his household with a firm hand. Some said he needed to be stern with four sons and three daughters to launch into the world. Three of them were already married and Bess would soon be the fourth. He had successfully negotiated with the factor for the tenancy of farms for his two married sons and it was common knowledge that he was presently arranging the tenancy of another farm for his daughter and his prospective son-in-law. It was to replace Bess that he had hired Emmie Greig.

As a boy James Sinclair had attended the Locheagle village school, along with the other lads and lassies from the surrounding farms and the village. He had known Bert Greig and Eliza since childhood, although they moved in different circles now. They were a decent God-fearing couple and they had reared their family accordingly. The two men had met by accident outside the cobbler's and enquired for the well-being of their respective families. Bert had mentioned that his youngest, his only daughter, was almost ready to leave school.

'We shall be needing a maid at Bonnybrae,' James Sinclair said. 'Bess is getting married so we shall need one to live with us. She'd need to work in the dairy as well as the house.'

'That would suit my Emmie,' Bert said immediately. 'I don't want her to go into the factory, or work at the tannery. She's small for her age but she's a tough wee thing. She has to be with three older brothers.'

'Send her up to Bonnybrae when she finishes at the school then. I'll tell my wife to expect her. She deals with the women and their work.'

'I'll do that. Thanks, James.' Bert had grasped the opportunity to settle Emmie's future without hesitation. He whistled all the way home. He felt fate had guided him when he'd offered to collect the boot repairs from the cobbler that morning, instead of leaving them to his wife as he usually did.

The youngest Sinclair daughter, Agnes, had married at eighteen against her mother's wishes. She already had two children but she was happy looking after her husband and his father on a sheep farm seven miles to the south. Robin and Jack and their wives were grateful to have farms of their own. They neighboured each other and worked together for hay and harvest or thrashing. People assumed that Maggie, the eldest daughter, was content to remain at Bonnybrae along with her elder brother Jim, since neither were married.

William was the youngest, and most like his father with his blue eyes and reddish brown hair and a temper to go with it if provoked. He had also inherited his parents' desire to be in control, rather than accept orders. At twenty he frequently rebelled. He was impatient to hold the reins and rent a farm of his own and make the decisions, but he had no desire to tie himself down with the 23-year-old daughter of a neighbouring farmer, however amiable she was reputed to be. Her father was a widower and a friend of James Sinclair. If William married the girl, he would take over the tenancy of the farm one day without needing the help of his overburdened father. William was adamant he would not consider such a union for the sake of a farm. He thought Laura Baird was passably good-looking but she lived in her father's shadow. She never expressed an opinion of her own. He was convinced she would never have a passion to match his own and she would probably be as strait-laced and puritanical as his mother when she was older, but he was wise enough to keep that opinion to himself.

'Your mother and Maggie have spoiled you or you'd be glad to marry Baird's lassie and set up home with her,' James declared after one of their arguments. 'You'll have to take my orders while you continue working at Bonnybrae.' The similarity of their characters often led to heated discussions but it also forged a bond so neither ever bore malice.

It was Maggie who drove the Bonnybrae trap down to Locheagle to collect Emmie and her few possessions the day after she left school. Her father and brothers were at work so there was only her mother to witness her tears and Emmie clung to her, unable to hide her emotions. Over her head, Eliza saw the concern in Maggie Sinclair's eyes and knew instinctively that she would treat her bairn kindly.

'Come now, lassie,' she said briskly and held Emma away from her. 'Dry your eyes and don't keep Miss Sinclair waiting.'

'Please call me Maggie.' She smiled and Eliza wondered why folks said she was plain. She had such a sweet smile and gentle grey eyes.

'There now, Emma,' her mother said firmly, using her proper name, 'you'll be fine. Miss Maggie will teach you to be a good housewife and dairy maid. Do you have any other maids up at Bonnybrae?' she asked, to give her daughter time to control her tears.

'Not now. We had two when we were all young but since my sisters and I grew old enough to work, we have only had Mrs Edgar. She comes in three days a week and helps with washing and ironing. She's a kindly soul, Emma. You'll like her.'

Emma nodded, sniffed hard and blew her nose.

'Away into the scullery, lassie, and wash your face. We mustn't keep Miss er Maggie waiting any longer.'

'We're to call for extra groceries today. We had so many visitors with Bess getting married that we're running short of flour and sugar and a few other things.' Emma returned and her mother hurried her out to the trap so that she would have no opportunity to cling to her again.

Maggie did her best to put Emma at ease but she looked no more than a child. She wondered whether her father had even met the girl before he hired her or whether he had simply acted on impulse after meeting his old friend, Bert Greig. Both her father and William were prone to acting first and ruing later. She wondered what her mother would think when she saw her diminutive new maid. Bess's wedding had taken a lot out of her and Maggie knew she was hoping for a big strong girl who could do a good day's work. Twenty years ago, she had almost died giving birth to William and she had been in delicate health ever since.

Emma helped Maggie carry the provisions from the trap. They went straight from the farm yard through a green painted door into a large scullery with a flat stone sink which had a pump at one end. Maggie explained the door to the left was the kitchen and the one in the corner was the pantry. She undid the sneck with her elbow and pushed the door with her foot since her arms were full of packages. Emma followed with a large basket. Her eyes widened as she took in the rows of shelves along two sides and the assortment of jars and bottles of fruits and jams, chutney and pickles. Above her head were four huge hooks and from two of these hung a large ham, swathed in white cotton, and a side of bacon. On one wall there was a mesh covered door and she guessed that was into the outside meat safe like the one they had at home. In front of them was a long stone table which held bowls of eggs and two large shallow bowls full of milk.

'We set the milk at night and skim off the cream in the mornings,' Maggie explained. 'We have two favourite cows which we keep for the house. Father takes the rest to the station each morning. It goes to Glasgow on the train and from there the creamery sells it round the houses. If you milk the house cows you must remember to bring their milk to the house.'

'M-milk the c-cows?' Emma echoed faintly. She had only seen cows from the other side of a fence, safely penned into fields.

'You've never milked a cow?' Maggie asked. 'Och, you'll soon learn,' she said reassuringly, but Emma shuddered at the thought. She felt sick. 'We churn the butter twice each week. Come on, we'll bring in your box now. The maids' room opens off the kitchen. I'll show you where it is.'

When they came into the scullery a second time Emma asked, 'Where does that door lead?'

'The one in front of us is the washhouse. There's a copper boiler in there and we light it every morning to get hot water for washing the dairy utensils, as well as for washing clothes. There's a door from there directly into the dairy. Father had it made to save us carrying hot water through the scullery. There's a door at the back of the washhouse to the clothesline and you'll see the closet near the gate into the orchard.'

'I hope I shall remember everything,' Emma said nervously.

'Och, you'll soon get used to things,' Maggie said. 'Come on and we'll take these to your room. Live-in maids always sleep next to the kitchen.' She gave a slight frown; she didn't enjoy giving orders, especially to such a young girl. 'You'll be expected to get up first and rake out the range and kindle the fire to boil the kettle. We all like a hot drink before we start the milking, then Mother boils up the porridge when she comes through. Bess used to light the fire and boil the kettle so we're missing her now she's married. I'll do it for a couple of days to show you until you settle in. It's important to clean the flues properly or the fire doesn't draw to make the oven hot, then Mother gets cross.'

How would she manage? Emma wondered. How would she remember everything and how would she waken? Dad always called her brothers to get ready for work and she got up for school when they left.

'Don't look so worried, Emma,' Maggie teased. 'You'll soon get used to things.'

'But what if I don't waken in time?'

'I'll lend you my alarm clock to waken you, then you can come and knock on my door. My room is at the front of the house, and Mother and Father sleep in the other front room. My brothers all slept upstairs. Only Jim and William are still here, and there's only me in the room I used to share with Bess. It seems quiet without her. She was always singing as she worked. Can you sing?'

'N-no, at least I don't think so. I-I sing hymns in the kirk.'

'William will try to coax you, for sure. He plays Father's fiddle when he can get it, and Jim's quite good on the penny whistle. Come on, we'll wash our hands at the pump, then you can help me make the tea. The men will soon be in for theirs before we start the milking.'

Emma turned pale at the thought of milking a cow, and she felt too sick to eat anything when the three Sinclair men came in, followed by the ploughman and a young man whom Maggie called an orraman. He grinned at Emma.

'That means I'm Jack of all trades,' he explained.

'Aye and master o' none, even though his name is Jock,' his companion teased.

'It means he's a general worker,' Maggie explained, 'and John mainly looks after the horses and helps with the ploughing. They sleep in the bothy so they eat with us. The other men are married and live in the three cottages we passed on the road up.'

'We all have to do whatever work is needed,' James Sinclair said sternly, 'and we shall expect you to do the same.' He eyed Emma for the first time and a frown knit his bushy brows together. 'There's not much o' ye.'

'That is exactly what I was thinking.' They all turned towards the door leading from the front hall. Mary Sinclair surveyed them, seated around the scrubbed kitchen table but her eyes rested longest on Emma before she turned her gaze on her husband and her fine brows lifted. James knew she was asking what had possessed him to bring this stray kitten into her household. He shrugged.

'There's not much of her but she'll soon grow when we get some good meat into her. Come on, lassie, ye'll have to eat more than that. We expect everybody to work hard at Bonnybrae but we dinna grudge any man or maid their meat.' But Emma was feeling more queasy by the second.

'What age are you?' Mrs Sinclair demanded as she took her seat at the end of the long table behind the big brown tea pot.

'I — I shall be fourteen on the 10th July, ma'am.'

'Fourteen in a week's time,' William whistled. 'You look more like a ten-year-old to me,' he grinned. His father scowled at him.

'It isn't how big people are, it's how willing they are that counts,' Maggie declared, also frowning at her youngest brother. 'Emma has never been near a cow so maybe we should give you the job of teaching her to milk since you think you have such a great understanding of cattle.' Now it was William's turn to glower. Emma shrank even further into her seat.

'I think you had better show her what to do the first time,' Mary Sinclair said to Maggie in a milder tone. 'We all know William is not noted for his patience. Did you collect the material to make her some working dresses and aprons?'

'Yes, I did. Miss Wilkins already had Emma's measurements from making her a dress to go to church so she has cut out the first one with a little extra at the seams to allow for her growing.'

'Can you sew?' Mrs Sinclair asked with a note of resignation.

'Oh yes, ma'am,' Emma said, brightening. She had won the sewing prize at school, and one for knitting. 'And I can knit socks on four needles,' she added eagerly.

'Well, that's something at least,' Mrs Sinclair said dryly.

'Can ye darn stockings, bairn?' Mr Sinclair asked. 'There's always plenty o' that to do, or so the women keep telling me.'

'Yes, I can darn neatly,' Emma said. 'I could do everything at school but — but I've never milked a cow — and — and I'm not sure if I c-can.'

'Don't let them sense you're nervous,' Mrs Sinclair warned. 'Keep your feelings well-hidden and under control . . . '

'With animals and with men,' William quoted, causing his mother to glare at him.

'Don't be facetious, William.'

'It's what you're always telling Bess and Maggie,' he grinned.

'And don't interrupt, either,' his mother scolded, while Emma chewed her lower lip and struggled to hold back tears.

'You'll soon learn, lassie,' John the ploughman whispered in her ear.

'It's not as bad as ye think and they're a canny lot, the old cows. You leave the heifers to William and if ye've any bother with the pigs ask Jim, or Master Sinclair and ye'll dae fine.'

'The — the pigs?' Emma turned startled eyes to him, reminding him of a nervous colt.

'Didn't ye know we have pigs as well? Bonnybrae has a bit of everything and the mistress is a fine cook. Ye'll not get a better training.'

Maggie was patient when she took Emma to the dairy and showed her where the milking pails and stools were kept, how to set up the milk cooler with the pipes in the right places and the D pan on top with its brass tap.

'Make sure it's taken out and cleaned when you're washing the dairy dishes and turn it off when you put it back until we're ready to cool the milk. You must put a milk can underneath, like this, to catch the cooled milk.' She demonstrated, deftly rolling the heavy churn on its rim and placing it beneath the ridged cooler. 'Remember that or you'll be in big trouble if the milk runs down the drain.'

Emma nodded. There was nothing difficult about that. She was not stupid but she was in terror of sitting next to one of the huge Ayrshire cows with their long pointed horns. Maggie seemed to understand.

'It's always best to confront the things you fear most, Emma,' she said firmly. 'Things are not half as bad as you expect, and even when they are they have to be faced.' They were words which came back to Emma many times in the years ahead and when she looked back to her first year at Bonnybrae, she cringed at her ignorance of life beyond the village school.

2

Eighteen months later, Emma remembered how homesick she had been so she had a lot of sympathy for 14-year-old Billy Watkins, the boy who had come to live in the bothy to replace Jock.

'You'll get used to it, Billy. I was scared to death of the cows when I first came. Now I love all the animals, especially the wee pigs and the calves.' She sighed. 'William's collie bitch had some puppies last spring and they were beautiful.' She didn't tell Billy she had wept into her pillow when all but one had gone to other owners. 'You'll enjoy helping with the lambs when they're born in the spring.'

In spring, the ewes and lambs were moved back to the higher pastures but any motherless lambs, or a sickly ewe with lambs, would be brought to a nearby shed for the women's attention. Emma loved to care for them and in the evenings, Billy came to help her when there was more than one lamb to be fed from a bottle.

'I'll not cry if the Master shouts at me,' Billy said. He was small for his age and he seemed more like a 12-year-old but Emma told him they had all teased her about being too small.

'He'll not shout when you get used to things and Jim doesn't shout at you, does he?'

'No. He's a good sort. William's all right but he gets impatient because I can't reach the horse's head to get the collar on.'

'You'll grow if you eat your porridge and cream every morning.'

'Of course you will, Billy,' Maggie said, smiling as she came into the kitchen, 'then you'll harness the horses as well as anyone.'

Whenever Emma went home, Eliza and Bert were delighted by her smiling face and healthy colour.

'It was fate the day I ran into James Sinclair in the village,' Bert Greig declared. 'Our bairn has fairly thriven since she's been up at Bonnybrae.'

'She has but she's grown out of her best Sunday clothes,' Eliza sighed. 'I've had a word with Miss Wilkins about making her a new dress and maybe a jacket. I do wish Bonnybrae had been in our parish, then they would have come down to our wee kirk every Sunday instead of going over the hill.'

'She wouldn't have had time to come home if she had,' Bert said. 'The animals have to be fed and milked on Sundays, the same as every other day. Let's be thankful she's happy up there. I never hear her coughing now.'

* * *

At fifteen-and-a-half, Emma was still young enough to feel shy in the presence of the Sinclair men. James Sinclair was sometimes abrupt, though he treated her kindly enough. Jim and William rarely seemed to notice her, or so she thought. They had been used to the farm since the day they were born and sometimes they teased her, at others they were irritable when she didn't understand, or couldn't do things they took for granted. Fortunately she had grown taller since her arrival at Bonnybrae, and she was proud of her five feet four inches.

In one of his more mellow moods, Mr Sinclair had made her blush when he declared she was filling out nicely and she would make a good wife for some lucky man in a few years' time. Out of the corner of her eye she had seen William and Jim exchanging glances. She was used to her brothers exchanging silent messages and mischievous grins and she wondered what the Sinclair brothers were thinking. She didn't know they had also recently remarked on her pretty face and developing curves.

'You'd better keep your eyes to yourself,' Jim warned his younger sibling. 'She's developing into an attractive young woman but Mother would send her packing down the road if she caught you admiring her.'

'There's no harm in looking.' William grinned, but Jim knew his youngest brother was restless.

Since he reached his twenty-first birthday, he had pestered their father to enquire about farms to let. It was accepted that, as the eldest son, Jim would take over Bonnybrae when their parents grew too old for the work. William knew his father had arranged tenancies for his other brothers and he was impatient to start farming on his own too.

It was usual for neighbours to help each other by sending men for a day's work when the thrashing mill was in the area. Jim and William enjoyed these occasions. They were strong and fit so the work didn't trouble them, and they enjoyed the company of the other men and the gossip at the end of the day when they gathered for an evening meal. It had been at one of these gatherings a year or two earlier that the brothers had overheard some of the older men discussing Bonnybrae. They learned that their father had been a dashing young man and could have had the pick of the girls in his younger days, although he had settled down when he married.

'Ye're the image o' your father when he was your age, young William,' one of them declared.

'Aye, and no doubt he'll have inherited his father's eye for a bonnie lassie.'

William had been eighteen at the time and he'd seen little of the wider world. He was fair-skinned and he hated when the colour stained his cheeks like a blushing girl. The men had roared with laughter at his expression and embarrassed him further with exaggerated tales of his father's prowess as a youth. After that, the brothers regarded their father in a different light. They realized he still had an eye for an attractive woman when they accompanied him to the kirk or the market, though they were fairly sure he was never unfaithful to their mother.

'I'm sure he loves her,' Jim said. 'I was eleven when you were born and the doctor thought Mother was going to die. I can still remember being frightened because Father was distraught. I have never seen him show so much emotion as he did then.'

'I always wondered why Mother seemed to love me less than the rest of you,' William said, unable to hide a faint bitterness.

'Och, that's your imagination and you've

always got into more trouble than the rest of us.'

Now, a couple of years later, William had gained a new understanding of what the men had meant that day at the thrashing mill. His experience was broadened unexpectedly by the wife of a farmer over the hill from Bonnybrae. He had been rebuilding a stretch of the stone wall which marked the boundary with the neighbouring sheep farm. He had watched the men who were trained to build the loose stone dykes and found it was a task he enjoyed, at least for short spells. There was satisfaction in choosing the right stones and placing them with care, knowing a well-constructed wall could last a lifetime. It was the highest and furthest point of Bonnybrae where the fields met the open moor and he was content to work alone with Mick, his faithful collie for company and the birds and the rabbits. Often he sang at the top of his voice, believing there was no one to hear. He brought his piece bag with bread and cheese and a bottle of cold tea to save the long walk home at midday. It was on one such occasion his solitude was disturbed by the approach of a woman on a sturdy pony.

'I've seen you working up here for several days,' she greeted him. 'It must be lonely on your own. You are alone?'

'Aye, I am, but I'm never lonely when I'm up here,' he said cheerfully. 'I enjoy the beauty of my surroundings and this job needs concentration.' He straightened his aching back and looked at her.

'I'm Eva McGuire.' She smiled and slid from the horse's back. 'A little company now and then can be er — satisfying, I think?'

Inexperienced though he was, it didn't take William long to recognize the invitation when Eva McGuire made her desire plain. He knew she must be at least ten to fifteen years older than him but she was attractive and her figure was nicely rounded in all the right places. She came again the following day and William needed little persuasion before he succumbed to her wiles. She hadn't laughed at his fumbling, indeed she seemed to enjoy teaching him things he had never guessed about a woman's body. He had no regrets about losing his virginity, indeed he had enjoyed the experience and repeated it on several more occasions when she appeared while he was working alone on the hill. He never arranged to meet her but she always seemed to know which part of the boundary to find him.

He had taken all she offered but when the repairs to the boundary wall were finished he made no move to see her again. The episode was over. At the time he felt no guilt for taking his pleasure with another man's wife but several weeks later, he was sitting between his mother and Maggie in church. He was sure the Reverend Jamieson was looking down from the pulpit straight at him as he intoned the words, 'thou shalt not commit adultery,' and 'thou shalt not covet thy neighbour's.' He squirmed inwardly, convinced the sermon was aimed at him. Afterwards he elected to walk home. He needed to think but Maggie decided to join him, leaving Emma and Jim to go in the trap with their parents.

'Are you well enough, William?' Maggie enquired. 'I didn't hear you singing the last hymn and you're looking unusually grim.'

'I'm fine. I was thinking, that's all.'

'Oh no,' his sister groaned softly. 'I expect you saw Mother's letter from her cousin Florrie. Has it made you restless again? Are you wondering when Father will speak to the factor about setting you up in a farm of your own?'

This was the usual reason for her youngest brother's moods, generally after an argument with their father. Although it was William's burning ambition to rent a farm of his own, it was the last thing on his mind for once, but he couldn't tell Maggie the real reason for his uneasy conscience so he went along with her supposition.

'Cousin Drew seems to be doing well since he moved south to farm.'

'He is only a second cousin. His mother and our mother are cousins.'

'What difference does that make? He rents a farm of his own, even if it is down in Yorkshire.'

'He's older than you. He's at least as old as me. I hope you're not contemplating anything wild, like leaving the glen, William?'

'Would you miss me?' he teased.

'You know I would. We all would. Mother wasn't going to tell you she'd had a letter from her cousin Florrie. I shouldn't have mentioned it.'

'She left it on the kitchen table and it was open so I read it,' William admitted. 'Drew seems happy. He's getting on well with his new factor, or land agent as he calls him. He says some of the neighbouring farmers only cultivate the fields around their farm steadings. Think what an opportunity that would be for a young fellow like me, Maggie.' As he talked William half-convinced himself, as well as his sister, that this was the only reason he had been brooding. 'I wouldn't mind visiting Drew and his wife. We always got on well when he lived up here.'

'We were younger then, but that's exactly what Mother feared you would say,' Maggie declared, pursing her lips.

'Don't worry, I'm only teasing you, big sister. We-ell, mostly I was teasing. We have too much work to do at Bonnybrae right now for me to journey to far-off places.'

'Thank goodness for that,' Maggie said with relief as they approached the farm yard. No more was said about going to Yorkshire to visit.

The following autumn, the thrashing mill arrived at Bonnybrae, along with several men from neighbouring farms. Maggie and Emma had been busy for several days, plucking and boiling a couple of old hens for a huge pot of soup, peeling vegetables, cooking a ham and setting out pickles and chutneys, baking bread and scones, churning the butter and bringing out jars of homemade jam.

'You're making a fine wee cook these days,' Mary Sinclair said to Emma as she watched her taking loaves from the oven at the end of a busy morning. Emma flushed with pride. The mistress rarely gave praise. Maggie beamed at her.

'Aye, Emmie is quick to learn,' she said, 'and willing too. There's not much she hasn't tried since she came to Bonnybrae.'

'You're a patient teacher, Maggie,' her

mother said, 'and a good one. I admit when I first saw you, Emma Greig, I didn't think you'd last five minutes, so small you were, aye and timid as a mouse. I thought Sinclair had taken leave of his senses hiring such a puny maid to replace Bess, but you're a good lassie and you've proved your worth. Keep it up.'

When the thrashing was finished at Bonnybrae, Jim and William spent several days following the thrashing mill to the neighbouring farms. It was then William overheard one of the other men mention Eva McGuire. Although it was some time since he had seen her, and he had no desire to see her again, he listened to the lewd comments and heard the guffaw of laughter. He cringed inwardly. What a fool he had been to believe she had singled him out for her attentions. It was clear she was the type who would go with any available man. He felt sickened. He looked up and saw Jim's eyes on him. The blood rushed up beneath his fair skin but he bit on his lower lip and thrust out his jaw, unaware that it gave him an air of arrogance. It did not fool Jim who could remember him in nappies.

As they made their way home in the darkness Jim said quietly, 'You're not the only one to be tempted by the wiles of women like Eva McGuire, Billy boy. If you've learned what you wanted to know, then forget about her.'

'How did you know?' William stopped in his tracks, glad of the darkness to hide his burning face.

'I saw you listening to that lot gossiping about her and I saw your expression.'

'Did she try it on with you as well then?'

'Not Eva McGuire, but there's other women like her, eager to teach young sprogs like us a thing or two. I learned my lesson when I was younger than you.' He grinned in the darkness, remembering.

'God, Jim, and I thought you were a saint.'

'I don't reckon there're any saints alive in this world,' Jim said easily, 'but I've no desire to rake round the towns to pick up a woman. I've no plans to marry, but if ever I do, I should want a woman with pride and dignity, and I'd expect her to be a virgin.'

'Even though you're not one yourself?' William laughed. 'Eh man, ye're as bad as Father.' William felt closer to his brother than he had ever been, but he still loathed himself for using another man's wife. Deep down he knew he resented being one of many. Even as a child he had always wanted to be in control of any situation or game, and it irked him to know it was Eva McGuire who had decided he would share her favours, and when and where. He vowed he would never fall into that trap again but he was honest enough to admit he didn't envisage living like a monk for ever. He had too much spirit and a zest for life.

Emma was developing into an attractive young woman with her brown wavy hair, her fair skin and wide, green-blue eyes. Her features were not the finest but her high cheek bones and her ready smile, with a dimple in one cheek, made up for the youthful look of her rounded chin. She kept herself clean and neat. Her hair was always well-groomed, but otherwise she paid little attention to her looks. She would be seventeen next summer but she had never been to a dance. Bonnybrae was too isolated for her to go to the village dances which she might have attended with her brothers had she still been living in Locheagle. Despite her innocence of life in the world beyond Bonnybrae, she was now skilled in most aspects of house and dairy work. She enjoyed the cooking and baking, and she and Maggie made a good team together.

'You'll be seventeen next year, Emma. I shall be sorry if you decide to leave us,' Maggie said one day as they worked together at the spring cleaning.

'Leave Bonnybrae?' Emma echoed. 'Why should I do that?'

'Your father had ambitions for you to find employment in one of the big houses, or so he told Father when you first came here. You must find it quiet up here. Except for young Billy, we are all so much older than you and you'll soon be wanting to go to dances and meet other young people.'

'I don't want to live in a town, or work in a big house,' Emma declared. 'I love it here. I'd miss all the animals.' She chuckled. 'I'd even miss the cows now.'

'I'm glad to hear it.' Maggie smiled. 'Did you ask Jim to tie a cart rope between the apple trees? We must lift and turn the sitting room carpet but it will need a good beating before we put it back down.'

'Yes, Jim tied the rope and he said he would come and help us lift the carpet when we get it rolled up. He even promised he and William would help us beat the dust out when they come in at noon.'

'That would be a big help. We could beat for ever and still the dust comes out, or so it seems. Anyway, we have plenty to keep us busy if we are to wash and polish all this furniture before we bring it in again. Mother suggested we leave churning the butter until tomorrow.'

'We shall need to bake bread tomorrow,' Emma reminded her.

'So we shall, I'd forgotten. You know, Emma, you will soon be able to run this house as well as I can.' Maggie smiled again.

'I only know what you've taught me, Maggie. Mother says I've been lucky to have you to show me what to do.'

She was down on her hands and knees, scrubbing the floor when Jim and William came to take the carpet out to the orchard.

'You're only just in time.' She grinned saucily up at them. 'One more strip of floor to scrub and I shall be up to the carpet.'

'Cheeky young minx,' William teased. 'I reckon we should give you a beating along with the carpet.' These days they treated her as her own brothers did and she no longer felt shy in their presence.

'It would take a real man to try that!' she quipped, holding up the wet floor cloth as a threat if William dared to come closer.

'Now then, you two,' Jim cautioned. He lowered his voice but his eyes were sparkling. 'Here's Mother coming with her chamber pot. You'd better behave or she might empty it on the pair of you.'

After dinner, James Sinclair suggested Jim should take a turn with the plough to give him a rest so it was Emma and William who ended up beating the carpet. It was not often it was just the two of them but William chatted pleasantly as he wielded the cane beater.

'When will the first lambs be born?' Emma asked. He grinned at her.

'You love the lambs, don't you, young Emmie? They'll be starting any day now. I was up on the hill gathering up the stragglers yesterday. You'd love it up there. All the world seems to be spread out before you. You can see for miles on a clear day. It's so quiet and peaceful with only the birds and a fox or two, and the rabbits of course.'

'I think Mistress Sinclair would have something to say if I went wandering off to explore the hilltops.' Emma smiled. 'But it sounds wonderful.'

'It is. You'll have to come with me sometime when it's your day off. Would you like to do that, Emmie?' It always gave her a warm feeling when any of them called her Emmie instead of Emma, and William often used the name these days.

'I'd love to explore and stand on the very tops of the hills and look down on everything,' she said as eagerly as a child.

'Then we'll do it sometime when you have a day off and I'm doing the shepherding up there.'

The lambing started and ended. The turnips were sown and hoed and hay gathered for another summer but William never mentioned taking her to the top of the hills and Emma felt disappointed, thinking he had forgotten.

Later she would learn that William rarely forgot anything — good or bad. Bonnybrae had one field of oats to harvest every year, and Maggie and Emma were always called upon to help with stoking the sheaves.

'Maybe when these are all gathered in we'll take that walk to the top of Bonnybrae.' William grinned as he worked beside Emma. 'Or have you changed your mind about walking so far?'

'Of course not. It can't be any further than walking home to Locheagle.'

'It's not as far but it's a lot steeper, especially when you get near the top.'

'Are you trying to put me off, William Sinclair?' Emma demanded primly. 'Maybe you're afraid I shall climb up the hills quicker than you.'

'What? With legs scarcely bigger than matchsticks?' William teased.

He broke off as his father moved into the row next to theirs. Although she had learned to regard Jim and William as surrogate brothers, teasing when they teased her, scowling at them when they scolded without good reason, she was always in awe of Mr

Sinclair. He gave her praise occasionally when she had done a good job, or a kindness for his wife, but he always seemed stern. Of all the family she was most at ease with Maggie. She was always patient and kind and she had taught her to do things she had never dreamed she could manage.

The September days were getting shorter when William came into the dairy where Emma was singing 'Bringing in the Sheaves' as she churned the butter.

'It's the last day of the month tomorrow. Is it your day off, Emmie?'

'Yes, it is.'

'How about that walk up the hill if the weather is dry? Do you still want to come?'

'Yes, I'd love to, if the views are as magnificent as you promised.'

'Well, I think they're worth the effort, but you can please yourself. I shall be gathering up the ewes and lambs anyway.'

'Ah I see, you're just wanting me to help!' she teased. 'All right, I'll come then. When and where?'

'I'll meet you where the track branches. If you change your mind, you can continue down to Locheagle to see your folks but if you want to come with me, we'll follow the burn up from there to the bottom of the hill land.'

'I'll be there,' Emma said firmly. She vowed she would not slow him down and maybe she could even help him round up the sheep. She lifted the ridged wooden hands and began to work the butter, humming happily as she worked the water out and fashioned the blocks as Maggie had shown her. It never occurred to her that her parents might object to her going into the hills alone with the son of her employer. He was just another young man like her brothers.

3

Maggie always gave Emma a few provisions to take to her parents on her day off and she had left them in a carrier on the kitchen table. Afterwards, Emma wondered why she had not mentioned to Maggie that she was going with William but she expected she would have time to go home for a short visit when she returned from the hill. She lifted the bag and peered inside. There was a loaf of bread, a bottle of fresh milk, a piece of boiled ham and a pat of butter. Maybe they could have some of it for a picnic high on the hilltop, she thought, with all the eagerness of a child.

'What's that you've got?' William asked with a smile when he saw her walking towards him. He was leaning against the fence, wondering whether Emma would have changed her mind and he was surprised how pleased he felt when he saw her. He enjoyed her company and the banter they shared. Now that she was used to him and Jim, they had discovered she had a ready wit and a fine sense of humour, something, he realized, his mother did not possess and did not encourage. His spirits rose.

'Maggie left these for me to take to Mother.' She blushed rosily. 'I — I suppose I should have told her I wasna going home yet. I — I wondered if we might eat some of it for a picnic if there's time?' she said diffidently.

'We'll make time,' William promised with a grin as they began their walk. 'I picked four apples from the orchard as I came by. I thought we might get a bit hungry before tea-time, but that will be even better.' He took the apples from his pockets and slipped them into the paper carrier, then took it from her. 'I'll carry this. It's a glorious autumn day. I'll cut you a good stout stick like mine when we reach the clump of hazel by the burn. It will help when the going gets steep. We should get a good view today. We might even see the Clyde in the distance if we get to the top of Muckle Torr on the neighbouring hill.'

'Where's Mick? Isn't he coming to help round up the sheep?'

'He got a thorn in his paw and it's festered a bit.' William frowned. 'I don't want him to make it worse.' Emma knew he thought a lot of his dogs. 'Queenie will have to manage today. She's young but she's coming along nicely. I'd have brought Misty but she's getting old for a long run.' Queenie wagged her tail at the sound of her name and Emma bent to pat her. ‘Right then, Emma Greig, this will be your first lesson in shepherding. You’ve had a go at nearly everything else since you came to Bonnybrae.’

‘I haven’t tried ploughing and I can’t harness the Clydesdales,’ Emma said. ‘They’re so big. I can harness the pony to the trap now though, and Maggie let me drive him home the last time we went to the village.’

True to his word, William took out his knife and selected a stick for her with a small knob at one end, which he shaped for her small hand to grasp. After a while they crossed the burn and left the lower fields behind. The ground grew rougher as they climbed. There were marshy patches and sometimes little shelves where bare rock jutted out of the hillside.

‘I love the little patches of wild flowers sheltering in the crevices,’ Emma said with delight, ‘and the heather is beginning to bloom.’

Her pleasure and enthusiasm pleased William but he didn’t forget they were there to shepherd and as they climbed towards the peak, he stopped a couple of times to take a closer look at a lame sheep, and one which he saw was infected around her tail with maggots from the blow flies.

'We must take a closer look at that tomorrow when we get them gathered. We'll start at the top and Queenie will help us bring them down.'

Emma was young and fit but William had longer legs and he was used to walking up the hills. Mr Sinclair had insisted that all his sons should be able to do every job there was to do on Bonnybrae, from milking to ploughing, and shepherding to killing and plucking a goose or curing a pig.

'I think we'll have something to eat in the shelter of the boundary wall,' William suggested. 'If you still have enough energy, we'll climb to the top of the Torr before we start gathering the sheep.' He knew his father would not approve of him wasting time going higher to get a better view but he was enjoying the fine day and Emma's cheerful company.

'I'd love to go to the top now we've come this far,' Emma said, 'but I love the view from here. The cows in the Bonnybrae field look like toys, and the farms and the cottages across the glen look tiny tucked into the folds of the grassy slopes. I can even see the kirk in the village in the distance.'

She turned slowly round in a circle, drinking in the sights and sounds. She gazed up into the sky as she watched a skylark soaring high above them and William admired the pale smooth column of her neck and smiled at her pleasure. She was like a child on an unexpected holiday. He was glad she shared his appreciation of the wild beauty of their native countryside.

'It's always a bit cooler when you get this high up,' he said, choosing a sheltered knoll for their picnic.

Queenie lay down obediently to wait for them to eat, looking up hopefully for a tit bit every now and then. They tore chunks of bread from the loaf and William wiped his knife on his clean handkerchief before cutting each of them a slice of ham and a knob of butter. He insisted Emma should have the first drink from the bottle of milk before he took a good swig himself. They sat propped against a smooth rocky slab munching their apples, then had a competition to see who could throw the core the furthest.

'I never knew food could taste so wonderful,' Emma sighed.

'It's the fresh air and the exercise,' William grinned. 'Now I'll lift you over the wall and you can relieve yourself if you like before I join you.' He laughed when Emma blushed. 'Nobody would guess you have three brothers, Emma. I promise not to look.'

He lifted her as though she was no more

than a sheaf of straw and let her slide out of his arms on the other side of the wall. Shortly afterwards he joined her and they climbed higher still. It grew more hazy as they climbed higher. The sky seemed to be coming down to meet them.

'I hope it's not going to rain,' Emma said. 'It was so beautiful when we set out. I didn't think it could change so quickly.'

'I don't think it will rain,' William said slowly, standing still, looking all around. A small frown creased his brow. 'But I hope the mist doesn't come down. It can happen swiftly up here. Maybe we shouldn't go any further today, Emma. I'm sorry. I know I promised to show you the river Clyde in the distance but maybe you'll come with me another day, in the spring. I think this may be an autumn mist rolling down on us.'

Emma was disappointed but they turned and began to make their way back down towards the Bonnybrae boundary.

'I hope we manage to get most of the ewes and lambs gathered before the cloud thickens,' William muttered anxiously.

'Oh look! The peak of the Torr has disappeared already!' Emma said, looking behind.

'Aye, the mist is coming down right enough. We'd better get a move on. It will probably be clear down in the bottom.' But the ground was rough and steep and it was not easy to hurry. Queenie kept running on ahead and then coming back as though to make sure they were still following. Emma noticed it didn't take long for her to become invisible in the gathering gloom. It was hard to believe the sun could still be shining only a few hundred feet below them.

'We shall be in terrible trouble if we don't get the sheep gathered and down to the yard,' Emma said.

'Aye, Father will have some choice words to say.' William grimaced, but a more worrying thought than the sheep had occurred to him. 'Once, when I was about twelve,' he said, 'I came shepherding with him. It was about this time of year and the mist came down fast.' His brows were knitted together and he was speaking slowly. Emma realized he was genuinely concerned now. She wished they hadn't come further up into the hills so she could see the view.

'What happened?'

'We couldn't find our way back. When the mist is thick you lose all sense of direction. Mountain mists are nearly as bad as a snow storm for that. We didn't know whether we were going round in circles or east or west. In the end, we ended up further along the boundary wall instead of further down the hill. We settled down in a hollow to wait but I went to sleep, cuddling one of the dogs. Father stayed awake and when the wind came up the mist cleared but it was daybreak by then. I hope that's not going to happen today.'

In his heart he feared that was exactly what was happening and he wished he had never suggested bringing Emma. His father would be furious if he ever found out he had brought his mother's maid up here on her own, and he worried what Emma's parents would think.

'I hope you'll not be in trouble if we don't get the sheep to the low pastures before evening. Your father will blame me.' She chewed her lower lip. 'It will be awful if he — he sacks me.' Her voice wobbled.

'Don't worry, Emmie. It hasn't come to that yet. I'll see you back safely if I can. The sheep can wait for once. But it would be better if none of them miss you.' He reached out and took her hand. His own was large and calloused, but Emma found it warm and comforting. 'What time do you usually get back when you've been home, Emmie?'

'Oh, anytime in the evening. It's usually late evening in summer so I come through the orchard from the closet and in through the washhouse. I never disturb anybody with my room being off the kitchen. When it's winter, Richard or Father always walk to the bottom of the Bonnybrae track with me.'

'Aye, they take good care of you, your family.'

'Richard says it's because I'm a girl but Joe says I'm spoiled because I'm the youngest.'

'Aye,' he chuckled, 'that's what Bess and the others used to say to me, but Maggie always defended me. I think that's our boundary wall we're coming to,' he added, peering through the swirling mist.

'It's really getting thick,' Emma said anxiously.

She had long since lost her awe of William and Jim but she never forgot they were the sons of her employer. Now, in the isolation of the thick damp mist, they were just two people lost on the hills. It was impossible to think the sun might be shining down below. She shivered.

'At least we'll be on home ground once we're over the wall again, but I don't think there'll be any sheep gathered today.' William paused and took out his silver-coloured pocket watch and clicked it open. 'It's half past two. We shall be lucky if this lifts before evening.' He turned to lift Emma over the dyke and felt her trembling. 'Are you cold, Emmie?'

'N-not really, but I'm afraid. I keep thinking I can see a sheep and it's just a rock and Queenie keeps disappearing.'

'She'll not leave us. We'll make our way home as fast as we can. We'll head in the direction of the sheep fank.'

'Is that the stone circle we passed on the way up?'

'Aye, it gives the sheep a bit o' protection in a snow storm. I know we're heading towards home and not our neighbour's place if we reach it.'

Long before they reached the stone circle, the mist had closed in like a wet grey blanket. Queenie stayed close to them now. Emma had been wearing a thick shawl tied around her waist for ease of carrying it but she untied it and wrapped it tightly around her shoulders and chest. She was glad of her stick to prod the uneven ground. They seemed to have walked for a long time when William stopped and peered through the mist in every direction.

'I can't see a damned thing,' he muttered.

'We are going downhill, though,' Emma said tentatively but she had no sooner spoken than a slight incline appeared before them. William clasped her hand in his again.

'We'll keep going for a wee while longer but I reckon we've missed the sheep fold.' He bent and stroked Queenie's head. 'Home, girl,' he urged. 'Take us home . . . ' but the young collie refused to leave his side. She gazed up at him with trusting brown eyes. Emma had often heard tales of dogs refusing to leave their masters during snowstorms or after an accident and Queenie obviously intended to stay.

Quarter of an hour later, William stopped again and peered around.

'We don't seem to be getting anywhere. If we've walked in a straight line, we should have reached the fence between the low pastures and the hill by now. We could be anywhere.'

Emma sighed. She was tired and hungry. William looked down at her.

'I'm sorry, Emmie. This is not how I meant it to be. I thought you would really enjoy being out on the hills and seeing Queenie working. It's a marvellous sight to see the dogs gathering sheep. They're so intelligent.'

'I was enjoying it until the mist came down,' Emma said, 'and no one can help that.'

'I suppose not. What do you say to us settling down for a while and eating the rest of the food in the carrier bag?'

‘I think that’s a good idea. I’m hungry.’

‘We shall know better where we’ve walked when the mist clears,’ William said dryly. ‘Come on then, we’ll find a mossy patch of grass or a bit of a hollow.’

A few minutes later, he chose a spot and they settled side by side to eat the rest of the bread and ham and take a drink of milk.

‘We’ll save the apples in case we’re still here when night falls.’

‘Do you think it will be that long?’ Emma shuddered.

‘It could be,’ William said, and he gnawed his lower lip, cursing himself for bringing Emma now the day had changed so dramatically. He looked down at her small hunched figure. She was not wearing her maid’s cap today and the damp mist was making dark curls all around her face. ‘Don’t worry, Emmie. We’re quite safe, you know, even if it is a bit damp and uncomfortable. It’s better to sit it out than wandering for miles in the wrong direction, or even worse, spraining an ankle or breaking a leg.’

‘I suppose so.’ Emma nodded. William moved closer and put his arm around her, drawing her against him. He commanded Queenie to lie at her other side.

‘We’ll keep you warm between us, Queenie and me,’ he said gently and Emma snuggled against his long thick jacket.

They talked quietly. William asked about her family and she told him about her brothers, especially Davy who had enjoyed school and won a prize when he left.

'He let me borrow it when I first came to Bonnybrae. It was a book of poems by Robert Burns. I've seen your father reading from a similar book.'

'Yes, he likes reading poetry. So do I, especially about nature and the countryside. Robert Burns seemed to understand such things.' He began to talk of his own childhood when they were all at home. His voice was deep and soothing and Emma felt warm and safe snuggled up against him. She drifted into sleep. William looked down at her curled in his arm. He'd never had a younger sibling and his eyes were tender. She was so soft and warm. There couldn't be a greater contrast between Emmie and Eva McGuire, the woman he had last held in his arms up here on the lonely hillside. He laid his cheek against her hair and fell into a doze himself.

Sometime later, Emma stretched and mumbled in her sleep, then curled into him as instinctively as a lamb curls against its mother. Only William was not a mother. He was very much a man and he was rapidly becoming aware of Emma lying half on top of him, one leg flung across his body as she burrowed into his coat with her head on his chest. He was half-sitting, half-lying against the grassy knoll and there was no denying the emotions which Emma's pliant young body was awakening. He tried hard to control his desire. He wriggled, easing her down onto the grass at his side but she mumbled a sleepy protest and clung to him.

'Emmie,' he groaned in protest.

At the sound of her name she opened her eyes sleepily.

'Where am I?' she muttered, then remembered. 'Oh, the mist. It hasna cleared at all.' She shuddered and pressed closer to William, unaware of the effect she was having on him.

'Emmie.' William's voice was firmer, more urgent now. 'You can't be so innocent you don't know what you're doing to me!' She blinked and looked up at him with bleary eyes. He moved and she felt the hardness of him against her thigh. Her eyes widened.

'What's that?'

'You don't know? Don't you realize you're — you're tempting me?'

'Tempting? Do you mean like Eve in the Bible?' She shook her head and frowned. 'Does that mean I'm wicked, William?'

'You're not wicked, Emmie.' William sighed and eased himself away a bit. 'Women are wicked when they deliberately make men want them, then run away. That makes them frustrated and angry. I don't think you intended to make me feel like this, did you, Emmie? Have you ever been with a boy?'

'No,' she said unhappily, thinking this was a fault on her part. 'Most of the time I'm working, here at Bonnybrae. Father says there'll be plenty of time for boys when I'm a woman. I-I didn't mean to make you angry.'

'Och, I'm not angry, Emmie,' William said gently.

'I hate this fog and being lost, but you make me feel safe.'

'I know, lassie. I don't like the fog either, but I can't keep on cuddling you like this . . . '

'Why not? Don't you like being close to me, even though we're warmer?'

'I do like feeling you close to me, Emmie. I like it a lot. Don't you understand anything about women's wiles?'

'I don't think so. I might know more if I had a sister instead of three brothers. I would like to know how it feels to be a proper woman.'

'I don't think you're ready for that yet.' William looked into her upturned face and wide serious eyes. She aroused more than desire in him. He felt protective and tender as he cuddled her closer. Blast the fog, if only it would clear and let them gather the sheep as he had intended. Emmie was in his mother's employ, in her care. She would fly into a real rage if she knew they were up here together, however innocently they behaved. He ought to have considered that. He wanted Emmie to enjoy the walk and see the views.

'Would — would it make me feel good, being a proper woman?'

'It certainly makes a man feel good.' William laughed softly. 'I suppose it must make women feel good too.' He thought of Eva McGuire's insatiable desire. He stroked Emma's hair gently back from her face and felt a longing to be the one to teach her everything, to make her his. He tangled his fingers in her hair and she lifted her face to his.

'You're so sweet, so very innocent, Emmie, but I must take care of you.' He thought of Jim saying he would want a virgin if ever he took a wife. He felt a twist in his gut at the thought of some other man teaching Emmie what it was like to be a woman, maybe hurting her if he was a brute. His arms tightened instinctively. Emmie would be a good wife when she was older, and she would be older by the time he got a tenancy of his own. Maybe he could marry her then. He sighed, frustrated as always when he knew he might need to wait for years before his father helped him get a farm on his own.

'I'm tired of everyone treating me like a child,' Emma said, unconsciously pouting her lips.

Her mouth looked like a pink rosebud and William bent his head and kissed her. Her lips parted in response, taking William by surprise. He knew he should push her away from him before things got out of hand, but Emmie was pressing closer, enjoying the warmth of him. She liked the feel of his mouth on hers and the way the blood seemed to tingle from her toes to her head and back again.

'God, Emmie, you drive a man wild.'

'Do I? Because I liked your kiss?'

'Yes, and because I like kissing you,' he said gruffly.

She pressed her mouth to his again, soft and yielding, and oh, so desirable in her innocence. William returned her kisses, growing more demanding when she responded so eagerly. Almost automatically, he found his hand stroking the curve of her hip and her leg, which was pressed against his own. His own desire intensified. He slipped his hand beneath her skirt and found the naked skin above her stocking.

She gasped against his ear, tickling it with her warm breath.

'God, Emmie, we shouldn't be doing this,' he breathed and drew away but she clung to him.

'I like it,' she said artlessly. 'Don't you?'

'Of course I do. What man wouldn't? But you're so young, so innocent, and you're in my mother's employ.'

'Oh.' He heard the flatness in her voice and she pulled back, the happy lilt gone. 'You don't like me because I'm only a maid.'

She remembered the gossip she had overheard John the ploughman telling the odd job man. He had said Mistress Sinclair was a snob and she had intended to marry the landlord's son, but he had married a girl of his own class. She'd had to make do with James Sinclair instead. Now, she intended all her family should marry well. William couldn't help pulling her close again when she sounded so sad and forlorn.

'That's not what I meant, Emmie. You're very pretty and my mother would expect me to take care of you and — and be responsible for you.'

'I don't want you to be responsible for me. It's bad enough having three big brothers, as well as my father. Kiss me again if you really like it.'

She lifted her face to his like a child and William's resolve melted away. His kisses grew demanding. He was surprised and delighted by Emmie's generous and passionate response. His fingers traced the shape of her leg, now lying across him, arousing him, filling him with desire. He found the warm flesh at the top of her stockings again. His hand moved higher. He glanced at her face, knowing he ought to stop. He saw her eyes widen and darken as he awakened feelings she had never thought possible.

'I — I think it may hurt if . . . '

'Don't stop, don't stop, William,' she said breathlessly. 'You make me feel — wonderful . . . '

'Mmm, me too . . . ' He groaned and tugged at his trousers. 'I'll try to be gentle, Emmie.' He wasn't sure she heard. She was so sensitive to every touch. He heard a little gasp and felt Emmie tense beneath him. He stroked and soothed and knew he was in control as she relaxed again, meeting his passion with a joyous exultation which surprised him and filled him with tender satisfaction

Later they slept, wrapped in each other's arms for warmth and comfort. When they wakened it was too dark for William to see his watch and the mist was thicker if anything.

Emmie stirred in his arms and raised her head a little. She moved stiffly.

'Are you . . . are you sore, Emmie?' he asked gently, filled with remorse in case he had hurt her.

'No, but it's cold.'

'It's the mist. It's miserable and — '

'Hold me close. Love me again, William?'

Love? He stiffened slightly. Was this love? Certainly Emmie was the most loveable girl he knew. She cuddled closer, her fingers moving to his thigh.

'You really are a temptress,' he chuckled softly. 'Are you sure, Emmie? It will not hurt this time.'

'I liked it,' she said simply.

'I would like to think you remember only the pleasure of being a woman.'

Eventually they dozed fitfully until a short sharp bark from Queenie wakened them. They sat up, stiff from sleeping on the hard ground. There was a sickle of moon and the wind had risen, driving away the mist. William pulled out his watch and peered at it in the faint light. Nearby, a ewe grazed contentedly, ignoring Queenie.

'It's twenty to four,' William announced. He stood up and looked around, trying to get his bearings. In the distance, further up the hill and to their right, he saw the dark shape of the stone circle of the sheep fank. 'If we walk down and diagonally we should reach the wire fence between the hill land and the pastures, Emmie. From there I'll direct you back to the house. I think that would be better if no one sees, don't you?'

'Yes,' Emma said gratefully. 'It would be terrible if I lost my job for being late back.'

'With any luck you'll be able to creep into bed and get an hour's sleep before it's time for the milking.'

'What about you, William?'

'I'll come back up here and Queenie and I will start gathering the sheep and bringing them down as soon as there's a bit more light.'

'You'll be very tired.'

'I'll be fine.' William smiled down at her. 'This way we shall not have lost a day's work if the sheep are penned and ready for Jim and Father.'

William drew Emmie close and gently kissed her soft lips one more time before he lifted her over the fence. He pointed out the hedges she must follow to bring her into the bottom end of the orchard at the back of the house. She turned to look at him anxiously.

'You — you'll not tell anyone I stayed out all night? Not ever? Promise? I mean my brothers or — or Maggie . . . ?'

'No, Emmie. This is our secret. I shall not tell.' She smiled at that and gave herself a mental hug. She was a real woman now and all her woman's instincts told her William was as pleased and happy as she was herself.

4

Emma positively bloomed in the weeks which followed. She felt on top of the world. Even her mother remarked on her daughter's glowing skin and jaunty step.

'I am happy,' Emma said. 'Usually I hate gathering potatoes but the weather has been crisp and bright, and even Mr Sinclair was in fine humour. He says he'll send you some potatoes next time somebody is driving the trap down this way.' She didn't tell them that William Sinclair sometimes teased her, or winked at her to make her blush, or that the twinkle in his blue eyes made her heart sing.

'That's very good of Mr Sinclair. I remember he sent us some last year.'

'It's part of my wages, I think. The men in the cottages get six bags each and as many turnips as they want and they get a can of milk every day and a dozen eggs each week. When there's a pig killing, Mistress Sinclair always gives something to each of the men in the cottages. I never thought I could eat liver but I love it when it's fresh, and Maggie fries it with a bit of bacon.'

'Aye, I'd always heard Sinclair fed his

workers well, even though he's known to be a hard man when it comes to expecting a good day's work,' her father said. 'That's more than I hear about a lot of the farms.'

'Mrs Sinclair is going to stay with Bess for a few days next week. I'm not supposed to know but Maggie told me it's because her sister is expecting a baby and she's been ever so sick. Her mother is going to help her.'

'Some women are bothered that way,' her mother said. 'I never had any problems until after you lot were born, then I felt low in spirits. I suppose we're all different.'

Emma would have liked to ask her mother more about how you made babies when you got a husband but Eliza Greig had never been one to discuss such things and she was too shy to ask questions when her father was present.

The autumn turned to winter and in December, Mrs Sinclair went to stay with her youngest daughter again, fearing she might be unable to see her for some time if the cold intensified and they were snowed in.

'Bess is keeping a lot better now,' Mrs Sinclair said to Maggie on her return. 'The sickness has stopped.'

'That's good,' Maggie said. 'The baby is not due until spring, is it?'

'Bess thinks it will come about mid-May,' her mother said. 'I must get on with knitting the shawl. And you, Maggie, Bess tells me you promised to crotchet three woollen blankets as well as some wee jackets.'

Emma was skimming cream from the large shallow bowls of milk in the pantry and the door was ajar so she listened intently to the two women and wondered how they knew when the baby would be born. Although she was expected to help with almost every task there was to do at Bonnybrae, the women were never present at the mating of the boar with the sows or a cow being taken to the bull and she was astonishingly ignorant of such matters. Had she been working in a factory with groups of women of all ages, her education in such things would have been broadened.

When Maggie saw her letting out the seams of her dresses, she teased her. 'I noticed you're beginning to fill out at last, Emmie. I'd begun to despair of ever putting any meat on your bones. It must be all the Black Bun you ate when you went home at New Year.'

'I did enjoy it,' Emma grinned. 'Mother always makes two or three because my brothers like it so much.'

'Aye, it was a pity we got word that the thrashing machine was coming the next day or you might have had an extra night at home.'

The winter days were bitter and they all got throbbing fingers after breaking ice on the water so that the animals could drink. Eventually the frost and snow melted, and spring slowly emerged with the appearance of dainty, green-tipped snowdrops and the golden celandines beneath the trees in the orchard, and the copse at the end of the track. The ice on the pond where the men had enjoyed curling melted and the spring work progressed.

'It will soon be time to start spring cleaning again,' Maggie said cheerfully on a bright day at the end of February when the wind was blowing strongly. 'If it stays like this, we'll take a blanket from each bed and make a start on washing them.'

Many of the woollen blankets had been woven by Mrs Sinclair before her marriage and they were washed with care, turned with the wooden dolly in the wash tub, then rolled through the heavy wooden rollers. It was heavy work, whether turning the handle or lifting the sodden blankets to guide them through the rollers. Maggie and Emma usually took it in turns unless Mrs Edgar was there to help Emma do them. They were rinsed at least twice in cold water and put through the wringer again before being lifted onto the clothes line in the orchard where the March winds blew away the moisture and left the blankets soft and dry. This was a ritual which was followed every year, and Emma remembered how tired she and Maggie always felt by the time they'd had several days of blanket washing, but she didn't remember feeling quite so exhausted as she did by the end of their second day with the blankets. Fortunately for her, the weather turned showery and it was ten days before they proceeded to wash the rest.

They were on the last blanket of the day and Emma was winding the handle of the mangle with Maggie close beside her, guiding the blanket evenly between the rollers. She had felt peculiar little spasms in her stomach for some time now but a particularly painful thump made her gasp and let go the handle. She clutched her stomach.

'What's wrong, Emmie? Are you ill?' Maggie asked.

'N-no, I'm not ill. It's just, I felt as though I'd been punched. Punched from inside. It was worse this time. It took my breath for a second, that's all.' She was standing, smoothing her dress over her stomach and Maggie stared. Her eyes widened in disbelief.

'Emma!' she cried. 'Why didn't you tell me

you're expecting a baby?'

'Wh-what?' Emma gaped at her as though she was speaking in a foreign language. Maggie's mind was in a whirl but even while she gazed in dismay, several things were falling into place.

'You are expecting a baby, aren't you, Emma?' she said.

'I d-don't think so. I havena got a husband.' She stared at Maggie in bewilderment.

'I should have guessed,' Maggie said dully. 'So that's why you haven't had any monthly rags to wash lately . . . '

'No, I haven't and I'm glad. I hate the monthly times. Mother said I'd get more regular as I get older.'

'Your mother knows?' Maggie stared at her. 'She knows about the baby?'

'What baby? O-oh!' she gasped again and pressed her hand against her stomach.

'I think that's the baby kicking. I believe that's what they do. No wonder you've put on weight, especially round your waist. You've hidden it well but we all wear so many layers in winter. You've never been sick, have you, Emma?'

'Sick?'

'Yes, like my sister. Bess was sick in the mornings.'

'But she's got a husband. Mother says girls need a husband and boys need a wife before they can have babies . . . '

Maggie chewed her lower lip and gave her a pitying look. Emma was far from stupid but she seemed to be totally ignorant of the facts of life. She had no sisters to tell her things and it seemed likely her mother was as reticent as her own mother when it came to such things. Maggie was the eldest girl in her family but she remembered Agnes explaining to her and to Bess about babies. Maggie still felt quite ignorant on many aspects.

'Who is the father, Emma? When do you meet him? Does he walk back here with you when you go home for the day? Is that when it happened?'

'When what happened?' Emma asked with a frown. 'Dad or Richard always bring me back when I've been home.'

'I know you don't have much spare time for boys.' It was Maggie's turn to frown. 'So who is the father?' she asked gently. 'Can you tell me, Emmie? I promise I will do my best to help you, but I'm afraid we shall have to tell Mother. I think she will send you home to your parents. Did someone force you, Emmie?'

'I — I dinna ken what ye mean, Miss

Maggie,' Emma's eyes were round and frightened now. Her voice shook and she was near to tears as she stared at Maggie. 'Wh-why will the mistress send me h-home?'

'When is the baby due?' Maggie asked kindly.

'How do you know it's a baby? Do you mean when will it come out? How would I know?'

'Oh Emmie . . . ' Maggie bit her lip. 'I think it's time you talked to your mother. She should have warned you. These things can't just happen, whatever it says about the Virgin Mary in the Bible. You must have slept with a boy.'

'No, I never.' She clapped her hand to her mouth, remembering the night she and William had fallen asleep on top of the hill in the mist.

'Emmie?' Maggie said softly. 'You must tell me. I promise I'll help you, if I can.'

Emmie stared at her then shook her head. She couldn't tell Maggie she and William had fallen asleep on top of the hill. They hadn't meant to sleep and they had agreed it was their secret. Maggie was getting more agitated and she sat down on the low stool and bowed her head with a groan. Emmie felt frightened by her reaction.

'It takes nine months to make the baby,

Emma. Nine months from the time you went with the boy. You must know who . . . when . . . ' They heard footsteps approaching.

'The mistress is coming,' Emma whispered. 'She'll be angry when we haven't got the blankets out to dry.' She began to turn the mangle as fast as her strength allowed, far more worried about a scolding from Mistress Sinclair than by her own predicament. Slowly Maggie got to her feet and guided the blanket through the rollers.

'We shall have to tell Mother, Emmie,' she said dejectedly, her voice low.

'Tell Mother what?' Mary Sinclair demanded. They both spun round to face the door to the kitchen. 'Haven't you got the blankets out to dry yet? The day will be over before . . . '

'Oh, Mother . . . ' Maggie said in distress. She turned to Emma. 'Hang these, Emma. I'll tell her.' Emma eyed them both fearfully, then gathered the blankets into the large wicker basket and carried them out to the orchard.

'What is it, Maggie? What's the matter with you?'

'Emma is — she's expecting a baby. She doesn't . . . '

'She's what?' Mary Sinclair stared at her daughter as though she had taken leave of her senses. 'Are you sure? When did she tell you? When?'

'She doesn't seem to realize. She's so — so innocent about th-things,' Maggie said desperately. She saw the patches of indignant colour staining her mother's cheek bones and her heart sank. Her mother was even more strict about morals than her father.

'Innocent! Don't talk rubbish.'

'Well, ignorant about — about how babies are made and it does say in the Bible . . . '

'How can she be innocent if she's expecting a child?' Her mother went to the washhouse door. 'Emma, come in here this minute! Maggie, you finish hanging the blankets. I shall deal with this.'

'But you don't understand. The father . . . '

'I don't want to know who the father is. That's no business of ours. A girl is responsible for her own actions. It's her body.' Standing white-faced in the open door, Emma gulped. She had never seen Mistress Sinclair so angry, not even the time when she over-churned the butter and made it into a greasy yellow football.

'Emma, pack your things and leave this house this minute.' Emma stared at her in stunned silence. 'Well, get on with it, girl! You're a disgrace. You're not fit to stay under my roof. Maggie, don't stand there. Get on with the blankets.' Emma gave a sob and ran from the washhouse, through the kitchen and into her own room.

'Mother! You don't understand.'

'Enough! Get on with the blankets. We shall have to ask Angus Taylor's wife to help until we can train another maid. She used to work for me before she married. Her children are all at school now. She will be glad of the money, I expect.' Mary Sinclair's first priority would always be the smooth running of her household.

Sobbing, with tears running down her cheeks, Emma pushed her clothes into a carpet bag and the remainder of her belongings she tied in her old shawl. Mary Sinclair watched in grim silence, thwarting any ideas she may have had of talking to Maggie.

Eliza Greig was in her garden, bringing in some of her washing when she saw Emma toiling up the road. She knew at once that something was wrong. This was the middle of the week and she was carrying her carpet bag and a bundle of her belongings. She had been getting on so well and was happy up at Bonnybrae. Three years she had been there so why was she coming home now? It was still three months to the term day and the hiring fairs when men and maids moved to other farms. She met Emma at the gate and relieved her of her bag and bundle when she saw her tearstained face.

'Come away in, my lamb, and tell me what's wrong.'

'Oh, Mother!' Emma sobbed and clung to her mother. 'I've I-lost ma place. M-Mistress Sinclair . . . sh-she says I'm w-wicked and-and . . . '

'Why are ye wicked, ma bairn? What can ye have done?' Eliza asked, uncertain whether to be indignant or alarmed.

'Maggie told her I'm going to have a baby and she . . . '

'A baby? Emma!' Her mother took her by the shoulders and held her away, staring into her daughter's face. 'How can she say such a thing?'

'Because it keeps punching inside me and Maggie felt it and she says it's a baby.'

'Oh dear Lord above,' Eliza whispered and she dropped onto a chair the moment they were into the cottage, her face white. 'Oh Emma, how could you do such a thing? Your father and me are struggling to bring all of you up in a decent home.'

Emma sobbed uncontrollably. The full implications of her situation still hadn't registered.

'Surely ye canna have been with that new

laddie in the bothy up yonder? He's no more than a schoolboy.' Emma shook her head. 'Did somebody force ye, lassie?' Again Emma shook her head, but she was beginning to see there were going to be a lot more questions. Fear clawed at her insides. She clamped her mouth tight shut and stared at her mother. Eliza stared back. 'Do you realize the shame you've brought to this house, Emma? There's Richard keeping company with a lovely girl from a decent God-fearing family. And Davy has begun walking out with the minister's younger daughter,' she added with a note of pride, 'and the Reverend Jamieson is helping him with his books, encouraging him to better himself. Now this!' Anger and anxiety vied with each other. 'What will your father say? What decent girl will want any part of this family when they hear of the disgrace you've brought?'

Still Emma didn't speak. She had been up since dawn for the milking, she was exhausted with the blanket washing, then the long walk home, carrying her baggage and now the knowledge that her own mother was as angry as Mistress Sinclair had been was devastating. Her mother sighed heavily. She could see the exhaustion in the slump of her shoulders and her pinched pale face, so different to the blooming girl she had been on her last visit. In her heart, Eliza knew she should have warned her daughter about men and their desires and what happened if you gave in to them, but it wasn't something she'd ever discussed with anyone. She hadn't known what to expect until she married Bert. It had been something of a shock but at least she had been lucky because Bert cared deeply for her and he was not a rough man.

'Go to your room, Emma. I'll bring you something to eat and drink. You'd better stay there. I don't know what the lads will say when they hear about this. If they don't kill the fellow, they'll beat him within an inch of his life for doing this to you.'

Emma stared at her mother, her eyes wide with shock. She shuddered. Her mouth opened and shut, but she made no sound. She would never tell them she had slept with William Sinclair if that's what they would do to him. She would never tell, even if they beat her to death. She was sure William had not meant to harm her. It was true he had hurt her a little but he had been gentle and he had made her feel so wonderful. She went to her room, her head bowed.

When she had eaten she undressed and climbed into bed, weighed down by the traumas of the day.

'You'd better stay in here, out of sight,' her

mother said through tight lips. 'I'll wait until the lads have gone up to bed and then I'll tell your father. He'll decide what's to be done. If the baby is moving as ye say, ye must be well on, and to think I never guessed.' She shook her head in disbelief.

Exhausted and bewildered, Emma curled up like a child and slept.

There was little sleep for Bert and Eliza Greig that night. Bert had guessed there was something troubling his wife as they ate their evening meal but it had always been their way to wait until the house was silent and they were snuggled up together in the box bed on one side of the kitchen range. At first Bert couldn't take it in. He loved all his family but he'd always had an extra tender spot for his wee Emmie. She reminded him of his mother with her thick wavy hair and wide blue-green eyes, her high cheek bones and pert nose. How could she have let him down so badly? It was nearly rising time when he decided on a plan.

'You'll have to tell the lads I'm not going to work. I'll stay here with the curtains drawn. Tell them I'm ill. When they've gone, I shall take Emma to the station and we'll go to my brother Dick's. She can stay with them until . . . until it's born.'

'Dick's?' Eliza echoed.

He was Bert's younger brother and she liked him well enough but his wife was the meanest, miserable and complaining woman Eliza had ever met. She sighed. Poor Emma. Even now Eliza couldn't believe her bairn had meant to be wicked or bring shame on them all.

'Aye, I know Vera is as mean as they come but if I pay for Emma's keep, she'll take her in. They're far enough away to prevent any gossip and Emma is used to the farm so Dick's boss might find her some work with the milking and the hens, and she'll help Vera with the bairns. We'll get her up as soon as the lads leave for work. If we go by the back roads we can walk to the station in an hour and a half. Thank God for the new railway line. It should take us to within a few miles of Dick's place and maybe somebody will offer a lift. I'll stay overnight and come back in the morning.'

'You mean to leave her in Vera's care to have the bairn?' Eliza's lip trembled and she bit down hard. This was no time for tears and Bert was doing his best to find a way and avoid gossip for the sake of the lads.

'What else can we do? Dick will call in a midwife when the time comes.'

'What about the babe?'

'That's up to Emma. If she won't say who

the father is, or if he's married and canna wed her . . . ' He broke off, lowering his eyes. 'It will have to go to an orphanage.' He gabbled the words because he didn't want to say them. 'That's what I'll tell her anyway.'

Eliza struggled to keep back her tears. Surely Emma would tell them more when she came to her senses and realized what she had done.

'I shall have to buy some wool and post it to her. She'll have to knit some clothes for the poor mite.'

'She'll not need a lot if she's not going to keep the bairn. She'll need to find work as soon as she's over the birth. If I could get my hands on whoever did this to ma lassie!'

'Aye, I darena think what Richard and Joe would do to him. As for Davy, he was getting on so well with the Minister and his lassie but this could ruin everything.'

5

That evening William trudged home beside his horses, tired but satisfied with his long day behind the plough. They had two pairs of Clydesdales at Bonnybrae, as well as an elderly mare who had proved herself to be an excellent breeder and was presently rearing another filly foal. They also had two young geldings which he and Jim were breaking to the cart, ready to sell to a Glasgow brewery. He was proud of his father and the way he ran things but he longed for a place of his own so that he could breed his own stock, make decisions and plan for the future. He had to admit that he and Angus Taylor, their horseman, were making better progress with the spring ploughing than most of their neighbours. He had a competitive spirit and Bonnybrae was the largest tenanted farm on the estate. It had always been an example since his grandfather first took it on as a young man, but he enjoyed variety and he could turn his hand to any task on the farm.

The farm yard at Bonnybrae was arranged in a square with an entrance from the road at the northern corner. There was a long horse trough along the wall between the back door to the house and the stables, and it was always kept full with a pump which brought water up from a deep underground well. The horses instinctively made for the trough as soon as they entered the yard; they too had earned their food and rest. Once they had been groomed and fed, both Angus and William returned to the trough and each filled a bucket of fresh clean water. Stripped to the waist, they were glad to dip their heads into the bucket to rid themselves of dust from the newly turned furrows. Maggie always left a coarse towel ready for them in the washhouse.

After a hard day's work, sustained by a short lunchtime snack of cheese and scones and a bottle of cold tea, William longed for nothing more than a good plate of food and bed. As usual, Maggie had left his meal ready and he was thankful to eat his supper and fall into bed after a long day behind the plough.

He was always up at dawn when they were ploughing or sowing, especially when they were working in the more distant fields. Consequently he was completely unaware of the turmoil in the house.

Jim noticed Emma's absence from the milking that first afternoon but he assumed she was helping his mother with other tasks. He liked the cheerful young maid and she was a hard worker so when she was still absent at the midday meal the following day, he became concerned.

'Where is Emma? Is she ill?' Even as he posed the question he noticed the stern demeanour of his mother, the stiffening of her erect posture. He glanced at Maggie. Her face was pale and pinched. There were circles under her eyes as though she had not slept. 'What's wrong, where is she?' Jim persisted. 'We missed her at the milking last night, and again this morning. Is she ill?'

'Emma has gone home in disgrace,' his mother said abruptly. 'You will not mention her name again in this house.' Jim raised his eyebrows but his father frowned him into silence.

It was evening before William returned from another long day's ploughing and Jim waylaid him on his way from the closet. He drew him into the pantry. He knew Maggie was in there skimming the cream.

'What are ye doing?' William asked with a grin and a look of surprise as Jim shut the pantry door.

'Mother has sent Emma home. She says she's in disgrace,' Jim announced.

'Sent her home? But why? Emmie is the

best maid I can remember us having here at Bonnybrae.'

'Mother sits there regal and grim-faced and insists we're not to mention her name.' Jim was the most tolerant of the Sinclair family but there was a note of irritation in his voice now. 'Father scowls us into silence. We're not bairns to be hushed without explanation. Maggie, do you know what's wrong with Emma? What can she have done for Mother to turn her off like this, without a character reference and months before term day and the hiring fairs?'

Maggie turned from skimming the cream and glanced at her brothers.

'She's expecting a child,' she said flatly. 'She didn't even realize what was wrong with her,' she added with a catch in her voice. 'It's all very well reading in the Bible about the Virgin Mary but Emmie's mother should have explained about — about things. She's intelligent and quick to learn everything about the house and the animals, she can add up a row of figures quicker than I can, and she's good at spelling, yet she's unbelievably ignorant about life. She's never experienced anything outside the school-room, and then her life here. She barely believed me when I told her the movements in her stomach were a baby kicking. Her mother told her girls only have babies when they have a husband.'

'Good God!' William muttered, his eyes widening. 'When is the baby due? Did she say?'

'She had no idea. I'm no expert on such matters but from what I know of Agnes and Bessie I should think June or July.'

William knew better than anyone how innocent Emma had been.

'I feel sick at heart and so sorry for Emma,' Maggie went on in troubled tones. 'She seemed bewildered. Mother was dreadfully harsh. She told her to pack her bags and get out. We were in the middle of washing blankets.'

'So much for the milk o' human kindness,' Jim muttered. 'Sometimes I think morals are all that matter to Mother.'

'Oh my God,' William said again. 'It's . . . '

'What are you all doing in here?' Mary Sinclair demanded, pushing open the pantry door. Her eyes moved from one to the other of her three remaining offspring. Her own face was pale and strained. She had liked Emma Greig and she wondered where she had failed the girl to let her go so far off the straight and narrow. 'I've told you, I will not have that girl mentioned in my house.' They followed her into the kitchen with varying expressions of exasperation, pity and determination.

'Mother, listen to me,' William demanded and grasped his mother's arm, turning her to face him by sheer pressure.

'Come and eat your supper and leave your mother be, William,' his father commanded sternly. 'Can't you see she's troubled enough?'

William's mouth tightened and his own face paled beneath his weathered tan.

'Not as troubled as she's going to be,' he muttered through gritted teeth and sat down in his place at the table. He met his father's eyes unflinchingly. 'If Emmie is expecting a bairn in June I reckon it's mine.'

Maggie caught her mother in her arms and lowered her onto a chair. Her face was chalk white and she was opening her mouth to speak but no words came. She moved her head from side to side in denial. William's eyes moved from her to his father, who had jumped from his chair and was towering over them.

'You young fool!' he spat out angrily. 'Do you see the shock you've given your mother? You nearly killed her when you were born; now you're trying again. The girl was in our employ. She lived under my roof. She should have been safe here.'

'I know, I know . . . '

'Well!' Jim muttered, shaking his head in disbelief. 'I never thought you'd play on your own doorstep, Will.'

'It was. I was not er,' William broke off. He had no doubt the baby must be his. It had never occurred to him it could be so easy to have a baby. Eva McGuire had never had a child in her life. 'I must talk to Emma . . . We must get married.'

James Sinclair looked at his wife's white face. He knew Emma's plight had upset and dismayed her but neither of them had dreamed one of their own sons could be involved. This was ten times worse.

'I refuse to listen,' Mary Sinclair whispered. 'I never thought my own son would take advantage of an innocent maid . . . ' She began to shake.

'Come, Mother,' Maggie said gently. 'You've had a shock. Let me help you to bed.' She drew her mother to her feet and helped her to her bedroom.

'I must talk to Emma,' William said, watching them leave the kitchen.

'There's nothing you can do tonight,' his father said sternly, 'and I might tell you it's not a good start to marriage so you'd better think about it.'

'Don't go out tonight,' Jim said with

concern. 'If you go anywhere near Emma's family, those brothers of hers will half-kill you. In fact, it's a wonder they weren't up here looking for you last night. You know how protective they are. One of them always saw her back safely when she's been home.'

'I need to speak with her,' William insisted.

'Not tonight.' His father's tone brooked any argument.

'You know how we'd have felt if somebody had taken advantage of Agnes, or Bess or Maggie,' Jim said. 'We'd have pulverised him. You'd be better to go tomorrow when there's only Emma and her mother at home.'

'Maybe you're right,' William muttered, but his thoughts were going round and round. He had no money of his own. James Sinclair had never paid wages to any of his sons but they had all known he would try to establish them in farms when the time was right. William knew there was no hope of his father getting him a farm of his own to rent now, and there were no spare cottages on Bonnybrae. He couldn't suggest bringing Emma here to live. His mother would never tolerate the scandal. And Emmie, how would she be feeling, cast out without a job?

It was a strained meal, eaten in silence.

'I'll speak to you later, William,' James Sinclair said, pushing his chair away from the table. 'Don't go down to the village, nor off to the ploughing in the morning. This affects all of us, whether we like it or not. I hope you realize that,' he added grimly. 'If you're going to marry the lassie you'll need to put a roof over her head and be able to support a wife and a bairn. We need to decide what's to be done.'

* * *

Emma's family were every bit as keen to avoid local gossip and the disgrace of having a bastard child in the family. As soon as she had washed and dressed and eaten a meagre breakfast, her father bid her gather up the clothes she needed.

'You'll be staying away until the baby is born,' he said grimly, avoiding his wife's tear-filled eyes.

As much as she hated gossip, Eliza loved her daughter and she hated the thought of her going away to stay with Vera. She busied herself making them a pack of sandwiches to eat on the journey. Emma had never even seen a train, let alone ridden on one, and in different circumstances she would have been excited. She remembered Uncle Dick visiting them often when she was a child but they had hardly seen him since he married and went to work in a village nearer Glasgow. As for her Aunt Vera, she had only met her once and she knew her mother and aunt didn't get on.

She had slept almost round the clock, and in spite of her bewilderment at the sudden changes in her life, there remained a small fount of happiness deep inside her which nothing could quench.

They were not expected, and when Bert Greig arrived at the door of his brother's cottage after a four mile walk from the railway station, he thought Vera was going to shut the door in their faces. He had not even had a chance to explain the situation or ask for their help at that stage. Fortunately Dick and the worker from the adjoining cottage were coming up the road, and he almost ran the last few yards in his joy at seeing them. Vera scowled.

'Ye'd best come in then,' she said ungraciously, 'but if ye're expecting me to make ye a meal ye're barking up the wrong tree. Arriving here and not so much as a letter to warn folks.'

'Och Vera, dinna be like that,' Dick pleaded. 'We've plenty eggs and milk, and there's the piece o' bacon Mistress Donnelly sent up yesterday. Ah but it's good to see ye, Bertie.' He clapped his older brother on the back and grinned widely. 'And this'll be wee

Emma? My, ye've grown into a fine-looking young woman since last I saw ye.' He smiled at her then called to three grubby children playing in the garden. 'Hi, you lot, come and say hello to your Uncle Bert and cousin Emma.'

The three children came running, eager to hug their father around his legs, but they were shy when he introduced them.

'Millie is nine and Bobby is seven. They go to school in the village. Peter is four so he will go to school next year.'

Emma bent down to greet them and Dick's eyes widened as her dress pulled tightly across the swelling of her stomach. Emma liked children but she was already feeling homesick. The cottage was much the same as her own home but it was dirty and the smell of stale cooking turned her stomach even before they stepped through the door. All three children smelled of urine and their hair needed to be washed. Over their heads she met her father's eyes briefly before he looked hastily away. She saw him gnaw his lip and she wanted to cry, 'Take me home with you, Dad,' but she swallowed hard and lifted her chin. Since yesterday morning, she felt she had aged twenty years. At least she knew how to keep a clean house and how to cook and mend and be thrifty. She had Mrs Sinclair and Maggie to thank for that.

While the children led her shyly into the dark kitchen, her father and Uncle Dick moved out of earshot down to the garden and she knew her father was explaining her situation and making arrangements for her to stay. They had had a railway carriage to themselves for most of the journey and he had explained what was to happen.

'I've saved nearly all my wages. I will pay for my keep,' she said when she understood. She was amazed to see tears shine in her father's eyes before he blinked and looked away.

'Emmie, you've always been such a good lassie. I still can't believe . . . Tell us who the father is and we'll deal with him.' But Emma pursed her lips and shook her head. Her father sighed heavily. 'Well, I'll pay Vera. She'll get her pound o' flesh out of both of us if I ken her, but try to put up with her, for all our sakes, because I canna think what else to do. We have to live in the village and the lads will suffer from the gossip if they hear what's happened to you.'

'I know. I dinna want to be a burden. Maybe I'll be able to earn my keep.'

'If I know Vera, she'll see ye do that anyway,' he said glumly, 'and she'll take my money and ask for more. You keep your own money safe. You'll need it before you can get back to another job.'

Her father had explained things but he had omitted to tell her the baby would be taken from her, and sent to an orphanage so that she would be able to earn her living again.

* * *

William was keen to see Emma without further delay. He had been so busy ploughing all day in the far field he hadn't even known the day she'd left Bonnybrae and he'd gone to plough before the rest had come in from the milking yesterday. This was the third day she'd been gone. He wondered how she was bearing up. He was not afraid of her brothers. He knew he deserved their anger.

He ate his breakfast quickly and waited impatiently for his father to say whatever he had on his mind before he went down to Locheagle. He was surprised when his parents came into the kitchen together, his father supporting his mother. He knew she was anaemic but she looked deathly white and there were dark rings beneath her eyes.

'Your mother and I have talked things over,' his father began sternly, 'and we don't need to tell you how disappointed we are, aye and disgusted that you have taken advantage of a young maid under our roof. There'll be no end to the scandal, whatever we do. Whether you marry the girl or not, folks have long memories. They'll never let her forget her shame, or your part in it.'

William wanted to cut him short and tell his father he had gone over and over all this in his mind but he held his tongue, his head bowed.

'You've always wanted the adventure of a train journey to see your relations in Yorkshire. We've decided that's the best thing for you to do now. I'll send them a wire and you'll go tomorrow. The sooner you're away from the district the better for all of us.'

William's head jerked up.

'Wh-what do you mean? Go tomorrow? This will not go away even if I stayed away for a month. There'll be a bairn. Mine. People will still talk when I come back.'

'You'll not be coming back. You'll have a hundred pounds. That will be your share and you can count yourself lucky. It's up to you to make your own way in the world now.'

William gasped, then he looked at his mother. She was sitting straight backed as always but she was still as a statue, her grey hair tightly drawn back into a severe bun and topped by her white cap. Only her hands gave away her agitation, clasped tightly together.

'I see,' he said slowly. 'Well, if that's what you want, but to leave so soon . . . '

'There's no use delaying,' his father interrupted harshly. 'Whether you send for Emma when you've found work and a place to live, it will be up to you. We'll send on a trunk with your belongings when you give us an address. I shall send the wire off to cousin Andrew today. You'll go into Glasgow with the milk train tomorrow morning. You should be able to get a train south from there on the Glasgow and South Western Railway.'

'I see,' William said. His family were putting him out. He rose and went out of the back door. Maggie followed soon after. He guessed she had been in the pantry and overheard everything when he saw her strained face and the tears running down her cheeks.

'Oh, William . . . ' She came towards him and hugged him tightly, as she had when he was a small boy. 'I wish you didn't have to go, and so soon . . . so far away.'

'I must go down to the village and see if they'll let me talk to Emma,' he said. 'I've made a mess of both our lives, it seems.'

'I'll come with you. I never got to say goodbye to Emmie. I can go to the door first and see who is at home. They may be more likely to let me speak to her. We got on so well.' Her mouth trembled.

'All right, if you want to see her anyway. We'll take the trap. If I'm to leave tomorrow there's things I need to do first.'

It was Mrs Greig who answered the door to Maggie's knock. Her face was pale, her eyes red-rimmed as though she had been weeping before she answered the door.

'Can — can I speak to Emma please, Mrs Greig?' she asked in her gentle voice.

'Oh, Miss Maggie, it's you,' the older woman said tearfully. 'Emmie's not here. Her father took her away yesterday to stay with his brother and his wife and children. He didna want the folks in the village tae ken the shame she's in. He says I'm not to tell her brothers but I dinna think I'll be able to keep it from them. They'll want to know why she's not been home on her day off.'

'Oh, Mrs Greig, I'm so sorry . . . ' Maggie said helplessly, near to tears herself.

'I know it's a shameful thing she's done but I hate to think of her away among strangers and having the bairn and — and everything.' The tears came freely now. 'M-my sister-in-law, sh-she's not a kindly woman. Emma wouldna tell us who the father is so we think he must be married already.' In her distress she didn't notice Maggie catch her breath. 'Bert says the babe will have to go to an orphanage or into the care of the nuns.'

'Oh no, no!'

'She'll need to earn her living, Miss Maggie. And he says nobody wants an unmarried woman with a bairn at her skirts.'

'I — I didn't manage to say goodbye to Emma, Mrs Greig and — '

'She often told us how kind ye were to her, Miss Maggie, and I was grateful for that.'

'Could you give me her address so that I might write to her, please?'

'You still want to write to her, Miss Maggie?'

'Yes, I do. I don't think she knew the risk . . . '

'That would be good of ye. I reckon she'll need a few kind words frae somebody, for she'll get none frae her Aunt Vera. I'll write down the address for ye.'

Maggie felt a hypocrite. What would the Greigs say when they found out her own brother was the father? She shuddered. Emmie was very loyal. It was more than William deserved.

William was growing impatient and on the point of tying up the pony and joining Maggie when he saw her hurrying down the garden path.

'Can I speak to Emma now?' he asked urgently.

'She's not here. Her father has taken her away to his brother's house near Glasgow. They're as concerned about scandal as our own parents. Emma told me they go to the Kirk every week.' William winced. He had never for a moment considered such consequences when he had taken Emmie up to the Torr.

'When I have work and a place to live I can send for her, but I need to get in touch.'

'I've got her address. They have no idea you are the father, though. Emma refused to tell them. Mr Greig says the baby will have to go into an orphanage or into the care of the nuns when it's born.'

'What? They can't do that . . . '

'Poor Emma. She loved the collie pups and she didn't want to part with them so I can imagine how upset she will be at the thought of parting from her own child. You must promise to keep in touch and let me have your address as soon as you have one, William. Meanwhile, I think you should let me write to Emma until we know whether she receives the letters or not. Mrs Greig doesn't seem to trust her sister-in-law. She sounds a horrid woman so I shall be careful what I say.'

'Thank you, Maggie. I know you must feel as ashamed as Mother does but at least you're willing to help.'

'I always liked Emma and I know she was not a bad girl. She was ignorant about many things. You're far from blameless.'

'I know,' William said wearily, 'but I've given myself enough lectures, not to mention the way Mother and Father are going on. I feel like a leper, or as though I've committed murder.'

'Emmie may not have been the woman you would have chosen but she'll make a good wife with a little help. You've always wanted to be in control of everything so perhaps it is as well to have someone younger who will not resent you giving orders.'

William glanced at her and saw a faint smile on her lips. He sighed.

'You're the only one who is trying to see some good in this sorry mess,' he said. His lips tightened and he lifted his chin. 'I'll show everybody yet. I don't intend to be a worker all my life. I shall look for a farm to rent at the first opportunity.'

'I think Father knows that, and I'm sure he believes you will do the right thing by Emma too. It is Mother who doesn't want you to contact her. I heard her saying should the baby be born dead then no one need know.'

'Born dead!' William gasped. 'Sometimes I wonder if Mother has a heart.'

6

Even in her worst nightmares Emma could not have believed it was possible to be so unhappy. She was bewildered by the way her life had turned upside down, yet deep within her there was a little well of hope, even joy, which even Aunt Vera could not quench. She continually told her she was a gullible little fool and what did she expect when she had played with fire. As soon as Uncle Dick left the house to go to work, her day became one long rant from Vera. She was used to being up early and to working hard. Everyone at Bonnybrae, with the exception of Mrs Sinclair, had worked the whole day long so it was not the washing and scrubbing and mending which made her miserable. In fact, she longed to bring some sort of order and cleanliness to the smelly little cottage. It was Aunt Vera calling her awful names which made her unhappy, especially when Peter repeated them. He was too young to understand and she didn't always understand either.

'Don't think you'll get away here to cast your big eyes at every man in trousers. You're to go no further than the garden or you'll find yourself back where you've come from, whatever Dick might say. Just because your father once helped us out of a bit of a scrape, he thinks he can use us how he pleases.'

'I'm sure Dad doesn't mean to use you,' Emma protested. 'He told me he would pay for my keep.'

'Ugh, he told you that, did he? Well, don't think that means you can sit there acting like a lady, doing nothing. I've enough to do without looking after the likes of you.'

'I'm used to working if you tell me what you want me to do,' Emma said firmly.

It hadn't taken long to discover her aunt was slovenly and lazy with no method to her housekeeping, and whatever anyone did to help she was never pleased. Emma remembered there had been a girl in her class at school like that and she had tried to bully everyone else. Davy had told her to stick up for herself and she would find the girl was all right underneath. He had been right. Emma was beginning to think Aunt Vera was a bully too but it was not so easy to stick up for herself when she was here in disgrace. She shared Milly's bed in the same room as the boys, and each night she wept into her pillow when the children were asleep.

One morning the postman brought a letter for her but Vera snatched it out of her hand before she could open it.

'But it's from Mother,' Emma protested.

'So *you* say, you little slut. I don't trust you. I'll see who it's from.' She was not the best of readers and the page was closely written so it seemed to Emma that it would take for ever. Vera looked up. 'There's no need to stand there gawping,' she snapped. 'Get that washing hung on the line. You can read this tonight when you've finished the day's work.'

Vera had a high-pitched screeching voice which carried through the open door. The postman heard her raging. He saw Emma carrying the big basket of washing down to the clothesline which ran alongside the wall of the long narrow garden. He paused out of sight of the house and gave a low whistle, beckoning Emma while keeping hidden by two gnarled apple trees.

'Can I help you?' Emma asked politely, brushing away her tears. She longed to read the letter from home.

'Nae, lassie, I dinna need any help but you might be glad o' mine if you've come to stay wi' yon woman. I pass this way every day on my way to the farmhouse. Mistress Donnelly makes me a cup o' tea, see, before I deliver the letters over the hill.'

'I — I see,' Emma said uncertainly. He was

a man older than her father and he had a cheery, weather-beaten face. She couldn't help responding to his grin with a faint smile.

'If you write a letter, private like, put a stamp on and hide it beneath one o' these stones on the corner.' He poked at the wall. 'See, here's a nice big flat stone that would keep your letter dry. You hide it under there and I'll take a look when I pass by.'

'Th-thank you,' Emma said, 'thank you so much.' She gave a huge sigh. 'I-I'm afraid Aunt Vera doesn't like me so . . . '

'Eh lassie, yon woman doesna care for anybody, even her ain bairns, the poor wee diels.'

This was true. Even the teacher in the village school remarked on the neat darn in Milly's stocking and the patch on Bobby's trousers.

'Yes, Miss Yates,' Milly said proudly. 'Cousin Emma has come to live at our house. She darned my stockings and patched Bobby's trousers.'

'Did cousin Emma wash and brush your hair too?' Miss Yates asked.

'Aye, she did,' Bobby said with disapproval. 'She made us sit in the tin bath then she poured water over our heads. It was horrible.'

'But you look clean and smart now, Bobby,' Miss Yates said encouragingly. 'You're like the other children now. I'm sure you'll be glad your cousin has come to stay.'

'Well, she did make a lovely bowl o' custard and a rhubarb pie,' Bobby conceded.

'Aye, and she made scones on a girdle. Our dad says they're like what Granny Greig used to make but Mother says Emma is wicked 'cos she's going to have a baby and she hasna got a husband,' Milly said.

'I — I see,' Miss Yates said. 'Well, I'm pleased your cousin is teaching you how to keep yourselves clean. Remember, 'cleanliness is next to Godliness' and I like all my pupils to come to school with clean hands and faces and neatly brushed hair.'

This was something the Greig children had never done and whatever her sins, Miss Yates considered the unknown cousin had brought a little bit of good into their lives.

Unfortunately, the more praise Emma earned from Dick or the children, the more Vera vented her spleen on her. It was spite and jealousy which made her hide the letter until night. When she handed it over, her expression was ugly as she recalled her sister-in-law's query to Emma.

Dear Emmie,

I do wish you could have stayed at home with me. Are you happy with Dick and Vera? Are they looking after you and feeding you well so you have a healthy baby?

Please, Emma, you must tell me who the father is. If he is single your father will persuade him to marry you. If you can't or will not tell us who he is, your father says the baby will have to go to the nuns so that you will be free to earn your living again.

Emma gasped at that and began to whimper softly. It was the first time she had really considered the future with a baby. She clutched her stomach with both hands as though cradling the baby and protecting it. She would never let them take her baby away, never. She read the rest of the letter but her heart was heavy, even when her mother mentioned the knitting.

I was going to send some wool to knit clothes for the bairn but it costs a penny halfpenny to post two ounces and another halfpenny for every extra two ounces so I'm knitting a wee set o' clothes myself while your father is at work. I can't bear the thought of my own grand bairn in the care of strangers, Emma. I pray you will tell us who the father is.

The following evening, Emma asked her aunt if she might have a sheet of paper to reply to her mother's letter.

'A sheet of paper to write letters?' Vera snapped. 'D'ye think I'm made o' money?' In fact, Vera could only just manage to write her name and address so she had no desire to write any letters. She resented Emma's request.

'I'll ask Mistress Donnelly if I can buy a sheet o' writing paper for ye, lassie,' Uncle Dick offered.

Later, Emma heard the raised voices and harsh words which passed between him and her aunt after she had gone to bed, and she guessed the quarrel was because he had offered to help her. She fingered the little copying ink pencil which she always kept in the pocket of her dress. It had a silver-coloured tin cover to protect the point. Davy had given it to her the first Christmas she spent at Bonnybrae so that she could write their mother a letter in the middle of the month. The writing turned purple if the paper got damp and she had thought it was magic. Davy explained it had been invented twenty years earlier by putting a dye into the graphite which made the pencil lead. It was one of her greatest treasures.

If only she had thought to bring a few

sheets of paper and an envelope. She had been too shocked to think of anything after being sent home from Bonnybrae at a moment's notice, then ushered away from her own home to be left in this wilderness with Aunt Vera. Her mother had told her to bring some money and to hide it under the mattress. She had brought four shillings and nine pence, and she would have welcomed the three mile walk to the village to buy her own writing paper but Aunt Vera never let her out of her sight.

Uncle Dick did not bring the promised sheet of paper. Emma never knew whether Mrs Donnelly didn't have any or whether he had changed his mind after the row with Vera. In desperation, she wrote up and down over her mother's letter and hoped she would be able to read it. She put a line through her address on the envelope and wrote her mother's address neatly in between, thankful the schoolmaster had insisted on neat handwriting when she was at school. She waited until Aunt Vera was outside haranguing the paraffin man, who called once a month with oil for the lamps. He sold candles, pots, pans, clothes lines and pegs. She had found a small stub of sealing wax, so it was an easy matter to melt it with a match in her bedroom and seal the envelope.

The following morning when she was hanging the washing, she put the letter under the stone with a three-penny piece. She used a piece of slate to scribble a message asking the postman to buy three penny stamps and stick one on her letter. She prayed he would understand. Rab Craig did understand. He showed his wife the letter.

'I know the lassie has gotten herself in trouble and that's a sin, but she doesn't deserve to be in Mistress Greig's clutches. I've never seen the door step washed and scoured before, nor the bairns bathed and their hair brushed. Every day she's hanging out washing.'

'Aye, Vera Greig has always been a lazy creature,' his wife said. 'So what are ye wanting me to do, Rab? I ken ye've some bee in your bonnet.' Her eyes twinkled as she looked up at him.

'She wants me to buy three penny stamps but I reckon she'll need paper and envelopes to go with 'em. Can you spare any?'

'I can. I wonder if the lassie can knit? She could borrow a pair of my fine needles and I've a skein o' lemon-coloured wool left frae when I knitted the pram set for oor Maisie's wee bairn.'

'I'm sure she'd be glad o' that. Miss Yates frae the school says she's the neatest darner she's ever seen and she patched young Bobby's trousers, so I expect she can knit.'

'I'll make up a wee parcel and we'll put the paper and envelopes and the two spare stamps inside, but ye'd best be sure to hand it into her ain hands. I dinna trust Vera Greig an inch.'

* * *

It was Jim Sinclair who drove the milk over the hill road to the nearest station to catch the morning milk train into Glasgow. Beside him, William sat silently, watching the passing fields and wondering if he would see them again. People of his acquaintance didn't travel much. They couldn't afford it. Under any other circumstances he would have rejoiced at the opportunity to go all the way to Yorkshire on the train. Cousin Drew had sent a wire back to say he would meet the train at Wakefield station. That seemed to reassure his father but breakfast had been a swift and silent meal with Maggie unable to hold back her tears. She had cared for William a lot when he was young and their mother had been so frail.

Together the brothers rolled the milk churns to the edge of the platform, then William seized his carpet bag from the cart and prepared to mount the train.

'I'll miss ye, Will,' Jim said gruffly. For a moment William thought his brother was going to clasp him in a farewell hug and he was relieved when he settled for a hearty slap on his back. They were not a family who showed their emotions. Their mother had seen to that. 'Have you got the sandwiches Maggie made for you?'

'Aye, they're in my bag. Tell her I'll write as soon as I'm settled.'

True to his word, Drew Kerr was waiting at the station when the train drew into Wakefield station. William was relieved to see a face he recognized. He had left behind everything that was familiar and he longed to know how Emmie was, and if she was happy in a strange place.

'You'll be tired and hungry after the journey,' Drew said. 'We need to move to the other station to catch the local train, but we could go into the Boy and Barrel for a pie if you like.'

'There's more than one station in the same town?' William asked in surprise.

'Aye. You'll see the cattle pens for the market when we get there. They've opened another railway line across country to carry coal and steel to the mills and to the coast for export. They finished building the cathedral recently. Wakefield is a city now. Everything is growing fast. We're in the midst of industrial development here but there's a lot of good land if you can get it, but Annie gets homesick for the peace o' the hills back home,' he added gravely. 'She's killed the fatted calf to welcome you. We try to speak our best English since we moved here so she'll enjoy hearing her own mother tongue again, and news of the folks we knew.'

He gave a sideways grin. At thirty-eight, he was fourteen years older than William but he still had a boyish smile and twinkling blue eyes. He was not wearing a cap and his thick mop of fair hair gleamed in the sunlight.

'You're picking up a Yorkshire twang yourself,' William remarked.

'Och, hardly that! But the locals canna understand me if I talk in broad Scots. What's more, you'll have a problem understanding some o' them when they talk broad Yorkshire. It's like a foreign language when they get together. You wait until you hear Tom Wright, the blacksmith. I've left the pony and trap with him in Wilmore village.'

'I can imagine what he's like frae what I heard o' the station-master,' William said.

They chatted comfortably with a carriage to themselves for most of the way as the train puffed its way from one small station to another. About six miles from Wakefield, they climbed down onto the platform at Wilmore and collected the pony and trap from the blacksmith a few hundred yards down the street.

'So tha's bringin' another Scots lad to these parts, eh?' the man said, eyeing William up and down. He stood feet apart, hands on hips as though planted there. He was not tall but his muscles bulged above his rolled up sleeves.

'This is a young cousin of mine,' Drew introduced them. 'He's here to visit but if you hear of any good farms coming to let, we might persuade him to come back and settle here, eh, William?' He gave a teasing grin and a wink.

'He should have been here afore Lady Day if he wanted a good farm. Tha's over late, lad. It was the best farm in these parts.'

'Oh?' William blinked, remembering that Drew knew nothing yet of his situation, or that he was here to stay. 'I would be interested to hear of any farms coming to let,' he said cautiously, 'but what's this about Michaelmas and Lady Day?'

'Och, they have some strange ways down here, William.' Drew grinned and looked at Tom Wright. 'We hold our hiring fairs at the end o' May and end o' November when the men and maids move to other places, and tenants take up their farms or give notice to the factor to quit.'

'Well, tha'll not change us, Drew Kerr. March an' September are the rent days in these parts. Mind, there's some landlords let at Whitsun. That'll not be much different to your May term. Maybe it's so they draw rent every quarter day.'

'Sounds strange,' William said.

'Aye, this cousin of yours thinks we're a queer lot but he's getting used to us. We reckoned he had some peculiar ways when he first came but they seem to work for him, leastways he pays his bills on time and he's not gone bankrupt yet, not like some folks near here.'

'Are you meaning the folks from Manor Farm? I heard they'd given up but that son of his didna deserve the tenancy. He never got out of his bed in the morning,' Drew said with disgust. 'And he ran after women half the night from what I hear. I'd have put him out long since if he'd been my laddie,' he added, turning to William.

He grinned at Drew, knowing they had both been brought up by stern fathers who commanded respect.

'Your bairn is halfway to being a farmer already, Drew, at least from what we read in

Aunt Florrie's letters. He's not yet ten years old, is he?'

'He'll make a farmer, I dinna doubt,' Drew smiled proudly. 'He milks his own cow night and morning, and he has a pig and a calf to rear.'

'Aye, he's a grand lad,' Tom Wright agreed. 'The way he handles them Clydesdales when he brings them to be shod, the lad puts many a man to shame.'

'Well, it's time we made for home or Annie will think we're lost,' Drew decided. Once they were in the trap and out of the village, he grinned at William. 'It's just the same as back home. You need to keep the right side o' the blacksmith. They know everything that's going on and they hear all the gossip. They can do ye many a good turn, or a bad one if ye get the wrong side.'

'Aye, so I should imagine,' William said. He swallowed hard. 'I should tell you why I'm here before I see Annie. You can explain my situation to her later.'

'Oh? Sounds serious,' Drew said, his eyebrows raised. 'Quarrelled with Uncle James, have ye? He always worried that ye wanted to spread your wings before the feathers had grown, I remember.'

'You could say that, I suppose,' William said. 'But I'm twenty-four now. I'm here to look for a farm of my own to rent. I hadna reckoned on waiting until September, though, but if that's the way things are done, I shall need to find work and have a look around the area until then.'

'You're serious?' Drew's eyes widened. 'Is this with, or without, Uncle James's blessing?'

'I expect Mother will be writing to tell your mother all her troubles so you'll hear about things soon enough,' William said with faint bitterness. 'I've upset her badly so Father is more displeased. I need to get married. Emmie was a maid at Bonnybrae . . . '

'Whew,' Drew whistled. 'That certainly will not be suiting Aunt Mary and her friends frae the kirk. You were playing a bit near home, though, weren't ye?' He glanced at William's brooding expression. 'What's she like, the lassie?'

'There's nothing wrong with Emmie except she was my mother's maid,' William said bitterly. 'She's seventeen, sweet-natured, innocent, pretty. She's from a decent family and she's a grand worker. It will make it easier for her when she arrives down here if folks think we're married already, though. The bairn will be born in June.'

'June? That's only two months away! Three if it's the end o' June. You're cutting things fine, aren't ye, Will?'

'None of us knew. I told you, Emmie was as innocent as a child.' He smiled faintly and not without pleasure as he remembered how trustingly Emma had lain in his arms up there on the top of the Torr.

'Set her cap at the boss's son for all, though, didn't she?' Drew said.

'No, she didn't do that. She's not that sort. She's been at Bonnybrae since she left school when she was fourteen. I hadna meant to do her any harm.' He flushed slightly. 'To tell the truth, I hadn't thought it was so easy to get pregnant.'

'I expect they all say that,' Drew said.

'It was fate, if you believe in such things.' William explained about being caught out by the moorland mist coming down.

'We had to spend the night up on the Torr. It seemed natural enough to cuddle close to keep each other warm. One thing led to another.' He shrugged.

'I see . . . ' Drew murmured. He was silent for a while then, 'You're sure you want to marry her? I mean it's not as though you're in love. Will she make a suitable wife?'

'I'm sure she will,' William said defensively. 'I don't know what love is but I like Emmie better than any other girl I know.' Drew hid a smile. 'She's a good worker and she can do anything in the house and dairy. She can read and write and she's thrifty.' He hesitated. 'Maggie and Jim like her. They think Mother treated her too harshly. They think we shall do well together.'

'Mmm, well, if Maggie approves I don't think there's much to worry about. She was always a good judge and a sensible woman, or so my mother reckoned. She felt Maggie was wasted staying at home to look after your mother instead of getting a home and husband of her own.'

'I agree, but she's terribly loyal to the parents. Mother has a subtle way of binding Maggie to her. Jim has no plans to take a wife of his own. He'll see Maggie is all right.'

'Well, Annie will be pleased if you stay in this area, and so shall I. I wish I'd known earlier. There was a grand big farm to let on this estate and the factor is a fair man. They don't call them factors down here, though. He's known as the land agent.'

'Aye, well, I'm not expecting it to be easy now that I don't have Father to speak to the laird for me. Most of the farms go to the families of existing tenants in our area.'

They turned off the road down a short track and into the farm yard. Almost immediately the door opened and Annie ran out to greet them, accompanied by three fair-haired children, so like Drew there was no doubt he was their father. For the first time William wondered what his child would be like. It was a sobering thought. He hoped Emma was being well looked after. He ought to have insisted on going to see her. Maybe he should have brought her with him, but where would they have lived? He had no place to offer a wife yet. An awful thought struck him as he saw the tears in Annie's eyes at the sight of someone from home. Maybe Emma wouldn't want to marry him? Maybe she wouldn't want to move so far from her family. He felt a pang at the thought of moving down here and never seeing her again. He couldn't let that happen.

7

Nearly three weeks had passed since Bert had taken Emma to stay with his brother and still they had not told her brothers what had happened. The weather was typical April showers, and Richard decided he would walk up the glen to meet his sister. He looked forward to her cheery presence at home.

'This is her day off, isn't it?' he said, seeing his mother and father exchanging anxious looks.

'We canna keep it frae them any longer,' Eliza said and burst into tears. It was something she was doing too often since Emma had gone to stay with Vera. It had grieved her terribly when she got the reply to her letter, using the same envelope and the same paper, telling her Vera had insisted on reading her letter and had made Emma wait until evening before she handed it over.

'Mother? What's wrong?' Richard asked with concern. 'Ye've looked pale for weeks now and I noticed you never seem to eat a proper meal with us. What is it?'

'All right, I'll tell you what's wrong,' his

father said gruffly. He hated to see his wife so upset but he thought he'd acted for the best for all of them, including Emma, by sending her away until the baby had been born and taken to the orphanage. 'I was trying to avoid a scandal,' he finished when he had explained, 'especially for you laddies when you live in the village and plan to marry decent lassies.'

'Emma, expecting a bairn? But why didn't ye tell us? Who is the father?' Richard demanded angrily. 'I'll kill him for doing this tae our wee Emmie! She's no more than a bairn . . . '

'Maybe she's a bairn in your eyes, laddie,' his mother sighed, 'but she's seventeen, a young woman. I should have warned her . . . '

'Who is he?'

'She willna tell us,' Bert Greig said unhappily. 'I didna want to send her away, specially to that whining slut, Vera. I did it for your sakes — '

'Our sakes, Father?' Davy interrupted indignantly.

'Aye, ye dinna think the minister will want ye walking out wi' his lassie if he hears your sister has brought shame on to the family, d'ye?'

'If he has the milk o' human kindness that he preaches about he'll know Emmie needs help, not blame,' he said with quiet conviction.

His mother stared at him. 'He'll not want his lassie marrying into a family like ours though, Davy, and we don't want you to suffer.'

'Suffer?' Joe joined in with a harsh laugh. 'It's the fellow who has done this to Emma who needs to suffer.'

'We don't know who he is so we think he must be married already,' his father growled.

'S-so your father says the baby will have to b-be taken to the nuns as soon as it's born,' Eliza said and broke into another storm of weeping. She had been knitting tiny garments in secret and she wept over every one.

'Oh Father, you canna mean it?' Davy said. 'It'll break Emma's heart if you give away her baby.'

'What else can I do?' his father demanded. 'She'll need to find work and how will she do that with a bairn to care for? Her life's ruined.'

'We'll all give a bit more money to help keep Emma and the bairn until she gets on her feet,' Richard said.

'Oh aye, and what d'ye think your ain lassie will say to that and you saving up to get a nest o' your ain?' his father demanded. Richard scowled but he knew it was true. He did want to get married and he and Lily had been tempted recently to do what Emma had apparently done.

'Leave it for now,' Eliza said wearily. 'I've written to Emma again this week. I sent her a sheet of paper and an envelope this time so maybe she'll send a reply. I have to be careful what I write now I know Vera reads her letters.'

'I don't like it,' Joe said belligerently. 'I've a good mind to travel up there and bring her back.'

* * *

William would not have been human if he had not appreciated Drew's warm welcome and the fuss which Annie made of him, especially when he was feeling rejected by his own parents. There was no doubt they were pleased to see him.

'Drew's mother has visited us once. She stayed for a fortnight and even then she was homesick,' Annie said, 'otherwise we havena seen anyone from Ayrshire.'

Drew must have told her of his plans to settle in Yorkshire after they retired to bed because the following morning, she was full of enthusiasm to get him settled as near to Blaketop farm as possible. In the days that followed, she plied him with questions about the folks back home but most of all she wanted to know about Emma. Her questions made William realize how little he knew about Emma as a person in her own right. He knew she was as innocent and genuine as a child in comparison to women like Eva McGuire, and the thought made his heart ache for her, wondering where her parents had sent her and if she was happy.

He wondered how they would get on together living as man and wife, sharing the same home, the intimacy of sharing the same bed. He recalled her soft, yielding young body and that prospect was a welcome one. He had seen Emma every day for three years but living together as man and wife would be almost like marrying a stranger. What if Emma felt the same? Was that the reason she had refused to tell her parents he was the father of her child? Why, oh why, hadn't she confided in him? Surely they could have worked out a solution?

It troubled him that Emma might not want to marry him, especially now it would mean moving so far from her family. His parents had made it clear he was on his own now. His father had been fair about giving him his share of capital but that was not the same help as he would have got if he had rented a farm near Bonnybrae. He knew his mother wanted him out of the area where he had been born and reared. He had wanted to be independent but he had never envisaged it like this. He thought it would be better for Emmie's sake, if he gave the impression they were already married. He sought Annie's advice.

'I think you're wise,' she agreed gravely. 'If you and Emma are to set up as tenants and you are expecting her to help you with the milking and dairy work, and possibly a man to lodge with you, then she will need a maid to help when she has a baby to care for. It will be hard enough, turning her whole life upside down. It's essential she should have respect from the men and maids you employ. People thrive on gossip. What would they say if they discovered Emmie had been your mother's maid and forced you into marriage — '

'She isn't forcing me into anything,' William interrupted. 'We haven't even had a chance to discuss our situation. Mother got her out of the house with all speed and her parents whisked her away to God knows where. We never had a chance to talk. Now I'm banished down here.'

'Whatever way things happened, it wouldn't help your image either, William, handsome fellow though you are,' Annie said with a smile.

'I know.' William sighed heavily. 'Mother always claimed you had a wise head, Annie. My parents consider that I've shamed them but perhaps they think it will be easier for me to start a new life down here, but for all her moralizing, Mother doesn't want me to marry Emmie, even though she must see it is the decent thing to do.'

'I'm flattered if Aunt Mary thinks I'm wise. She never gave praise lightly. I suppose it's the religion and the way she was brought up. Religious people can be very cruel sometimes, though. You must follow your own conscience, William, and do what you think is best for both you and Emma, as well as the baby.'

'I know marrying Emma will be the best thing for all of us,' he said firmly. 'Mother hates scandal so much she's not thinking clearly.'

He decided to write to Maggie without delay and ask her to send Emma's address. He would ask her to mention the possibility of marriage and living in Yorkshire, then it would not be such a shock to Emma when she received his own letter. He and Drew had an appointment at the estate office with Sir Reginald Wilton's land agent but he vowed to write directly when they returned.

William had always been impatient to make things happen once he had made up his mind, so he was bitterly disappointed when the land agent informed them that there was no prospect of any of the farms on the estate falling vacant by Michaelmas, but there was a possibility of a small farm being to let by Lady Day as the tenant was in poor health and he had no family.

'Nothing until March 1899?' William repeated with a sinking heart.

'That's right. I'm sorry, Mr Sinclair, because if you're as good a farmer as your cousin here, I would have welcomed you as a tenant. If I hear of any farms on other estates around here, I'll ride over to Blakemore and tell Mr Kerr. Meanwhile, if you're looking for temporary work, we are needing a man to help with the dairy herd here at the Mains. One of the men was injured by a bull last week. He hopes to return to work in a few weeks. He is a good worker and he has a young family so we're leaving him in his cottage until we see how he recovers. You would need to sleep in the loft above the stable with two other single men but you would be well-fed in the Mains kitchens. The cook is excellent and Sir Reginald doesn't grudge his men their food if they work well.'

'Thank you,' William said. He didn't relish the idea of sleeping in a loft or sharing it with two strangers. He grimaced wryly. He could imagine his father saying it would be a lesson to him. 'I shall have to earn my living one way or another. Can I let you know?'

'Don't delay too long. The foreman would prefer an experienced man but he needs someone now. He has ten acres of turnips to hoe and sheep to sheer and it will be hay time before long. He can't spare the other men to help with the cows. In fact, if you have experience in sheep shearing you'd be doubly welcome. You would be paid extra for work outside the dairy. We have three women who churn the butter and make the cheese so they do all the washing up around the dairy. You would be doing the milking, helping with calving cows, feeding calves. I expect you know what's involved.'

William felt despondent when he sat down to write a letter to Maggie but he asked her to broach the subject of marriage and moving to Yorkshire with Emma.

He asked after Jim and his father and how things were going on the farm but he felt sick at heart when he thought of them all in their familiar surroundings. Surely creating a baby out of wedlock was not the criminal act his parents seemed to think. He wondered how

Emma was coping. She had been sent away from her family too and it was all his fault. His heart ached for her.

As Eliza Greig had hoped, Emma sounded more cheerful when her next letter arrived. She wrote about the friendly postman and how he kept her letters secret so Vera wouldn't see them. She told them his wife had loaned her some knitting needles and sent a hank of lemon-coloured wool.

I sat Peter down and showed him how to hold the wool in his hands, as we used to do for you, so I could wind it into a ball. Can you believe, none of the children had ever done that before. Aunt Vera never knits or darns. Miss Yates at the school has given Milly some thick needles and a ball of wool so that I can teach her to knit.

I had a lovely letter from Maggie Sinclair. Her mother has been ill and she's still not very strong. I do miss Bonnybrae and all the animals and Maggie. She says William has travelled all the way to Yorkshire on the train to visit his cousin.

Emma had stopped writing there and chewed the end of her pencil for a long time.

In the end, she didn't tell her parents Maggie had hinted that William would come to get her and the baby. If only he would, she thought with longing. She assumed Maggie meant William would take her back to Bonnybrae as a maid again, especially when Maggie had so much extra work to do caring for Mrs Sinclair. But would she be able to keep her baby there? She could never let any of them take her child from her. She wondered when he was due to return from his travels. It never occurred to her that William planned to ask her to marry him and settle in Yorkshire.

As time passed Richard, Davy and Joe urged their father to bring Emma home to have the baby. They knew it was what their mother wanted. She didn't trust Aunt Vera to look after their sister. After weeks of family discussions Bert agreed. Jubilantly, Eliza wrote to tell Emma her father would come to collect her the first Saturday in June. Emma was so overjoyed when she received the news that she blurted it out to her aunt and uncle.

'How do' ye know that?' Vera demanded. 'I never saw the postman here with any letters.' Emma flushed guiltily. In her excitement she had forgotten about keeping her letters a secret.

'H-he saw me hanging the washing and he

handed it over the garden wall,' she said.

'Oh, aye? Same as he did with the wool, eh? If you ask me you're too friendly with yon postman.'

'Oh for goodness sake, Vera,' Dick muttered in exasperation. 'Rab Craig is old enough to be Emma's father, if not her grandfather. He and his wife were only being kind to the lassie.'

'You're a man. Ye dinna ken anything,' Vera scorned. 'She's wicked where there's men. She'd have been making sheep's eyes at you if ye hadna been her uncle.'

'You do talk rubbish,' Dick said, and stomped out of the cottage and down the garden to shut himself in the closet. Emma had often heard him say it was the only place he could get peace when Aunt Vera started to nag. Vera's eyes narrowed and her mouth thinned.

'Tomorrow you'll clean out the loft and move the boys' mattress up there. You'll need the bedroom to birth the bairn, whatever your mother has written in her letter.'

'But Father is coming to take me home before the baby is born. I'll not need it.'

'*If* he comes,' Vera laughed harshly, 'and if the baby waits that long.'

She eyed Emma's bulging stomach spitefully. 'He told us to get the bairn away to the nuns as soon as it's born.'

The change of plan had come as a surprise to Vera and she was not pleased. She hadn't wanted Emma in her house but now that she would be leaving, she realized how much of the work she did each day. She was determined to get as much out of her as she could before she left. Although the loft had once been used as a bedroom by the sons of the previous occupants, Vera had never cleaned it since she and Dick moved into the cottage when they married.

The following morning, she asked Dick to put up the wooden step ladder before he went to work.

'It's time the boys slept up there away frae Milly,' she said.

'Surely there's no hurry to separate them yet,' Dick protested, 'Milly is only nine and Peter isna five yet.'

'Milly will be ten soon. Anyway I dinna believe that brother o' yours will come. He insisted we get rid o' the bairn as soon as it was born so that his precious Emma wouldna be upset. Look at the size o' her. You mark my words, she'll be here for the birthing.'

'Bert will come if he says will,' Dick said. 'He must have changed his mind about sending the babe away. After all, it will be his first grand bairn and it would break Emma's heart to give it away. You can see how good she is with our three rascals.'

Vera gave a scornful sniff and turned away. Dick's eyes narrowed. He knew Vera well by now. 'You weren't thinking of sending Emma up there to clean, were ye? Not the way she is and the baby due in a week or two. I'll not have that, Vera.'

'She can do the washing and cook the dinner while I do it.'

'She does that every day.'

'Anyway, she doesna know when the bairn is due.'

'She said she thought it was sometime in June and you said yourself she's getting big now.'

'There's four weeks in June.'

'Aye, and babies can be early or they can be late,' Dick said. 'She can't be that far off and we're supposed to be looking after her. Remember, Bert has paid us for her keep, though I reckon she's earned it. I'll not have her climbing up into the loft,' he said sternly.

Vera's eyes narrowed and she pursed her lips.

'We'll see about that,' she muttered as he shut the door with a bang and went away to work.

Emma supervised the children as they washed and dressed, and brushed their hair ready for school. It had become her daily routine. As soon as they had eaten their porridge, she and Peter walked with them down the path to the end of the garden, where it joined the main farm track between the farm and the village.

'Take a brush and shovel up to the loft,' Vera ordered as soon as she and Peter returned to the house. 'Sweep out the cobwebs and the dirt then you can scrub the bed boards ready for moving the boys' mattress up there.' Peter was excited at the prospect of exploring the loft.

'Surely he is a bit young to go to bed up there?' Emma said.

'Just you do what I tell you.'

'I want to go into the loft now with Emma,' Peter insisted.

'No, Peter,' Emma said gently, 'you might fall down the ladder and break an arm or a leg. You stay with your mother until I get rid of all the big spiders and the cobwebs.'

He shuddered and his eyes grew round. She hated spiders herself but she knew it would be no use protesting. She had seen the determined set to Aunt Vera's thin lips and the glitter in her eyes. She would have to make the best of it. The thought of her father coming to take her home before the baby was born kept her spirits up.

After ten years of neglect, the loft was festooned with long black cobwebs and there was a thick layer of dust on the floor and the built-in bed boards. It made Emma cough. There were two tiny skylights in the steeply sloping roof so she brushed these first to let in more light. She discovered one of them could be opened by a rusty iron lever. It was stiff and creaked in protest but Emma was thankful for a breath of fresh air. It was going to be a hot day again and she knew it would be stifling up here later on.

She could see Peter playing in the garden and he looked up when he heard the creak of the protesting lever. He waved to her excitedly and she waved back. He was a lovely little boy but he was often left to his own devices.

Today she knew Aunt Vera had received a copy of *Harper's Bazaar*, and another women's magazine from the woman in the next door cottage who helped Mrs Donnelly at the farm. The magazines were passed on from Lady Chisholm's housekeeper to Mrs Donnelly, who sent them round. Vera was not very good at reading but she could spend all day looking at pictures.

At each end of the loft, platforms had been built about a foot off the ground to hold the mattresses. As many as four — and sometimes six — boys had slept in the cottage loft. There was a long wooden chest built under the eaves for storing clothes. Emma prised open the lid with an effort but even inside there was dust and cobwebs, and she realized it would take her all day and maybe longer to clean everything thoroughly.

At midday she climbed carefully down the wooden ladder, her throat parched with dust and her stomach rumbling with hunger. Aunt Vera was still sitting in the wooden chair, absorbed in the new *Women's Penny Paper*. She looked up at Emma's hot, dust-streaked face and the cobwebs clinging to her cap.

'You've finished then, have you? Peter is waiting for you to play with him in the garden. He's been whining for you all morning.'

'I haven't finished yet,' Emma said. 'I've cleaned all the dust and cobwebs away as much as I can, but the bed boards and the chest will need scrubbing before they can be used.'

'You'd better get back up there and do it then.'

'I shall, but not until I've had some bread and cheese and a drink of milk,' Emma said firmly. Vera opened her mouth to protest but Emma met her eyes steadily. The older woman had realized she could only push her so far when she gave that steely look.

'You're just like your father, you like your own way,' she grumbled.

'I've worked hard up there and I've earned some food.' In truth she would have loved to lie on her bed and rest. She felt hot and sticky and her back ached from continual bending to avoid bumping her head on the beams in the sloping roof.

'I see you didn't light the copper to do the washing so I'll boil the kettle to dissolve the soda for scrubbing the boards.'

'Suit yourself but make sure there are no spiders left up there or the lads will never go to sleep.'

Emma had almost finished by late afternoon. She looked around with satisfaction as she viewed the results of her labours. The loft smelled fresh and clean, and the summer breeze was blowing gently in at the open skylight. She had several bruises where she had bumped her head, though. She moved backwards towards the open trap door and carefully eased herself through. She would stand on the steps to scrub the last square of the wooden floor boards and everything would be ready when the wood had dried. If only Aunt Vera would stir herself to make a bright rag rug for the floor, it would make a cheerful room for the boys, like the one her brothers shared back home.

She had just finished scrubbing the last of the boards and she was wringing out the cloth to wipe them when Peter seized the bottom of the ladder and shook it impatiently.

'Don't do that, Peter! Stop shaking the ladder.'

'When are you coming out to the garden, Emma? How long before Bobby comes home?' he demanded, adopting his mother's whining tone.

'I'll not be long now,' she said soothingly. 'You go find your mother while I finish this last bit of floor and I'll bring my bucket down the ladder. I might spill the dirty water over you if you're standing there.' This was no deterrent to the impatient four-year-old.

'I want you to come now. Now!' he shouted and grabbed the ladder with all his puny strength.

'Don't do that, Peter!' Emma shouted in alarm, feeling the ladder wobble and settle again, but it was not as level as it had been before and as she reached for her bucket and began to descend it wobbled precariously. Peter giggled and grabbed one side of the ladder to shake it some more. The last thing Emma remembered was hearing his howl as she fell down the last half of the ladder, spilling the water over him as the bucket flew from her grasp.

8

Whatever his faults, William had never been idle and his pride would not allow him to remain as a visitor with his cousin indefinitely so he accepted the job at the Mains Farm. The work was familiar but he thought he would never get used to the strange Yorkshire accent of his fellow workmen, especially when they gathered around the long scrubbed table in the kitchen for their meals and gabbled away to each other. He would never admit it in his letters to Maggie but he was homesick for the familiar faces and voices, and the landscape he had known since he could toddle. He felt both he and Emmie had been banished and they were being made to pay a high price for one night of pleasure — carnal pleasure, his mother had called it. If he felt bitter, the experience hardened his resolve to make a success of his life. He would prove himself as good a man as his father and an even better farmer.

He did not relish his nights in the loft above the stables but at least it was warm enough in May. He had begged a sheet from the housekeeper and one of the maids had offered to sew it into a large bag which he filled with hay for a mattress. He swept away the cobwebs from his corner of the loft, and kept the floor around him clean and tidy. His work clothes he kept in a small tin trunk which Annie had loaned him. He had written to Maggie, asking her to send on his wooden trunk by train to Wilmore station where Drew had promised to collect it. He knew his fellow workers smirked when they saw him making himself a clean corner to sleep and when he washed each evening at the pump in the yard, stripped to the waist.

'I wish we had more men like him,' Cook said to Mrs Milne, the housekeeper. 'He brushes his feet afore he comes into my kitchen.'

Fred Black, the foreman, also expressed his approval when the land agent enquired how he was getting on.

'Grand, Mr Frame, we could do to keep him.'

'That good, is he?' Walter Frame asked with some amusement, knowing how dubious the foreman had been about taking on a Scotsman, and how rarely any man came up to his exacting standards. 'He is looking to rent a farm of his own, but even if he was content to stay with us, he would not want to stay in the stable loft. He has a young wife so he would need a cottage and we have none vacant.'

'So that's the way of it. I wondered why he didn't join the other lads and enjoy himself on a Saturday night. He told Mrs Milne he enjoyed a good dance. She says he can play the fiddle, but he hasn't brought it with him. Last Saturday night I saw him having a go at breaking one of the young 'osses. You can tell he's done that job afore. It seems him and his brother broke 'osses to sell to a brewery back home in Scotland. I hope he stays long enough to help with this lot. We've four to break in this year.'

'Mmm, so we have, so we have,' Walter Frame mused. 'Leave it with me. I'll see if I can do a deal with him before his wife comes down to join him. I understand she is expecting a child so she is staying with her parents until he gets settled. Pity we have no spare cottages. Allan is recovering well so he should be back to work in a few weeks.' He frowned. 'I had a feeling William Sinclair was hiding something, maybe a shady past, but he seems to be a hard worker and honest. I promised to let him know of any farms coming to let so I'm glad of this opportunity to get to know more about him before I recommend him to any of my fellow land agents.'

'Well, I've no fault to find with the lad. Even Cook has a good word for him.'

'Has she now?' Walter Frame chuckled. 'That's all the recommendation he will need then.' It always amazed him how swiftly gossip spread from one big house to another via the domestic staff.

'I reckon so. Ellen's never been easy pleased.'

'Walk over to the long paddock with me, Fred? We'll have a look at the young horses now. Sinclair might be willing to break them in his spare time now it's long light in the evenings. Maybe we could offer him the little filly in return for his labour as an inducement, provided he makes a fair job.'

'Aye, she is a little 'un even for a Clydesdale.'

'I expect that's because her mother died of the grass sickness before she was ready to wean. She might grow a bit yet.'

'Compared to the three Shires she's a midget, but Scotsmen seem to like their Clydesdales.'

'He will need a decent pair of horses if he takes on a farm tenancy. Perhaps Drew Kerr would keep it for him until he's ready for it.'

William was astonished at the foreman's proposal. If he had been given the choice he would still have chosen the Clydesdale filly, before the Shires, and in preference to money. He had no intention of letting the foreman see how he felt, though. He lowered his eyes and hid his excitement. Horses were the backbone of any farm. It could save him thirty of his precious guineas. Fred Black mistook his silence.

'I can't offer you money,' he said. 'It was Mr Frame's idea. He thought your cousin would keep her until you need her, if that's what's bothering you, lad.' He brightened as an idea struck him. 'Or you could sell her to him if you don't need her. Mr Frame says his are all Clydesdales. She has a pedigree. The stallion travelled from Scotland.'

'All right, it's a bargain,' William said. He looked up and smiled, giving the foreman a firm handshake. 'I might need one of the laddies to help with yon big Shire with the white splash on his side — just in the beginning until I show him who is boss. He'll make the best o' them all if I can break him without wasting his spirit, but I've seen the fire in his eye.'

'Aye, his mother's a bit of a devil, but she's a grand worker. Don't take any chances with him, though. We don't want any more accidents and the three Shire geldings are for sale to the brewery if you can train them to the cart. There's not a man on the estate who likes breaking 'osses in.'

* * *

Emma became aware that someone was slapping her face hard and shouting at her to wake up but her eyelids felt like lead and her head was spinning. She tried to move but pain shot though her. She became aware of Peter crying.

'I'se sorry, Emmie, I'se sorry. I didn't mean to make ye fall and spill the water.'

'Shut up and get outside!' That was Aunt Vera's voice. Emma tried to speak but although her lips moved, she didn't seem to be making sense.

Millie and Bobby came running in from school. They had seen Peter sobbing in the garden.

'What's happened, Ma?' Millie demanded.

'Run up to the farm and bring your father. Quickly now.'

There was silence for a few minutes then Emma became aware Bobby was trying to push a pillow under her head. She forced her eyes open.

'Wh-what happened?' she asked faintly.

'You might well ask,' Vera said grimly. 'You clumsy fool. See what a mess you've made spilling that filthy water everywhere.'

Emma closed her eyes, willing everyone to go away and leave her in peace. It seemed only moments later when she heard Uncle Dick's voice, speaking softly and kindly. He lifted her in his arms and carried her through to the bedroom. She groaned as pain shot through her. She clutched her stomach but in fact she seemed to be in pain all over.

'Where does it hurt, lassie?' Uncle Dick asked. 'I don't think you've broken any bones as far as I can tell.'

Emma opened her eyes and looked up at him, but the clenching pain in her stomach came again, making her catch her breath with its ferocity.

'The baby!' Uncle Dick exclaimed. 'I think it's the bairn.'

'It can't be,' Vera said sullenly. 'She's only wanting sympathy.'

Emma screwed her eyes tightly and chewed her lower lip, trying to stifle her moan at the recurring pain. Dick was looking down into her pale face. He saw the sweat beading her brow.

'The fall has brought on the baby. Vera, go and fetch Mistress Donnelly. She'll know what to do. Milly, find some towels and put the kettle on to boil.'

'Who do you think you are, ordering everybody about?' Vera protested.

'Get Mrs Donnelly now!' Dick shouted. 'If anything happens to Emma or the bairn, you will be to blame. Go on!'

Several hours later, a kindly woman bent over Emma and placed a tiny, dark-haired bundle in her arms. Emma felt the pain had gone on for an eternity. She couldn't believe it had stopped. It was true her back and hips were badly bruised from the fall but as she gazed down at the snuffling little bundle in her arms, a tender smile lit her face.

'My baby?' she whispered.

'Yes, my lamb. You have a wee boy. A pair of broad shoulders he has on him. He may be a bit small but there's nothing wrong with his lungs, is there, Doctor?'

Emma looked past her, and saw a man with brown side-burns and moustache and sparkling grey eyes.

'Nothing wrong at all that a good supply of milk willna cure and that will come in a day or so. You were a brave young woman, but let that be a lesson to you, no more climbing steps into lofts in your condition.'

Emma cradled her baby in her arms and her young heart swelled with love, until she remembered Aunt Vera's words somewhere in the mists of her pain.

'You willna let them take him away, will you? My father was coming to take me home before he was born.'

The doctor looked at Mrs Donnelly with

raised eyebrows, his eyes questioning.

'I think that was the plan originally but Dick told me his brother and his family have changed their minds.' Mrs Donnelly drew the doctor to one side of the room. 'Vera would have him away to the nuns immediately if she had her way. I think we should wait until her father comes to take her home. Let him make the decision.'

'It will be at least two weeks before she's up and fit to travel,' the doctor frowned, 'but the baby will benefit from his mother's milk whatever happens. He is obviously a bit before his time so he may turn yellow.'

'I think you should ask Mrs Mackie, the midwife, to check on them every day until the girl regains her strength. I will pay her,' she added. 'Dick is one of the best workers we've ever had but his wife is a harridan. She has no idea of cleanliness. We don't want the girl getting an infection. Young Milly has more sense but she's still at school.'

'Very well.' He moved back to the bed. 'Don't worry, Emma. I shall tell your aunt on no account is she to take your baby away. That decision will be up to your father when he comes to take you home.'

'Thank you, Doctor,' Emma said in a tremulous whisper. 'Thank you b-both for saving m-my baby.'

When they had gone, she noticed the little room seemed strangely empty, then she noticed Uncle Dick must have removed the boys' mattress up to the loft. In the dim light of the Kelly lamp she saw the clock. It was two in the morning. No wonder it was dark and the house so silent.

Several times in the next two weeks, Mrs Donnelly sent up a pot of chicken broth with Dick.

'She says it's the best thing for getting your strength back, lassie, so you're to eat it all.'

It was delicious but she didn't get the chance to eat more than one small bowl each time he brought up a pot. Aunt Vera saw to that. She grumbled constantly, and Emma was grateful for the visits and ministrations of the motherly midwife who came each day to make sure the baby was feeding and that she was recovering. She had been dismayed when she first saw the bruises which had turned Emma's back and hip black and blue and yellow, but Emma didn't complain. The bruises would heal and she was young and strong; she had her baby son and she felt better each day. She had written to tell her parents of the baby's birth and when she would be ready to travel home, and she couldn't wait for that day to come in spite of Uncle Dick's kindness and the way the children wanted to spend all their free time with her and the baby.

* * *

When the baby was nearly two weeks old and Emma was getting up each day, in spite of the midwife's advice that she should rest, Uncle Dick asked her if she could manage a walk into the village to register the birth.

'The blacksmith is the local registrar. I'll come with you, but it needs to be done here and your father will be coming for you on Saturday.'

'The station is twice as far as the village so it will be good for me to get into practice,' Emma said.

'Ye willna need to walk to the station, lassie. Mrs Donnelly has offered me a loan o' her pony and trap to drive you and your pa.'

'How kind she has been,' Emma said in surprise. 'How can I ever repay her? She paid the midwife to attend to me too.'

'Aye, she's a true Christian. She's had her own troubles but it hasna made her bitter. Her husband died when her two bairns were still at school. She kept on the farm for her laddie. He'll make a good farmer one day.'

Emma refused to leave her baby behind with Vera while she went to the village. She still had a fear that her aunt might find a way of taking him away from her. She felt she would die if anything happened to him now. Uncle Dick seemed to understand and he even offered to carry him.

'Have you thought of a name?' he asked.

'Yes. I intend to call him James Albert, but I expect he'll be Jamie.' She didn't explain that he would be called after his grandfathers or that she had another name to add if she could see the blacksmith privately. As it happened there were two men already talking at the forge, and Dick took the baby from her and stood talking to them while the blacksmith showed her through to the cosy parlour, where his wife was stirring a pot of broth over the fire. It was usual for the fathers to come to register the births of their offspring but George Irving knew all about this young niece of Dick's so he didn't ask any unnecessary questions; he simply wrote 'father unknown.' He looked up at her.

'Have you given the laddie a name?'

'Yes. James Albert Sinclair.'

'And your surname is Greig, the same as your uncle?'

'That's right.' Emma nodded. The entry in the book was blotted carefully and then Emma was given a birth certificate. She was happy to know her baby was now an official person with a name of his own. Since his birth she had given little thought to the man who had sired him, or even to Maggie. Consequently it was a surprise, and a welcome relief, when she and her father arrived at the little station three miles from their village of Locheagle, and found Maggie waiting for them with the Bonnybrae pony and trap.

There was a sheen of tears in Maggie's fine eyes as she gazed down at the tightly swathed bundle in Emma's arms.

'He's a beautiful baby, Emma,' she said softly. 'His dark hair is like yours.'

'The midwife said he would lose it and I think it is coming out already.'

'I see him smacking his wee lips and clenching his tiny fists. I expect he's ready for a feed so the sooner we get you home the better,' Maggie said, smiling as she bundled them into the trap.

All the way home, Albert Greig had been unusually quiet and his silence made Emma nervous but he had not mentioned taking her baby away from her or sending him to the nuns.

'We're very grateful to ye, Miss Maggie, for meeting Emma and the bairn with the trap,' he said formally when they arrived back at the house. 'Will you come in and take a cup of tea with us?'

'No, thank you, Mr Greig, not today,' Maggie smiled. 'I suspect there will be enough excitement when Emma's mother sees her first grandchild.'

'Aye, there'll be that all right,' he said gruffly, 'and then the gossip will start,' he added bitterly. 'I hope Eliza can cope with that.'

'I know,' Maggie said seriously, 'but I'm sure everything will turn out well in the end and all will be forgiven. I pray to God it will be so anyway.'

Bert Greig looked at her curiously, wondering why it should be any of her concern, but maybe she was just a good woman with a kind heart. As she helped Emma down from the trap, Maggie held the baby for the first time and her gaze was tender as she looked into his wondering eyes.

'I have a letter for you, Emma,' she said quietly. 'It is from William. I hope you will reply as soon as you can. It came a week ago. He does not know yet that he has a son.'

'Oh thank you, Miss Maggie. Is your brother not back frae Yorkshire yet then?' she asked in surprise, tucking the letter into the pocket of her skirt to read later.

'Oh no. He will not be coming back to

Bonnybrae. Maybe I did not make that clear in my last letter to you. I'm sorry. I think William's letter will explain everything.'

'I see. Thank you, Miss Maggie,' Emma said, but she felt as though a cloud had blocked out her sunshine. Had William Sinclair changed his mind and run away from her and her baby? Maggie had made no further mention of taking her back to work at Bonnybrae, either. She chewed her lower lip as she watched the pony and trap drive away, and the tears sprang to her eyes as they seemed to do far too easily since the baby was born. Her clasp on Jamie had tightened instinctively, and he began to struggle and whimper as she stepped into the familiar kitchen that was home.

Eliza immediately reached for the baby, crooning softly, smiling down at him, and Bert knew he had done the right thing in letting Emma keep him. It would have broken her heart to part with him and he could see already that Eliza would love the bairn. That would help her face the scandal mongers, although he knew of old how cruel village gossip could be. He prayed the wee fellow would not suffer too badly. He would have to learn to be tough when he went to school.

'Our first grand bairn, Bert,' Eliza said, softly holding the baby towards him, inviting him to take a better look.

'Aye, he seems a fine babe considering he came a bit early.' He looked into his wife's pleading eyes and smiled. 'We must be thankful that he's right and straight, eh, Lizzie?' Watching them, Emma gave a sigh of relief.

'I think he's ready for his feed,' she said.

'Aye, he will be, the wee soul. Ye've done more than your grandmother already, ma wee man, ye've travelled on the train and that's something I havena done yet.' She handed Jamie to Emma. 'I'll make some tea. I expect you're ready for it and your brothers will soon be home frae the football.'

Later that evening, all four of her menfolk went together to the Crown and Thistle. Usually Davy and Richard went courting on a Saturday night, or to a dance in one of the surrounding villages, but tonight it was as though they were joining forces in mutual support. Somebody would have seen Emma arriving home with the baby. She would be a topic for gossip in the bar until something else happened for folks to talk about.

Eliza seated herself beside the fire and looked across at Emma's bowed head as she fed wee Jamie. She wondered why she had named him James, but at least she had given him her father's name as well.

'Well, Emma, was Vera good to ye?' she asked. Emma compressed her lips and didn't reply immediately.

'Uncle Dick was kind, and Mrs Donnelly came when the baby was born and she paid for the midwife to come every morning for ten days and she sent chicken soup for me. I d-don't think Aunt Vera was very pleased at her making arrangements.'

'Then we ought to repay her,' Eliza said anxiously.

'Uncle Dick says we're not to worry because he'll repay her with his work.'

'Aye, he's a decent fellow, Dick. I dinna ken how he got a wife like Vera. I was surprised when Maggie Sinclair called again to hear how you were, and when I told her about the baby and that you were coming home, she offered to meet you with the pony and trap. That was real decent of her, I thought. Has she ever mentioned anything about ye going back to work at Bonnybrae?'

'No, no, she didn't. I almost forgot in all the excitement of being home again. She gave me a letter.' She handed the sleepy baby to her mother to rub his back in case he had any wind while she carefully slit open the envelope. It had obviously been folded inside one to Maggie.

She gasped aloud and the colour drained

from her face as she read William's letter.

'What's wrong, lassie?' Eliza asked in concern. 'You look as though you've seen a ghost. Is it bad news?'

'I . . . he . . . William Sinclair . . . He wants to make me his wife.'

'His wife? William Sinclair? He wants to marry his mother's maid?' Eliza stared at her. Then she took a deep breath. She wished Bert had been at home. 'Is he the father of this wee fellow, Emma? Did he come to your room at nights while you were a maid in his mother's house?' she asked angrily.

'No! No, he never. It was only one night because the mist came down and we were lost on the hill and we had to stay out all night. He kept me warm and . . . and . . . '

'And he's the father 'o your bairn? I suppose he must be, if he's asking you to be his wife . . . '

'B-but Mother, you dinna understand. Mr and Mrs Sinclair sent him away frae Bonnybrae. He's gone to live in Yorkshire. I-I'd have to live there if I was his wife.'

'Yorkshire? What possessed him to go so far away?'

'He must have told them — told them everything. I — I think they must have sent him away in disgrace too.' She shuddered. 'Mrs Sinclair would be very angry with him, I suppose, if he told them. I mean when they realized.'

'Realized he was the father of your bairn?' Eliza's lips tightened. 'So he's been banished frae his own home?'

'He-he says he canna send for me yet. He is sleeping in a loft with two other single men and working on an estate. He says he'll get a cottage as soon as he can b-but he hopes to rent a small farm someday.'

'At least it sounds as though he means to do the right thing by ye then, Emma,' Eliza said with relief.

'B-but Ma, ye dinna understand!' Emma wailed. 'I — I c-canna go to live in Yorkshire! It's miles and miles away.' She began to sob. 'It was bad enough going to stay with Aunt Vera. I didn't know anybody or where I was. I was a prisoner there. I don't want to go away. I willna go! I willna . . . ' She almost snatched the baby from her mother's arms as she ran to her bedroom, leaving the letter to flutter to the floor.

9

The Greig men returned earlier than usual for a Saturday evening. The atmosphere in the Crown and Thistle had been strained, and they all knew the rest of the men were waiting for them to leave so they could discuss the latest gossip. Bert Greig was a proud man and he thought he had brought his family up to be decent, God-fearing citizens but the blow Emma had dealt his family had shaken him more than he cared to admit. Yet in his heart he knew he couldn't have left the baby in the care of strangers, whatever the wagging tongues might say. The wee laddie would make a place for himself.

He hung his cap on the nail in the tiny lobby and went into the living room to find his wife staring into the embers of the fire with a sheet of paper in her hand. The boys followed their father in and seated themselves round the table.

'Any tea going, Ma?' Joe asked, striving to lighten the mood.

'Aye, I'll shove the kettle on,' she said absently.

'What's wrong, Ma?' Richard asked. 'You

look . . . sort of strange.'

'I know who the father o' Emma's bairn is.'

'Who is he?' they demanded almost in unison.

'It's William Sinclair . . . '

'William Sinclair! Why, the scoundrel! I-I'll kill him!' Joe declared.

'You'd need to travel a while first,' his mother said dryly. 'He's gone to live in Yorkshire.'

'Running away? By the devil, he can't hide frae us. We'll find him.'

'I think you'd better read the letter he's sent to Emma first,' Eliza said wearily. 'I think the Sinclairs have sent him away, the same as we sent Emma. Pride can be a sin. And another thing, Vera must have treated Emma badly. She doesna want to leave here, or go away anywhere, except maybe back to work at Bonnybrae. She doesn't want to go all the way to Yorkshire.'

'He's asking her to join him?' Davy asked.

'Aye, as his wife.'

'I'd say the lad had no more warning than we did about what was going on,' his father said with a frown, looking up from the sheet of paper, neatly covered on both sides. He handed it to Richard. 'He doesna sound a bad fellow. I can't understand why Emma didn't tell him. Why didn't she tell us earlier?'

'Because she didna know herself,' Eliza said. 'She was blooming and in the best of health. We have never talked about things. I blame myself. She thought a woman didn't have babies until she had a husband.'

'That's the way it's supposed to be,' Bert said gruffly.

'Emma might have been ignorant about such things but William Sinclair would know well enough what he was doing, taking advantage of a young innocent maid, and under his parents' roof,' Richard said grimly.

'Emma says it was only one night. The two of them got lost on the hill when the mist came down. If she'd been sick in the mornings, or unable to do her work, he might have guessed.'

'At least he's offering to marry her now,' Davy said pacifically, 'and he intends to make a home for her and his bairn.'

'Aye, Davy is right,' Bert said firmly. 'Eliza, you'll have to make Emma see sense. It's only right she should go to him. They both owe it to the bairn to give him a father and a home. He says he has not got a place for them yet so she'll have time to get used to the idea. She'll come round so long as you don't encourage her to think she can stay here for ever.'

'I know that, Bert,' Eliza said wearily. 'I've thought o' nothing else since I read the letter.

Emma ran off to bed sobbing her heart out. I know it's right for her to go, but it grieves me sorely. My only lassie and going so far away. I might never see her again if she goes to live in Yorkshire.'

'Of course you will, Ma,' Richard said soothingly. 'There'll soon be trains the length and breadth o' the country.'

'But think of the cost!' his mother protested.

'Then you'll have good reason to put a bit extra in your tea caddy to pay the fare when the time comes,' he chivvied her with a smile.

'Look at it this way, Ma,' Davy intervened, 'William Sinclair is aware of what he's done and he's willing to make amends as far as he can. It's changed his life as well as Emma's, but he'll make an honest woman of her. What he needs to know is whether she's willing to marry him and live down there. So you'll need to persuade Emmie to write without delay. He needs to know what she intends to do before he makes plans. It doesn't sound as though he knows he has a son by the way he writes.'

* * *

Things were not moving as fast as William had hoped. In April it had seemed an age until September, but tenants usually gave notice when they intended to give up a lease and there had been no word of any tenants giving notice to quit from Mr Frame, or from Drew. He was beginning to despair of getting a farm even by Michaelmas. The man he had been replacing at the Mains Farm had returned to his work with the cattle but Fred Black, the foreman, had asked him to stay on as a general worker to help with sheep shearing, then the hay and harvest. Both he and the land agent seemed impressed with the progress he had made with the breaking in of the geldings, and he was secretly delighted with the Clydesdale filly they had promised him.

He knew they had a poor opinion of her because she was so small in comparison to the three Shire geldings, but he was convinced her lack of size was more due to the poor start she'd had, rather than inherited. He was almost certain she would breed well with the right choice of stallion, but even if she didn't, horses were essential to every farm and more valuable to him than a few extra guineas in wages, which is what he would have got anywhere else.

As a general worker, he earned fifteen shillings and six-pence a week after the half-crown a week deduction for his food. He paid sixpence a week to one of the maids to do his washing. He hated the idea of dirty clothes and earned some ribbing from the two men who shared the loft with him. He had learned from the married workers who occupied estate houses that a deduction of eight pounds a year was taken from their wages for the occupation of a house, plus other deductions for potatoes, milk and coal so he knew this is what he could expect if he took a job with a house when Emma came to join him. He also knew there would be little money left at the end of a week by the time he, his wife and child were fed and clothed. When he considered that he could save most of his fifteen shillings in his present state, it made his sojourn in the loft more bearable.

Subconsciously he already considered himself as a man with responsibilities so he had little desire to spend his hard-earned money by accompanying the other single men to the pub on Saturday evenings. The only socializing he did was to visit Drew and Annie, and go with them to church and share their Sunday dinner.

'I find the kirk service even more strict and formal than the one back home,' he remarked to Drew after attending his first service.

'Aye, but you get used to it. It's all set out in the book of Common Prayer. You just have to follow the order and join in with everybody else.'

'Good Lord! Is it like that every Sunday?'

His cousin's mouth twitched, knowing what stern Presbyterians William's parents were.

'I doubt Aunt Mary would approve of you blaspheming, whatever she thought of the English Church. There's worse to come, though.' His eyes glinted. 'They wouldn't accept Annie and me as members of the Church of England although we had both been joined as members of the Presbyterian Kirk back home since we were teenagers.'

'Why ever not?'

'They don't accept our religious ceremonies.'

'But surely a promise to God is the same wherever you make it,' William said incredulously.

'It seems not. If we wanted the bairns christened, we had to go to confirmation classes and make our vows all over again before the bishop. A very solemn ceremony it is. The young girls wear white.'

'Are ye telling me I'll need to do the same? And Emma? Her parents are as strict about the kirk as mine are.'

'Aye, well, if ye want to go to church it's what ye'll both have to do. There's some things we have to accept whether we agree with them or not.'

'I see,' William said. If he wanted to prosper in his new surroundings, he didn't think he could do it without God's blessing and his Bible, even though he had often railed against the strictures of his parents.

Two things happened which concentrated all William's thoughts on the future. He was not expecting a reply from Maggie so soon, so it was a shock when he opened it and discovered Emma had given birth to a son. The news made it more urgent that he should be able to offer her a home and make an honest woman of her. He was still awaiting her reply to his proposal and he felt a frisson of anxiety. Supposing she didn't want to marry him and move so far away?

The second surprise was when Drew rode over to see him one evening a fortnight later. It was mid-June and he had been mowing hay all day. He wanted to finish the field before dark. Cook had sent him out with a can of tea and thick slices of fried bacon, sandwiched between wedges of newly-baked bread. He had stopped to eat it in the shade of the tall thorn hedge when Drew cantered along the side of the field and sprang from his horse.

'Fred Black said I'd find you here.'

'You havena brought bad news, have you?'

William asked, preparing to get to his feet and nearly upsetting his precious mug of tea. Rivulets of sweat were running down his cheeks, making paler streaks in the dust. He rubbed it out of his eyes with the back of his hand.

'No, why should there be bad news?' Drew said. 'I was at the blacksmith with one o' the horses this afternoon and Tom Wright thought you might be interested in a farm to let, though we hope you'll not want it, or at least Annie does.'

'That's a strange thing to say,' William said. 'Well, spit it out!'

'Och, ye're the image o' Uncle James. He used to get impatient,' Drew laughed. 'It's not the best of places according to Tom, so we think you should wait for something better, that's all, and Annie would like you nearer to us. It's six miles the other side of Wilmore village and it's to let at Michaelmas. The tenant has gone bankrupt so he's giving up the lease.' Drew's expression was serious now. 'Annie and me — well, we hope you'll not rush into it, but we know how keen you are to rent a farm, rather than go on working for a wage, so she said it was only fair to tell you.'

'I should think so. How do I make arrangements to see it? You'll go with me to walk over the land, give me your opinion?'

'Of course I will if you want me there, but if you could be patient there's bound to be better farms come up, maybe even on this estate.'

'What's wrong with it?'

'It's called Moorend Farm. Tom's cousin is blacksmith in the village there. He says the farm is well-named. It's the last farm in the village before the moors. The gypsies often camp on the common land.'

'They wouldna bother me.'

'It's about ninety acres. Tom's cousin, Joe Wright, reckons the present tenant has only farmed the paddocks next to the house for the last five years or more. He's an old man. He's lost heart since his wife died a year ago. He's going to live with his widowed sister over Doncaster way.'

'Sounds as though it will take a bit of getting back into cultivation but I can't afford to miss an opportunity, Drew. I need to look at anything that's available. I've had a letter from Maggie. Emmie has had a baby boy. It's time I brought her down here.'

'Ah, ye're a father! Congratulations! Ye've got a son and heir, eh,' Drew teased. 'Well that does make a difference.' He clapped him on the back. William didn't mention that he had not heard from Emma. 'There'll be no holding ye back now,' Drew chuckled, then he sobered. 'But don't rush to take the first farm that's available and lose all your money.'

'I hope I shall have more sense than that.'

'How about showing me the Clydesdale filly you're to get? I heard Mr Frame is well pleased with the geldings you've handled. He would keep you in this area if he could. I think you should bide your time.'

'I want to finish mowing this field before dark. Fred Black brought me a change of horses specially. I might ride the filly over to your place on Sunday, if that's all right?'

'Aye, of course it is. She can graze with our horses until you're ready for her. I might find her a bit of light work to keep her fettled.'

⋆ ⋆ ⋆

Emma couldn't believe what a relief it was to be back home, sleeping in her own clean bed without Milly's gangly legs pummelling her in the back, or wrapping around her waist. The whole house smelled fresh and clean after Aunt Vera's, and her mother's cooking tasted like manna from heaven. The tastiest meal she'd had was Mrs Donnelly's soup, except when she had done the cooking herself.

Bit by bit, with a careful question or two, Eliza learned the sort of existence her bairn had had and she bitterly regretted sending her away. She hadn't the heart to insist Emma must write to William Sinclair and tell him she wanted to marry him and live in Yorkshire. Each night when the house was quiet, Eliza would tell Bert another tale about the misery of living with Vera.

'I ken what Vera's like and I dinna ken how Dick has put up with her, but Eliza, you have to tell Emma she must reply to William's letter.'

At the end of the second week, Bert could see his wife was growing more and more fond of her grandson, as they all were, but he had to harden his heart and speak out. He saw Emma carrying a basket of clothes to hang on the line and followed her into the garden. He couldn't afford to choose his words.

'Emma, lass, have ye replied to William Sinclair's letter yet?'

'N-no, Da. I — I dinna want to go away again.'

'And who do you think will feed and clothe you and the bairn?'

'I-I'll find work.'

'Now listen to me, Emma.' Bert had to look away from his daughter's pleading eyes and harden his heart. 'Your mother and me are not going to be here for ever and you'll find it hard to get a decent job when you have a bairn to look after. Either you marry

William Sinclair and do your best to be a good wife to him, or I shall take your bairn to the orphanage. Maybe Vera was right. Maybe we should have done that straightaway.'

'No! No, Da,' Emma shrieked, 'y-you couldna be so cruel.'

'I dinna want to be cruel. A bairn is better with his ain mother and his ain father. William Sinclair comes frae a decent family. I ken he shouldna have taken advantage, but it takes two. Ye're as much to blame as he is. He's paying a high price too, away frae his family. At least he's decent enough to offer you his name, and he's willing to make a home for you and wee Jamie. You're luckier than many a young maid in your situation. You might have ended up in the workhouse, or on the streets.'

'Dinna say that, Da!' Emma pleaded.

'Well, it's up to you to give your bairn a home and a father and a decent upbringing. Write a letter to William Sinclair.'

When her sons had gone to the Saturday football match and Bert was working at his vegetables in the garden, Eliza sat down with the baby on her lap and soothed him to sleep while Emma finished washing the dishes and putting them away. Every now and then, Eliza heard her give a sniff or a stifled little sob and her heart ached for her only daughter, but she knew Bert was right, even if he had been a bit blunt.

'Come and sit down for a wee while, Emma, if you're finished.'

Emma sat on the other side of the fire and picked up her knitting automatically. She was seldom idle, Eliza realized, and she had become a good cook under Maggie Sinclair's guidance.

'You know it wouldn't be the same as living with Vera if you marry William Sinclair, Emmie. You would be mistress in your own home.'

'You don't know that. He has not got a house yet.'

'No, but he is looking for one. He says in his letter he will send for you as soon as he can give you a home. All he wants right now is to know whether you will marry him and live with him in Yorkshire. Surely he deserves a reply to his letter? Many men in his position would have gone away and forgotten about you and your bairn. He didn't need to admit it was his in fact. You don't realize how lucky you are to have this chance to give your baby a name and a father.'

'Y-you're as b-bad as D-Da.' Emma stifled a sob. She couldn't understand why she felt so low and tired and out of spirits. All the time she had been expecting Jamie she had felt an inner glow, a feeling of optimism. Even Aunt Vera had never managed to quench her secret joy. If she hadn't felt so good, she might have realized earlier that she was having a baby, or so Maggie and her mother had said. She looked across the hearth and saw her mother watching her with troubled eyes.

'Emmie? D-did William, did he force himself on you that night on the Torr?'

'Oh no,' Emmie said, remembering. 'He cuddled me between him and the dog to keep me warm. I felt safe. Then . . . ' She broke off, colour staining her cheeks, as she remembered her night with William. He had shown her how good it could be between a man and a woman.

'So he was not cruel to you, Emmie?'

'Oh no, no, he's not a cruel man, Mother,' Emmie assured her quickly. 'Though he does lose his temper sometimes.'

'All men lose their temper sometimes, but you're not frightened of him? That's not why you don't want to marry him, Emma?'

'I was a bit frightened o' Mr Sinclair sometimes but I was never frightened of William.'

'I've heard he is like his father. I believe James Sinclair can be very impatient, but your father reckons he was always fair.'

'I suppose William is like him.' Emma nodded.

'Then you must be honest, Emmie. At least tell him about his son.'

Emma's eyes brightened as she looked at her baby, sound asleep in his grandmother's arms. He was beginning to lose the mop of dark hair and she thought the fine hair beneath would be reddish-brown like William's.

'All right,' she said. 'I'll tell him all about Jamie.' She looked up at her mother and smiled. Eliza heaved a sigh of relief. Any sort of communication was a start.

* * *

William opened Emma's letter eagerly, expecting her to tell him they could be married. She was a neat writer and she described the baby in detail, but she didn't say she would be his wife, or even mention marriage. He felt frustrated and more disappointed than he had thought possible. He longed for Emmie to join him, to talk together about the places and people they both knew. More than that, he wanted to feel her in his arms again, see the slumberous expression in her big blue-green eyes and feel her arms, soft and warm. He wanted to see her cheery smile and bright eyes. He needed her. He wanted to see the baby too — his son, the cause of his and Emma's troubles.

10

Drew arranged that he and William would catch the train to Silverbeck where Mr Rowbottom, the agent for Moorend Farm, would meet them and drive them to the farm. William was buoyed up with anticipation in spite of Drew's warnings about the farm's neglected state. His heart sank when they drove into the untidiest, most overgrown, farm yard he had ever seen.

'Good God, what a mess!' he exclaimed involuntarily, seeing a hen coop buried in weeds with grass growing through the wire netting, an upturned cart without a wheel and various other implements which looked as though they had been there for ever.

'Aye,' Mr Rowbottom sighed heavily, 'I have to admit it's a disgrace to the estate, though it only takes a couple of years for the weeds to take over. Old Ed should have given up when his wife died. Lord Hanley has been patient because the Dixon family have been tenants for generations but Ed has no family. He needed somebody to make his mind up for him. Now we have. He seems content to live with his sister now she's a widow.'

'Does he intend to have a sale?' Drew asked. 'It doesn't look as though there will be much to tempt folk.'

'There's nothing worth buying except his two milk cows and a decent mare. He has a gelding but I don't think he's paid for.' William was silent, his heart heavy. He had lived a dream since Drew mentioned the tenancy but this was worse than anything he could have imagined. What would be the point of putting all his energy into reclaiming a place like this if Emmie didn't want to marry him?

'I'll take you round the land and show you the boundaries, now that you're here,' Rowbottom said. 'The four fields around the farm yard are in fairly good shape but Ed hasn't enough stock to graze them now.'

'These three would yield a crop of hay if we got a good spell of weather,' Drew reflected. 'I wish they'd been nearer to me. We can always use extra hay.'

'The rest of the fields are down either side of the lane as far as the Common. Moorend has free grazing rights on the Common if the tenant has stock to graze it. These fields furthest from the farm have not been farmed for a good few years now. If it had been up to me, I'd have been asking Ed Dixon to give up the tenancy before his wife died.'

'I expect the house will be in a mess too then?' Drew asked.

'He only uses the kitchen. He reckons it's warmer sleeping by the fire. He hasn't changed a single thing since Doris died. He says we can put a match to it all once he's gone. The only thing that upsets him is leaving his two cows and his mare but he knows he can't take them with him.'

'Ye're very quiet, Will,' Drew said, 'but I did try to warn you Tom Wright's cousin said things were in a bad state.'

'I know, but I didn't think they could be this bad. Anyway, we may as well see what else there is now we've come.' William's mind was racing but he was not going to mention anything good or positive in front of the agent. He was not afraid of hard work and if it was possible to strike a good deal, the place might have possibilities eventually. If only he knew whether Emmie would marry him.

'If the tenancy doesn't begin until September things will be even worse by then,' he muttered.

Drew's comment about the hay had made him think it might have been possible to mow three of the fields and sell most of the hay to bring in some cash. The agent was shaking his head at Drew. He had misinterpreted William's morose expression and knitted brows.

'Your young relative is not impressed at all, Mr Kerr, but I can't blame him. The tenancies don't change until Michaelmas but Ed has not paid any rent for eighteen months. The sooner someone takes it on the better pleased we shall all be now he's made up his mind to go. As I said, the only thing which troubles him is sending his animals away. Whoever takes it on could move in as soon as Ed moves out of the house.'

'Would they pay rent? Or wait until the end of September?' Drew asked. William gave a harsh laugh.

'From what we've seen so far, I shouldn't think any tenant would be ready to pay rent until a year come September.' Rowbottom raised his eyebrows at William.

'At least it's an experience,' Drew said resignedly. 'Show us the rest of the fields now we're here.' They walked over the fields on one side of the lane. 'We'll see the other side on the way back.'

At the edge of the Common, there were several gypsy caravans and about half a dozen piebald horses tethered. Some half-naked children chased each other with glee round one of the larger caravans and several dogs ran around or lay sleeping. An elderly woman came towards them, offering to tell their fortune if they crossed her palm with silver but when she recognized Mr Rowbottom, she backed quickly away.

'I beg pardon, good sir,' she said. 'We were not expecting to see you.'

'It's not you or your men I'm after today, Rosa, but if I catch you poaching — '

'No, no, good sir, you know we would never be doing such a thing and you are so good to us. Can I sell the handsome young gent some clothes pegs to take home to his wife?' she wheedled.

'Not today, thank you,' William said politely.

'Butter wouldn't melt in her mouth,' Rowbottom muttered as they turned away from the boundary and made their way back along the lane.

'It looks as though the landlord will need to erect a new boundary fence,' William remarked.

'Oh, so ye are taking notice then, Will?' Drew chuckled.

'I couldn't miss the neglect if I was half asleep,' William said with some asperity. 'I haven't seen a decent fence anywhere on the farm, but I imagine the landlord is responsible for the boundaries.'

'Aye, he is, but there's been no point while we had a tenant who didn't farm the far fields,' Rowbottom said a little huffily.

'Some of the neighbouring farms don't look too bad,' Drew remarked.

'Oh, the land is pretty good on this part of the estate, that's why it has grieved me to see it so neglected. I'm sorry for old Ed but he needed to face facts. Most of our tenants are hardworking farmers.'

When they got back to the farm yard, Ed Dixon was turning his two shorthorn cows out to the nearest paddock. A light roan calf followed one of them on wobbly legs, clearly wanting to suckle.

'I didn't know you'd put your cows back in calf, Ed.'

'She done it herself, Mr Rowbottom. I 'spect she went to see Tindal's bull. Tis a fine calf though. Born last night. I 'spect you'll be wanting to see the house?'

The agent looked at Drew and William, thinking there was no use looking at the house since they were not interested in renting the farm.

'I'd like a look at the cowshed and dairy,' William said, 'and we ought to get some idea of what the house is like.'

Rowbottom brightened. Maybe the young Scotsman was more interested than he'd let on so far and if he was as good as Walter Frame said, he could be the tenant they needed. He thought it might give a better first impression if they went in through the front door but it took Ed Dixon a while to find the key and turn the rusty lock to let them in.

'It hasn't been opened since the wife's funeral,' Ed muttered. 'I thought I'd be next leaving this way.' He pushed open a door on either side of the passage but they didn't see much because the curtains were drawn across the windows, though they both looked big square rooms.

'The house may be filthy and I see there's cobwebs everywhere,' Rowbottom added quietly, brushing one away from his face, 'but the building is sound enough and I don't think it's damp. We try to keep the dwellings and buildings in good order. There's four bedrooms and another two up the back stairs where the single men or maids sleep. They're over the wash house.' He led the way into a large kitchen cluttered with a settee as well as a bed, plus the usual dresser, table and chairs. A fire smouldered in the grate but the range didn't look as though it had ever seen polish. William shuddered, imagining what his mother would have said if she saw it.

'The other doors lead to the pantry, a cellar, and a store room,' Rowbottom said, leading the way through the kitchen and down four steps into a large room.

It appeared to serve both as a wash-house and a dairy, judging by the copper boiler, washtub and wooden mangle at the near end and a row of unused milking buckets and milk churns at the other. A short passage led to a byre with stalls for eight cows in a single row.

'Dairy maids wouldn't need to get wet carrying the milk to the dairy with this arrangement,' Drew mused. 'It's a good idea.'

'This part of the farm yard is in good condition, and so are the cart sheds,' Rowbottom said. 'Lord Hanley insists on maintaining the roofs and buildings. So, gentlemen, I don't think there's much more I can show you. I see you're not very interested in renting it, Mr Sinclair, but if you do consider it, I think Lord Hanley might allow an extra six months' rent free until next spring, so long as the tenant agrees to get the place back into order.' William lowered his eyes so the agent wouldn't see his interest.

'I would need to write to my — my wife, and describe the conditions.'

'If you tell the truth it would put any woman off,' Drew said.

'I would need her cooperation before I could even consider taking a place in this state. I wouldn't ask her to come under false pretences.'

'I suppose you know best,' Drew said slowly. 'She will certainly be busy with a young baby.'

'I know that. There's a hell of a lot of work to do in the house and she would have a single man to feed and wash for if I could get one.'

'I wish we could offer something better, Mr Sinclair, but you know where to contact me if you want to discuss anything. I'd welcome a decent tenant and I'd do my best to draw up a satisfactory lease. Now, I'm sure you'd like a lift back to the station?'

'No, but thanks anyway,' Drew said. 'Our blacksmith at Wilmore is a cousin of the man here, Joe Wright. We have a parcel to deliver before we catch the train back.'

'I see. So that's how you heard that Moorend was to let?'

'Yes, he knew I was keeping my ears open for a farm to let for cousin William so he passed on the news. Blacksmiths hear all the gossip.'

'They do indeed but Joe Wright is a decent man. He'll know if there are any maids or single men looking for work, Mr Sinclair.'

Drew had guessed that delivering the parcel of fresh strawberries and a jar of newly made raspberry jam was Tom Wright's excuse to get them to call on his cousin, but William welcomed the opportunity to hear more about the surrounding land and farmers. Mrs Wright also provided them with cups of tea, a huge sandwich of fresh bread filled with slices of home-cured ham, a wedge of fruit cake, as well as apple pie and cheese.

'An apple pie without the cheese is like a kiss without a squeeze,' she chuckled, passing William a generous portion. 'That's what we say in Yorkshire and you'll be needing your bellies full if you're to walk back to the station and then the journey home.'

'So what did you make of Moorend Farm then?' her husband asked as he joined them at the table with a plate of food even bigger than theirs.

'I warned my cousin here,' Drew said with a grin, 'but it's even worse than we expected. Am I right, William?'

'It will certainly need a lot of work. I wouldn't give it a second thought if there was anything else likely to come vacant. As it is, I can't ask Emma to come without warning her how bad things are. The house seemed full of stuff as it was left by his wife. It didn't look as though it had been cleaned for years. Only the two milk cows and a nice-looking mare seemed well cared for.'

'Aye, you'll be right there, lad. The mare would be worth buying if you do take on the tenancy. I expect you prefer Ayrshire cows instead of Shorthorns, you being a Scotsman.'

'I would, but I would take over the two he had. They looked healthy and seemed to have plenty of milk. Emma is good with animals and milking, and she can churn the butter as well as any woman.'

'In that case, lad, I agree you need to tell her how things are. Don't condemn poor old Ed, though. Doris used to have some nice furniture and things and she was a good wife before she fell ill. There'll be lots of good stuff left if your wife can sew.'

'Oh yes, Emmie can sew well. Even my mother admitted that.' Mrs Wright guessed from his tone there was a bit of friction somewhere.

'Moorend Farm was not always like it is now,' she said. 'It was as good as any other farm round these parts when Ed Dixon and his wife were younger. Let us know what you and your wife decide. We have a niece leaving school in a month's time. She has everything to learn about housekeeping, but she loves kiddies and I hear you have a baby boy?'

'Yes, we do. Emmie might be glad of someone to help with the baby.'

'Aye, she'll need a maid if she's to tackle that place as well as milk the two cows and make butter,' Drew declared. 'I saw some hens wandering around. I expect she'll want some of them so she can sell the eggs. Most of the farmers' wives do that. Now, I think it's time we were leaving if we're to catch the next train.' They both thanked the Wrights warmly for their meal, promising to let them know of any developments regarding Moorend.

That evening William sat down and wrote Emmie a longer letter than he had ever envisaged writing to anyone. He didn't hide the fact that the house was filthy and neglected, or that they would have a lot of years of hard work in front of them to get the land back into a good state.

If we do take on the tenancy, we should be working for ourselves instead of putting money in the pockets of a boss, and we wouldn't be living in a tied cottage. Even if my parents had let us stay at Bonnybrae, a cottage is the best we would have got from them.

If you can face a lot of hard work I think we shall do well together. I haven't forgotten how wonderful it felt to hold you in my arms, Emmie, or how good we made each other feel. I really want you beside me and I shall not take the tenancy unless you agree. I expect we shall have some hard times but I promise I shall do my best to make it worthwhile for all of us.

I would need a man to help. They don't have bothies down here as we do in Scotland. The agent said there were two rooms up a back staircase where single men or maids slept. They would eat their meals with us so that would mean extra work for you too, but I know you're a grand wee cook and you'd be boss in your own kitchen. The blacksmith would like us to take on his niece as a maid. You would need to train her but her aunt says she likes children so I thought she might help you with Jamie.

He added a few more sentences describing the area and the people he had met, and telling her about the gypsy wanting to tell his fortune. When he had written the letter, he read it through and told her again how much he longed for her company. Then he remembered that Emma had not earned any money since his mother dismissed her without even a reference. He added an envelope and stamp and pleaded with her to reply as soon as she could, then he sealed the envelope securely with wax.

When he had finished, he sat for a while deep in thought and the more he considered, the more he thought he would relish the challenge of taking on the run-down farm of Moorend and bringing it back to fertility.

He wondered whether his father would let him bring Queenie. He loved his dogs. If he could mow the long grass, and gather it into hay to sell for cash, he might be able to take on some sheep to graze the fresh pastures for a few months. He would ask Drew if the Yorkshire men took on sheep for folding. He would certainly need a dog then and he had trained Queenie himself to his own ways. The more he dreamed, the more he hoped Emmie would marry him and come to live in Yorkshire.

He took out his pen and ink again and a clean sheet of paper, and began to write to her father, telling him of his plans for Emma and her baby, promising to do his best to take good care of them. If she agreed to marry him, he suggested he should travel up on the train and have a quiet morning wedding the next day so that he could bring her and Jamie back with him. He said he was sorry for the way things had turned out but he would do his best to make amends, and he considered the sooner they were married the better it would be for all of them, especially their baby.

Once he had finished the letter, he decided to write to Maggie and tell her about the farm and his dreams for the future, as well as his suggestions to Emma and her father. He knew Maggie would smooth the path for them if she could, just as he knew his mother would never forgive him for dallying with a girl who was her servant. William understood her well enough to know she was a snob and her pride would prevent her attending his marriage to Emma. She would never give them her blessing. His father had liked Emma and her family, though. Maggie might persuade him to attend if only Emmie would agree to marry him. He didn't blame her for not wanting to travel to Yorkshire and spend her life so far from her family, but the possibility that she might refuse filled him with dejection. He had never considered marriage to anyone until he knew he had given Emmie a child, and now he felt his life would be nothing without her to share it and help him on the unfamiliar path which lay ahead. It was a long time before he settled to sleep that night and even then he was troubled by dreams, and he wakened, unrefreshed.

Bert Greig was surprised when he received a letter. Few people had reason to write to him but he was warmed and reassured when he read it.

'It sounds as though William Sinclair really wants to marry Emmie,' he said, handing it to his wife. 'He doesn't sound like a man who is being forced into marriage against his will.'

'Mmm, he doesn't hide the fact that she will have to work hard, either,' Eliza demurred.

'Our own lives have not been easy, Lizzie. We've both worked hard and pulled together. I reckon Emmie is lucky to get a husband at all in the circumstances. He didn't need to write. And another thing, he says they will be doing the work for themselves and the wee fellow, not for his parents or some stranger. This is Emma's chance to make something of her life if you ask me, so long as she puts some effort into it.'

'But they will be so far away . . . ' Eliza broke off, her voice wobbling.

'Now Eliza, you're not to keep reminding the lass. You know it's the right thing for her to do. He gives his word that he'll treat her kindly and take care of her. He sounds a decent laddie to me, even if he did take advantage o' an innocent lassie.'

His wife remained silent, striving to accept that Emmie would live her life so far away from them. Her heart felt leaden and it was hard to put on a cheerful face when Emmie showed them the letter she had received from William. Her heart had beat faster when she read his words about making each other feel good and they would do so again when the two of them were together, and she longed to feel his strong arms around her again. She was sure she could never feel that way with anyone else. On the other hand, like her mother, her heart sank at the prospect of living so far away.

'He tells you a lot more about the place and the house than he has told your father,' Eliza said. 'It sounds a terribly dirty place.'

'Dirty?' Emma gave a sarcastic grunt. 'Nothing can be worse than Aunt Vera's, especially the loft. It had never been cleaned in all the years she had lived in the cottage. She made sure I would get it done when she heard Dad was coming to bring me home.'

'Emmie will manage fine,' Bert interrupted. He still felt guilty about leaving her with Vera. 'It will be your own home when ye've got it cleaned, lassie and nobody can give ye orders and tell ye what to do.'

'But she's so young and there'll be nobody to advise her,' Eliza protested. Bert ignored his wife for once and went on encouragingly, 'You might be able to use some of the furniture the tenant is leaving behind. I'm sure you'll make it look grand when it's cleaned and polished. That will save a bit of money and maybe ye'll be able to keep some hens and earn a wee bit for yourself. It sounds as though William is willing to pay a nursemaid to help with wee Jamie. Not every man would do that.'

When Emma's brothers returned from work and heard the news, Richard and Davy both felt William Sinclair was doing the decent thing by their sister and they told Emmie she was lucky, knowing he might have left her with a baby to bring up on her own.

'You should jump at the chance to have a husband,' Richard said bluntly.

Joe made no comment. He still blamed William for taking advantage of their sister.

As soon as he had eaten his meal, Davy washed and changed and went off to see Julie, his own paramour. It was a great relief to him that her family had not condemned him for Emmie's misfortune, but he knew some of the parishioners felt he was no longer good enough for a minister's daughter. If Emma married William Sinclair, it would restore some respectability to his family. He was sorry they would live so far away because he was fond of Emmie, but the distance would allow people to forget.

'I told the Rev Davidson about William's

letters and his proposal to come up and take her back with him,' Davy said to his parents when he returned later that evening. 'He has offered to conduct the marriage ceremony for them as early in the day as they find convenient. He had a suggestion to make about getting wee Jamie christened as well. He says things are a bit different in the Church of England and he would be happy to christen the wee fellow if that's what Emmie and William want.'

'Oh, I would like to see him christened,' Eliza said, clasping her hands together. 'What a good man the Rev Davidson is. He is a true Christian with a forgiving heart — not like Mrs Sinclair, sending her own son so far away because he's caused a scandal,' she added bitterly. 'I'm sure it says pride is a sin in the Bible.'

Maggie received her letter from William with a mixture of joy and regret. She had always loved her youngest brother since he was an infant and her mother was too ill to look after him. She was saddened that he would settle so far away, but she was glad he would take care of Emmie and their baby son. Her mother had refused to hear William's name mentioned since he left so she knew better than to discuss the letter. She was glad the postman had given it to her while she was out in the yard. She waited until the afternoon milking to tell Jim and her father of William's plans to travel back to Scotland to marry Emma and take her and Jamie back with him.

'He wants to know if he can take Queenie with him. He plans to rent a run-down farm and take on some sheep to eat the grass until he can buy his own stock. He trained Queenie after all. She's really missed him since he went away.'

'We've all missed him,' Jim said gruffly. 'One of us will need to take the pony and trap to the station and bring him home the night before the wedding,' he added eagerly. 'It will give us a chance to hear all about the farm and his plans, and about cousin Andrew and his family.'

This was an unusually long speech for Jim. Their father was silent for a while, then he shook his head and Maggie thought he looked sad.

'Your mother will not have him to stay here. She's vowed he will never step through her door again. I could put my foot down over this, but William will have gone and we shall still be here. Perhaps you could ask Bessie to give him a bed for the night, Maggie? We can't have him staying with the Greigs. It wouldna be right the night before he weds.' His mouth firmed. 'Emma was a good lassie and she's from a decent family. I shall attend the wedding service. I hope you two will come with me?'

'Oh yes, Father,' Maggie said, her eyes shining with tears. 'As a matter of fact, William hopes Jim will be his witness, or best man. But he was still not sure whether Emma will agree to marry him and go so far away from her family to live in Yorkshire.'

'I see,' James Sinclair said slowly. 'Maybe you should go to see Emma tomorrow and help her decide to do the right thing. She hasna worked for months. She will not have any spare money for a new dress. You could take her with you and choose some material.'

'Oh, Father, thank you,' Maggie said. 'Imagine you thinking of that. I'm sure Emma will be pleased and she is good with her needle. She will need a decent dress to go to church when she moves so I will choose material which will be suitable for a best dress. It will be better if they make a good first impression on the people where they will be living.'

'Ye're a good lassie, Maggie,' James Sinclair said. 'Get some material to make yourself a new dress as well while ye're there and bring the account to me.' He didn't add 'there's no need to tell your mother', but Maggie knew what he meant. Jim gave her a wink and a smile when he rose from milking one of the cows.

Later when they were alone he said, 'I'm glad Father is taking this so well. I reckon Emma will make a good wife for William and he always had a soft spot for her, even when she first arrived as a nervous wee lassie straight frae school.'

'I agree, but I do wish Mother could have accepted her as her daughter-in-law. After all, she is the mother of her grandson.'

'Aye, she's good at preaching about the Bible but she's not very good at doing what it says when it comes to forgiveness. Weren't they supposed to be Jesus's last words when they hung him on the cross? 'Father, forgive them for they know not what they do.' If you ask me, Emma didn't know what she was doing either, or at least she didn't realize the consequences.'

* * *

Bert Greig gave Emma no peace until she had sent her reply, but William felt he had waited half a lifetime hoping for a letter from her. He would not make any decisions until he knew whether she would marry him and move to Yorkshire. The men who shared the loft with him complained that he was irritable and even the housekeeper, with whom he had found favour from the day he arrived, was bewildered by his moods. When the letter did eventually arrive, he tore it open with such haste he tore the single sheet of paper but it didn't stop him reading the news he wanted to hear. It was true she didn't sound overly enthusiastic about living so far away from her family, and in her honesty she told him her father insisted it was the right thing to do for Jamie's sake. She told him Maggie had been to see her and she agreed with her father.

Emma didn't tell William about Maggie taking her to see Miss Wilkins to buy material to make new dresses for them both. Maggie's excitement was infectious. She had volunteered to be matron of honour and she said they would surprise him when he saw them at the church. Emma was happy until Miss Wilkins looked down her narrow nose and refused to serve her. She almost burst into tears but Maggie had intervened, firmly telling her Mr Sinclair was paying the account for the material. Emma had always got on well with the seamstress after she won the school prize for best sewing, so she was hurt by her attitude.

'She wouldn't have sold me a bag of rags if Maggie had not been with me,' she told her mother tearfully. 'She hardly spoke to me. She brought out some coarse grey cotton and said it would be very suitable for me, but Maggie insisted she get a bolt of material from the top shelf. That's where she keeps the quality stuff.'

'I know.' Eliza sighed. She didn't tell Emma she had suffered various snubs herself from Miss Wilkins and other local people since Emmie and her baby had returned to Locheagle. 'It's another of life's lesson's ye've had to learn, lassie, but I hate to see ye hurt. Don't let it make you bitter. Some people canna forgive, some are jealous, others are fickle. We have to learn to choose our friends carefully. Anyway, Emmie, this material is beautiful and the royal blue will suit you. You'll look lovely. I'm truly grateful to the Rev Davidson for being so kind and understanding. No one in Yorkshire will know your circumstances and the dress will be suitable for attending the kirk in the summer, as Maggie suggested. She has a heart of gold.'

'I know and she says she will come down and we can cut out our dresses together and then fit them on each other. She is going to bring a paper pattern from Bessie to guide us.'

* * *

William lost no time in replying to tell Emma how pleased he was. He wrote to tell Maggie they would be married as soon as he could see the land agent and reach an agreement over the tenancy of Moorend Farm. He also wrote a short letter to Mr Rowbottom to say he would like to meet him again on Saturday afternoon after he finished work, so that he could take another look at the more distant fields, and discuss a possible tenancy. It was short and business-like. He had always been good with numbers at school but he was thankful now that Maggie had made him pay attention to his spelling and practise his handwriting. He couldn't wait for Saturday afternoon, although he did not intend to let Rowbottom see how keen he was, or how urgent it had become as a place to live for his wife and son.

He was buoyed up with anticipation but his heart sank when the land agent told him they were to call on Lord Hanley before any discussions.

'He gave instructions that I'm to take you to the Manor. After all, he has known all his tenants and their families all their lives, as his father did before him. He said he would make enquiries about your cousin from the agent at Wilmore, since he is your only connection that we know.'

‘I see,’ William said stiffly.

Inwardly his spirits plummeted. He had intended trying to negotiate a whole year’s tenancy free of rent to help him bring the farm back into production. Now it seemed he might not even get the tenancy at all, and if he did they would have to depend on whatever income they could make from hens and pigs in the farm buildings and the nearby paddocks, while he paid a rent for fields too neglected to keep stock.

He had ridden over on his Clydesdale mare. Rowbottom admired her and suggested he turn her into the paddock with the two house cows and old Ed’s horses.

‘We’ll drive to the Manor in the pony and trap. Best not keep His Lordship waiting.’ William sensed an uneasiness in the land agent and his own tension grew. Back home he would have had his father’s influence and support behind him.

11

Lord Hanley greeted them politely and led the way into the estate office. He lost no time in telling William he had made enquiries about him and, as far as possible, about his relatives in Yorkshire.

'Walter Frame, the land agent, is impressed with Mr Kerr and his farming methods. Apparently he pays his rents on time and has a good reputation for paying his debts promptly too, though I gather he doesn't suffer fools gladly. However, that does not mean to say you will prove to be as good a farmer as he is, and you're younger than I would have liked, but at least you will have someone to give advice if you need it. I'm told you have proved yourself a hard worker, good at breaking in the young horses.'

'Thank you,' William said uncomfortably.

'Having relations in the area may help you settle. I assume you do mean to make your future in Yorkshire?'

'That is my intention but my — my wife has not seen the house yet, nor the farm and the countryside around here.'

'We understand the women have to be

happy if the men are to get on and do their job, don't we, Rowbottom?'

'Yes, Your Lordship, but there is not much we can do about the house. It is sound enough underneath the dust and rubbish.'

'Emmie doesn't mind hard work,' William said firmly, 'but she has just had our first child.' Privately he thought he was getting quite good at sounding like a married man.

'Mr Rowbottom tells me she can do milking and churn butter. Not many farmers' wives around here do that. You may be wise to get her some help when you have heard my conditions for granting you the tenancy.' William sat up straight. It didn't sound as though there would be any negotiating with the land agent at this rate.

'I suggest a trial tenancy of three years until we see what sort of farmer you prove to be . . . ' William opened his mouth to speak but Lord Hanley held up his hand. 'Hear me out first. I am well aware Mr Dixon has neglected Moorend but his family were good tenants for four generations. Mr Rowbottom considers I have been too lenient and it irks him to have the farm under his charge.' He raised a quizzical eyebrow as he glanced at the land agent. He grimaced in response.

'I feel responsible and I'm ashamed to see such neglect.'

'We agree the first thing we must do is erect new boundary fences,' Lord Hanley went on, 'but the tenant will be expected to maintain them. We will also fence two of the fields which are furthest away from the farm to prevent stock from the Common Land straying onto your land. If you are good at hedge-laying, several of the other fields could have a stock-proof hedge within a couple of years for the cost of your labour.'

William frowned. 'I have done some, but we had more stone dykes, stone walls that is, for our boundaries.'

'However you do the rest of the fencing will be up to you, as tenant. Ed Dixon is keen to move now so you can have immediate entry but your three-year lease will not begin until the end of September. Mr Rowbottom and I agree that you should have the first year rent free, provided we see some improvements at the end of the first six months. If you've made no improvement at the end of the first year, we shall terminate the tenancy without further notice.' He eyed William shrewdly.

'I understand,' William said, hiding his jubilation at being granted a whole year rent free without even asking. 'That sounds very fair, but I would like it in writing and granted a three year tenancy, though I would have preferred five years. In return, I guarantee to improve the fertility of the land and the farm itself without delay. Indeed, I could not live there and not bring some sort of order to the place,' he added wryly. 'I shall keep a note of all the changes I make, and the cost, and I think you will find my period without rent has been as much to your benefit as to mine.'

'Fine words, Mr Sinclair. All that remains then is to see whether you can follow them through,' Lord Hanley said. 'Anything to add, Rowbottom?'

'Can you tell me what you plan to do immediately? It is possible we may be able to help, though I am not promising anything at this stage.'

'I would like another good walk over the fields which have grown wild,' William said slowly. 'If I can employ a man to help, I would mow them and maybe make hay if the weather allows. It wouldn't be the best fodder, removing the rank grass would allow the pastures to freshen. It could even be suitable for grazing sheep since they don't like it long. Do you take sheep for folding down here? I don't want to use my capital to buy stock until I see how productive I can make the land. As it is, I shall need to buy a mower and some carts, as well as another horse. Folding someone else's sheep would help the fertility too.'

'That's true.' Lord Hanley nodded and looked at his agent.

'I agree with your ideas so far,' he said. 'I have a cousin who is a land agent in North Yorkshire. Many of his tenants have sheep on the moors. I should think some of them would be pleased to send ewes for grazing for a few months to preserve their own land for flushing the ewes in the autumn. I could ask him. He would know which of the farmers are reliable with healthy stock and able to pay at the end of the season.'

'What do you say, Mr Sinclair?' Lord Hanley asked.

'I should be glad of that sort of recommendation. I wouldn't like to herd sheep for the summer and autumn with nothing at the end of it. In fact, I think I will tell the farmer he has to pay when he collects his sheep or I shall keep enough to sell to make sure I get my money.' Both men chuckled.

'There speaks a Scotsman,' Lord Hanley said, but William felt he approved.

'Ed Dixon is hoping whoever gets the farm will take over everything,' Rowbottom said, looking doubtfully at William. 'Most of it is lost amidst the grass and nettles, and the carts will need some repairs. He has a mower but I don't think it will have seen grease for some time. He seems oblivious to the fact that he's still owing rent. He has neither the energy nor the inclination to organize a farm sale. He'll not be difficult to deal with but you'll need to pay for repairs. Joe Wright, the blacksmith, is an obliging fellow and good at turning his hand to repairing machines.'

'Yes, I met him with my cousin on our last visit.'

'Aye, so you did. Ed is hoping the new tenant will buy his two cows and his mare. The previous owner will likely claim the gelding.'

'When I've had another look at the land, perhaps I could have a talk with him, later this afternoon? Before I leave?'

'All right, I'll tell him,' Rowbottom said. 'If you're finished here, Lord Hanley.'

'Yes, I think that's all. I'll have an agreement drawn up.'

'Very well,' William said, 'and thank you for considering me as your tenant.'

'I have a feeling I shall not regret it, unless you make too many demands of course.' His tone held a warning, but he smiled and added, 'You must remember a Yorkshire man and his brass are not easily parted.'

'I'm finding that out already,' William grinned and his blue eyes sparkled.

* * *

Emma knew she was fortunate that William was willing to help her with wee Jamie and that she wouldn't have to struggle to find even the most menial jobs as an unmarried mother, but her heart sank when she read William's next letter telling her he had signed a three-year agreement for a tenancy of the Yorkshire farm, with the chance of a longer tenancy if he proved satisfactory. Secretly she had hoped he would not find a farm in Yorkshire and that he would come back and settle near her family. She didn't understand that without his family's backing, it would be even more difficult to get a tenancy in this area.

Part of her longed to see his merry smile and teasing wink again. Her insides trembled when she remembered the way he had held her in his arms out on the hill and she longed to feel the thrill of him again, but in other ways she still regarded him as the son of her old employer. Although they had lived under the same roof and eaten their meals at the same table for three years, they had never had private conversations, like lovers, or even as friends. There were lots of things she didn't know about him, and he didn't know anything about her own hopes and dreams and opinions. He was marrying her out of a sense of duty because of Jamie, not because he loved her as her parents loved each other.

Eliza found it a strain because she understood Emmie's doubts and fears, but she had promised Bert she would hide her own feelings and chivvy Emma along until William came to take her back with him after the wedding. Maggie had been down to see them twice more and she and Emmie had cut out their dresses and tacked the pieces together.

'What a small waist you have, Emmie, and you don't even wear corsets yet,' Maggie exclaimed. 'I wish I was as slender as you.'

'I've told her it's time she was wearing a corset,' Eliza said, joining the conversation, 'especially now she's had a child but she's even skinnier than she was before.'

'I'm not skinny here,' Emma said, struggling to tug the bodice of her dress higher to cover her full breasts.

'That's because you have plenty of milk to feed wee Jamie,' her mother comforted. 'That's a good thing. It keeps him content. Anyway, the curves suit you. Maggie has cut the dress beautifully.'

'I know,' Emma smiled, smoothing down the flat front with the pointed V just below the waist. She couldn't see the back while she was wearing it but Maggie had swept the material towards the back, almost like a small bustle. She said the back was as important as the front because other people would see it when she was making her vows at the altar.

'There won't be any other people,' Emma said.

'Your parents will be there and your brothers and my father. Bessie wants to come too, and Jim and I will be there. You will look lovely, Emmie. I'm sure William will think so too and that's what matters. Bessie is sending you her blue wool jacket and matching hat in case it is cold when you travel on the train. None of us have ever been on a train. It will be a big adventure.' Maggie seemed to sense Emma's anxiety, Eliza thought, and she was doing her best to encourage her and keep up her spirits.

'Please thank Bessie for me,' Emma said, her eyes watering and her chin wobbling with the effort of fighting her tears. 'You have both been so kind to me. I know Miss Wilkins thinks I don't deserve it.'

'Never mind what Miss Wilkins thinks,' Maggie said briskly.

Emma knew her mother had bought a big bag of wool and she was knitting her a warm shawl so she could hide Jamie discreetly when he needed to be fed on the train. This had made Emma blush. She hated the thought of feeding her baby in front of strangers, but her mother insisted she couldn't let him go hungry or it would upset him and make him cross. She didn't know Maggie had another surprise for her, although she would not see it until the day of her wedding.

Indeed, Maggie had been surprised herself when William had written to ask if she could give him an idea of Emma's measurements. He said it was Annie's idea that he should give Emmie a new dress as a wedding gift.

> *She is friendly with a woman whose husband owns one of the woollen mills so she has bought a length of material to make a dress and one of the long jackets which she says are in fashion. Annie says it will be suitable for travelling in. I told her Emmie has eyes the colour of the sea, neither green nor blue, so she has chosen a sort of bluish-grey material. She knows a seamstress who will make it up quickly if I pay her.*

Maggie's heart warmed to cousin Drew's wife, although she scarcely knew her. It sounded as though Emma would have one friend down there at least. Another thing which pleased Maggie was that Annie Kerr seemed to understand Emma would be exhausted after the upheaval of her wedding, taking leave of her family, and the long journey with a new husband and a young baby, as well as Queenie, William's collie.

Annie is insisting Andrew should meet us at the railway station, William had written. *He is to take us to Blakemore to spend the night with him and Annie and their children. Annie says it will be better for Emma if she has had a night's rest before she sees the house where we are to live. I hope they will get on together.*' He sounded anxious in his letter, Maggie thought, but he went on to say,

> *Of course, Annie is not at all like Mother. She has not uttered a word of condemnation about us having a child out of wedlock. She understands what it is like to feel homesick. She is hoping she and Emma will become friends, even though we shall be living several miles away. We shall need to set out for Moorend first thing next morning because I am taking over Ed Dixon's two milk cows, and he is staying at Moorend to milk them until I arrive. It is upsetting him more leaving the two cows than anything else. He is leaving all the things he and his wife accumulated over the*

years. Emma will have a lot of cleaning and sorting out to do. Annie says it is better if she sees it in the morning rather than arriving in the evening with no one to make a meal or prepare a clean bed. I do hope Emma will agree with these arrangements.

Maggie thought Annie sounded very thoughtful and considerate. She felt she should leave it to William to explain all the arrangements but she thought it would comfort Eliza Greig to read the letter.

'How kind of your cousin to invite them to stay, and how thoughtful his wife is,' Eliza said gratefully. 'I shall make sure I pack some clean bedding in one of the wooden chests. Bert says it will be all right to send all Emma's stuff and wee Jamie's because the railwaymen have a luggage van to store it all.' She shook her grey head in bewilderment. 'I can't imagine what it must be like travelling on a train.'

William was not looking forward to showing Emmie the place which was to be their home. He had never seen a place in such a state of neglect himself, and he was afraid Emma might be so overwhelmed she would burst into tears and want to go home. He didn't know that the house was the least of Emma's worries. It was the last thing on her mind as her wedding drew nearer and the parting from her family approached. In her own mind she had convinced herself that William was almost a stranger.

Jim greeted William warmly when he met him off the train late on the evening before his wedding. The two brothers talked eagerly until William asked, 'Why are we taking this road?' Jim flushed and his mouth tightened.

'I'm taking you to stay the night with Bessie and her husband but Father will be at your wedding tomorrow. So will Maggie, Bessie and I, and we're bringing Queenie with us so you can take her back with you.'

'I see,' William said stiffly. 'So Mother has not found it in her religious heart to forgive either of us,' he added bitterly. 'Well, so be it. We shall manage well enough without her blessing.'

'Don't be bitter, William,' Jim said gently. 'I'm sure Emma will make a good wife. Maggie has been down to Locheagle several times and she says you have a fine son, and Emma is a natural mother even though she is so young. Maggie is going to miss her but Emma has promised to write. Of course, Mother didn't approve of her 'fraternising' as she calls it and she wouldn't allow her to do any baking for a wedding breakfast tomorrow.

Father told her to buy extra groceries and take eggs and milk to Mrs Greig and she would see to everything. He has a great respect for the Greigs, I think. He doesn't quarrel with Mother, he simply does what he wants to do and ignores her grim looks. Mother has not come out of this well. He asked her in front of Maggie and me if she would accompany him to the kirk. She pursed her lips and didn't reply. We know she will not be there.'

'Never mind. I'm glad you and Father will be there to support me.'

'Do you need support?' Jim asked in surprise. 'Emma's a grand lassie. Aren't you sure about marrying her?'

'Oh, I'm sure I want to marry her, I'm not so sure she wants to marry me. I need her beside me, Jim. It's lonely in a strange place where you don't know anybody. It will take the two of us, working together, to make anything of Moorend Farm. Mother wouldn't approve of the place at all. I pray Emmie will not take one look and want to run home.'

'Well, Father and I will not be there to support you over that.'

'Of course not. It will be up to me to make Emmie happy. Remember, she has three big brothers! Mind you, I don't know if they will take time off work on a Saturday morning to attend their sister's wedding in the circumstances. I haven't had any details in Emmie's letters about the wedding but I'm pleased she has arranged to have the baby christened before we move to Yorkshire. She hasn't said much at all about getting married. Most of her letters are taken up with Jamie. We shall have to change his name to Jim before he goes to school. I don't want him to be a sissy boy.'

'At least she chose a good name,' Jim grinned, 'after two good men — Father and me!'

'Aah-ah,' William mocked.

'Maggie says he looks like you now he's lost his dark hair and he's getting gingery brown hair like yours.'

The following morning, William was doubly glad to have Jim at his side. He was surprised how nervous he felt. What if Emma changed her mind and didn't turn up? He was almost relieved to see her three brothers arrive. Lily — Richard's girl — and her parents had come too so they were obviously not as prejudiced as his own mother. Then Davy was introducing him to the Reverend Davidson and his wife and daughter before he and Jim were ushered into the vestry for a word with the minister before the service began. When they came out he saw that

Emma's mother had arrived. He knew who she was because he had seen her at the cottage door when he and Maggie had called. She looked like an older version of Emma too.

'Stop fidgeting,' Jim hissed softly. 'Ye're as nervous as a kitten.'

'I should have talked to Emmie last night, even though it was late,' he whispered back.

There was a stir and everyone stood up. William couldn't believe his eyes when he saw Emma — his Emmie — walking down the aisle on her father's arm. She looked beautiful in a dress of shimmering deep blue which suited her fair colouring and emphasized her curves — more curves than he remembered. Her lovely wide eyes looked more blue than green. She was wearing her hair on top of her head with a small matching blue hat, and she seemed taller and older and very pretty. He saw at once that she had lost her rounded schoolgirl cheeks and his conscience smote him when he remembered all she had come through in the months since he had last seen her. She gave him a tentative half-smile as she reached him and he clasped her hand tightly and smiled back at her, his eyes shining with admiration and relief. She was trembling slightly and he tried hard to reassure her with the pressure of his fingers and a tender look in his eyes.

'Emmie.' He breathed her name softly. 'I was afraid you might not come,' he whispered almost under his breath, but she heard and her eyes widened in surprise.

He looked so handsome, standing tall and straight at her side. She knew he didn't love her. He was marrying her because he felt it was his duty, but her heart filled with gladness, for surely he could have had almost any girl for miles around. William lifted his eyes and saw Maggie. Her eyes were luminous with tears but she gave him a smile and a little nod, and he was sure things were going to be all right after all.

After the wedding service and signing of the register, the Minister's daughter, Julie, stepped forward, cradling a baby in her arms in readiness for the christening and William saw his son for the first time. As they made their way outside afterwards, Emma and her family were even more surprised to see a small group of people had gathered to see the newly-married couple. Eliza tensed. Had they come out of curiosity, or to cast nasty remarks? But no, they had come to offer their good wishes to the young couple. William was surprised when he realized his father and Emma's parents knew them all, until he remembered his father had attended Locheagle village school. If only his mother had been here to see their smiling faces and hear their greetings, he thought.

They all paraded down the village street to the Greigs' cottage where Eliza had a table groaning with food and to William's joy, he saw Queenie tied to the garden fence. As soon as she saw him and Emma, she barked and wagged her tail energetically, straining at the leash. Both he and Emma bent to greet her, hugging the little dog in their shared delight.

'Mind your good clothes, both of you,' Maggie urged. 'I hope Queenie will not be frightened of the noisy train.'

'She'll be fine when she's with us,' William said jubilantly and turned to his father. 'Thank you, Dad.'

'Aye, she's a grand dog. We might need to send the next litter down to you to be trained,' his father answered gruffly and William knew that was his father's way of saying they would miss him.

12

All too soon it was time to leave. Bessie had driven down with the pony and trap, bringing William with her that morning. Maggie, Jim and their father had come in the Bonnybrae trap. Emma's brothers planned to walk ahead to the station to see their young sister off on her journey.

'I'll walk with you if you dinna mind,' William said. 'There's a long time to sit on the train and I'd appreciate the walk with Queenie.'

'Ye're welcome,' Richard said jovially. He felt cheered that things were working out so much better than any of them had expected. He felt he would have liked both William and his elder brother if they'd had time to get to know each other and in better circumstances.

'Maybe I'll walk with you,' Jim said. 'It will give us chance to talk a bit longer. You can tell us all about this farm ye're taking. I don't think there'll be room in the trap for more than Maggie and Emma with so many boxes.'

'Have all these to go with us?' William asked in surprise. 'What are you bringing, Emmie?' he asked, looking at the two wooden chests as well as two bulging carpet bags and a basket of food for them, plus baby essentials for the journey.

'If the house is as bad as you said in your letters,' Eliza said, 'Emma will need some clean bedding. I would have sent the pair of you more of this food but I dinna think ye'll be able to carry anything else, as well as the wee fellow and the dog.'

'Ye're right, Mrs Greig. Thank you.' William smiled his appreciation. 'I hadna thought of that side of things.'

'Men never do,' Eliza said wryly, shaking her head, completely won over by his smile.

'We thank you for whatever you're sending. The railway wagon will deliver the boxes at the other end.'

'Are you coming to the station with us, Father?' Davy asked. 'It's time we were setting out if we're to beat the pony and trap.'

'No, laddie, I'd better not.' Bert shook his head. He knew what a strain it was for Eliza saying good-bye. 'I'll stay with your mother. Things will seem quiet once Emmie and the bairn are away.'

'What about you, Father?' Jim asked James Sinclair.

'No, I'll leave the walk to you young folk. I'll take a lift back with Bessie and walk home across the fields frae her place. Maggie will have you for company on the drive home. She's going to miss Emma.'

'Come on, Emmie,' Maggie said, 'I'll help you change. You look so lovely in your dress. I know William thought so too. I saw it in his eyes when he looked at you.'

'D-do you think so?' Emmie asked wistfully. 'I know he is only marrying me because he — he feels it's his duty, but I would never want him to be ashamed of me because I was only a maid.'

'I'm sure he'll never be ashamed of you, Emmie! You made a wonderful job of sewing your dress. I will pack it carefully.'

Emma felt shaky as she struggled against her tears. Whatever Maggie said, she wondered if she had done the right thing in agreeing to marry William. He looked so handsome when he was dressed in his good suit. Her heart had given a little flip of joy, but she knew he would not have chosen her as his wife in different circumstances. Why, oh why was she going so far away?

'I have a surprise for you,' Maggie said softly, understanding Emma's uncertainty and not wanting her to burst into tears. Emma handed wee Jamie to her mother. She had such a lump in her throat she felt she would never be able to speak again.

She had laid out her best brown woollen

skirt for travelling in, and a new cream blouse which she had made herself with buttons, making it easy to open to feed Jamie on the train. She also had the lovely soft shawl her mother had knitted. Maggie saw them but she had previously hung up the new travelling dress and jacket which William had brought for Emmie. She turned her round to look.

'William had it made especially for you, Emmie. I think it was Annie's idea because she got the material from one of the mill owners. Isn't it lovely — almost the colour of your eyes. You will look so smart.'

'B-but how did he know my size, and how could I feed Jamie if I wore it? It is too good to travel in . . . '

'I think William might be disappointed if you don't wear it,' Maggie said gently. 'I suspect he thought you might want a new dress for the wedding. He had reckoned without Father buying material for both of us. Look, this dress opens at the front too. I expect Annie would know what's required because she's had babies of her own. You could always wear your shawl on top of the jacket to hide Jamie when he's feeding.'

'Oh, Maggie, I wish we didn't have to go so far away.'

'I know, Emmie, I know,' Maggie soothed. 'Just try on the dress. You don't have to wear it if it's not comfortable. See how the seams are sewn. William said the seamstress has got some kind of sewing machine which makes a very firm seam.' Maggie ushered a distracted Emmie into the dress and deftly folded the brocade one and packed it carefully in one of the large carpet bags. Swiftly, she added Emmie's skirt and blouse so that she wouldn't change her mind.

'It's a beautiful dress,' Emmie said, stroking the fine wool. 'I've never had two new dresses at once, except working dresses.'

'There's a little hat to match. William said Annie had made it herself. I'm sure you will like her.' Maggie organized Emmie as she talked, knowing there was little time to spare if they were to get to the train in time and unload the luggage.

Saying good-bye to her mother and father was even worse than Emma had feared, and in the end Bert Greig caught Maggie's anxious gaze and almost lifted his daughter and her baby into the trap, telling Maggie to get the pony moving or they would miss the train. He turned away abruptly but Maggie understood he was hiding his own emotions. The pony was well-rested and trotted at a good pace. The cool air rushing past helped to cool Emma's damp, flushed cheeks and the miles to the station gave her time to calm herself and wipe away her tears. Jamie seemed to sense the upheaval but Maggie was thankful when his whimpering demanded Emma's attention. Cuddling him close seemed to comfort her.

'You look really smart in your new outfit, Emmie. No one would think you have a baby only a couple of months old. Your waist is so small and not even a corset.'

'Oh, corsets! Mother was going on about that again. Ye're so kind, Maggie. You will write to us, won't ye?'

'I certainly will and I shall expect lots of details of your new home, the bad bits as well as the good. William does admit it is in an awful state. I think he feels a bit guilty at taking you to such a place.'

'Ma says we shall have to sleep Jamie in a big drawer until we can get a cot for him. I hope he settles all right.'

'I'm sure he will if you do.'

They were only just in time arriving at the station but the brothers willingly lifted the wooden trunks onto the platform, ready to load in the luggage van. William smiled warmly at Emma as he helped her down and took charge of the two large carpet bags, while keeping a tight hold on the leather strap he had fastened to Queenie's collar. 'Can you manage the basket as well as the bairn?'

'Yes,' she nodded, biting her lip and not meeting his eyes.

Then all at once, her brothers were hugging her and even Jim kissed her cheek as they ushered her into a carriage and slammed the door shut. William let down the window to call good-bye and Jim came closer.

'Keep him in order, Emma and don't let him boss you,' he grinned.

'I — I'll try,' Emma responded with a watery smile.

'Be sure to write, Emmie,' Davy called. Then the train was drawing away. Queenie cowered down at William's feet. She didn't like the loud banging of doors and hissing steam. William soothed her and patted her head. There were two other men in the carriage sitting near the window. After a brusque nod, they ignored the newcomers so William and Emma sat opposite each other, keeping their distance from them.

'Has he been good so far?' William asked awkwardly, nodding at Jamie now snuggling down in Emma's arms and ready to sleep.

'He senses things are — are different, I think, but perhaps he will have a good sleep now.'

'Annie says even young babies know when they're in a strange place,' William reflected. He looked at her anxiously. 'I didn't tell you before, Emma, but Annie is kind and she means well. She insisted we must go to her house to stay tonight. She said you would be tired out after the excitement and the long journey, and it isna right to take you straight back to a filthy house with no one to welcome us or prepare a meal.'

'I — I see,' Emma said nervously. She didn't know what else to say. 'You know hard work doesn't worry me . . . '

'I know that, Emmie, but you needn't be nervous with Annie. She's not at all like my mother. In fact, she's the very opposite. I think she wants us to stay because she's curious to meet you and to see your bairn. She's hoping the two of you will become friends. I think she still feels a bit homesick for Scotland.'

'He — he's *our* bairn.'

'Aye, I suppose so,' William said awkwardly. 'It will take some time to get used to having a wife and a baby,' he added. The two men looked up. One raised his eyebrows and eyed them more keenly, making Emma flush and chew her lip. William grimaced.

'I'd forgotten about them,' he mouthed silently. Emma nodded and they fell silent. The train made several short stops until they reached Carlisle.

'I think they change drivers here, or stock

up with coal, or something.'

'Aye, they do,' one of the men said. 'This is as far as we go.'

They squeezed past Emma and William, and jumped onto the platform as soon as the train stopped. Perhaps people thought the carriage was full when they saw William and Emma sitting near the door. Certainly no one entered. The porter came round, slamming all the doors and making poor Queenie jump. Jamie stirred and grizzled a little too but Emma was thankful he didn't waken. Queenie stood up then and went closer to look at him. Emma patted her silky head.

'You're a good dog, aren't you, Queenie? Maybe you'll learn to guard this wee fellow when he starts to move around.'

'Shall we move nearer the window?' William asked. 'Then you can see the scenery as we pass. I wouldn't mind having one of those sandwiches your mother packed for us now.'

'Are you hungry already?' Emma asked in surprise.

'Yes, the food looked lovely but I was too nervous to eat much.'

'*You* were nervous? I don't believe you.'

'I was. I didna ken what to expect with your three brothers and your father all watching over you. They love you very much,

Emmie. They all gave me a lecture on taking care of you. Joe says he's saving up for the train fare and he'll come down to visit and see that I'm looking after you.'

'Did he really say that?' Emma asked, removing the cloth from the top of the basket with one hand. She held it out for him to choose. He selected a thick ham sandwich.

'Shall I pass you one or can you manage with one hand?'

'Of course I can.' Emma gave a little laugh and he was pleased to hear it. Ever since she arrived at the station she had been wide-eyed and anxious. 'Ye'd be surprised what you have to learn to do while shushing the baby or carrying him around. Pass me a smaller sandwich, please?'

'They're delicious. I'm glad your mother thought to send some.'

'I expect she guessed we'd need them. The ham is frae Bonnybrae. Your F-father and M-Maggie have been so kind.' Her voice shook. She brushed a crumb from her skirt. 'Oh and I must thank you for buying me this lovely outfit.'

'It was Annie's idea,' William admitted. 'She asked an awful lot of questions about the colour of your eyes and your size. I asked Maggie for your measurements. Annie and her sewing friend did the rest, but she will be pleased when she sees you in it.'

'I thought it was too good to wear for travelling, especially when I shall have to feed Jamie on the journey.'

'Will you?' William sounded alarmed. 'Have to feed him while we're on the train, I mean?'

'Y-yes, of course. He likes a feed every four hours and sometimes more often. He's a greedy boy,' she added fondly, stroking his cheek with a gentle finger.

William was surprised to feel a pang of jealousy at her obvious love for the sleeping infant. She looked up at him and there was a glint of challenge in her eyes, reminding him of the old Emmie who had always responded to his teasing. 'If you need to be fed so soon, why shouldn't your son?'

'Mmm, I suppose that's something else I need to get used to. Let's hope we don't get any more passengers in with us then.'

'Well, I hope we don't get any more men in,' Emma admitted, her cheeks flushing. She already felt embarrassed at the prospect of feeding the baby in front of William, even though he was the father. They were a newly married couple and unused to each other.

Almost as if he had read her thoughts, William said, 'I have told everyone, except Annie and Drew, that we are already married and I had left you behind to have the baby until I had a home for you both. I thought it would make things easier, especially when we shall have a maid and a man living with us, at least in the beginning. The blacksmith is looking out for anyone available. Will you give Mrs Wright's niece a trial? She will have everything to learn when she's so young but Mrs Wright says she loves babies, and she has seven younger brothers and sisters so she is used to caring for them.'

'That will be a great help, I think. We put him to sleep in the clothes basket at home but Ma said we should look for a big drawer or take the lid off the big blanket box we are taking with us.'

'I'm sure we shall find something for him,' William said. 'I pray you will not be too dismayed at the dust and cobwebs. Old Ed, the previous tenant, is a nice, gentle old man, but I don't know how he has survived all on his own. He refuses to leave his two cows until he has met you and he's sure you will look after them well. I assured him you're very fond of animals but he wants to be introduced to you. They're like friends to him. He is staying to milk them tomorrow morning, then he's catching the train to travel to his sister's as soon as he's seen you.'

'I see,' Emma said. 'The cows should be

quiet then.' Jamie began to stir and then to whimper, shoving away the blanket in a determined manner. 'I think he's hungry.'

'This would be a good time to feed him when we have the carriage to ourselves, Emmie, and before we need to change trains for Wakefield.'

'We need to get on another train?'

'Yes, but don't worry, the porters will help with our luggage. Then Drew will be there to meet us at Wakefield with his pony and trap.' He tried to keep his eyes to himself as Emma, her cheeks growing pink with embarrassment, tried to arrange her shawl as she opened her bodice. Jamie was an eager feeder and needed little guidance to find her nipple with his soft, searching mouth. In spite of the stressful day, she had plenty of milk and Emma knew it would be a relief to have him take his fill but she couldn't bring herself to meet William's gaze when she felt him watching. She couldn't know how much he envied his young son as he kneaded the creamy skin of Emma's breast with his tiny fists. William had noticed the swell of her breasts as soon as he saw her at the kirk and he thought again how well motherhood suited her. She looked happy as she watched her suckling infant.

Queenie was getting restless and both Emma and William were eager to reach their destination after several hours of sitting still. Emma felt she had been on the moving train all day. It seemed impossible that they had had a wedding and a christening before they started their journey. William was relieved to see Drew was waiting for them at the station. He greeted them warmly, peered at the sleeping baby and patted Queenie.

'Can you keep a hold of Queenie for me a minute, Emmie,' William asked, 'while I arrange for the railway wagon to deliver the two wooden chests to Moorend?' Queenie was not used to being restrained by the lead for she was an obedient, well-trained dog. She remembered Emma well and she lay at her feet, looking up with reproachful eyes. Emma smiled down at her and bent to give her a pat. 'I know you're a good dog but this is a frightening, noisy old place for you and me. We're just making sure you don't come to any harm.'

'Do you always hold conversations with your animals, Emma?' Drew asked, his deep voice reflecting amusement. Emma looked up and her blue-green eyes sparkled.

'Of course I do. Sometimes they make more sense than people.'

'Mmm, well you could be right there. She's a fine young collie.'

It didn't seem to take them long before

Drew was turning the trap into a farm yard in the middle of a village. Her dark brows rose questioningly.

'Drew tells me most of the farms down here are situated in the villages with the land stretching out behind them,' William said, seeing her surprise. 'Moorend is at the far end of a village but it has an advantage in that we shall have a field on all sides, but it's only a short drive to the road.'

'I can't wait to see it. I'm sure it can't be as bad as you say.'

Annie welcomed them warmly and insisted on giving Jamie a wee cuddle while her own two children looked on shyly. She bent to let them see the baby and Hannah, a fair-haired 2½-year-old, came close and stroked his downy head with a gentle finger.

'We've maked a bed for him,' she said. 'It's in a basket.'

She had a slight lisp and Emma thought she was adorable. Her brother Ronnie came closer and looked down at the sleeping baby.

'Does he sleep all the time? I would like a boy to play with me when Mam gets a new one.' Annie gasped and stared at him, her cheeks colouring a little. 'It'll be all right,' he said innocently. 'Fran said I shouldn't worry 'cos you weren't ill and it's only a new baby making you sick.'

'Fran said that, did she?' Anna pursed her lips, but she looked at Emma, shaking her head in despair. 'She's our maid but she lives in one of the cottages with her husband. We inherited her. She's a good worker but,' she grimaced, 'she takes a bit of managing sometimes, the things she says. I hope you'll be better with a young maid you can train yourself, Emma, even if you do have to teach her everything at first.' She looked up at William. 'You have arranged for Emma to have a maid, haven't you?'

'Yes, if Emma approves. She's a niece of Joe Wright's wife. She's bringing her to Moorend tomorrow morning. He's also found me a man. Cliff, he's called. Apparently he has the strength of an ox but not much sense. Willing enough though, or so Joe Wright says. Anyway, he's the only one available until the hiring at Michaelmas.

'Come on, Emma, let me show you where you're to sleep tonight. I'll bring you a jug of warm water so you can freshen up after all that travelling, though I must say you do look smart and not at all travel weary.'

'I must thank you for your part in my new outfit,' Emma said.

'Och, William paid for the material and the seamstress. I only arranged it. Drew has promised to buy me one of these treadle sewing machines when the new baby is born but it's not due until January. Fran shouldn't have stuck her nose in and told Ronnie so early.'

Annie had prepared a lovely meal for them — roast chicken and new potatoes and peas from the garden, followed by rhubarb pie and cream as well as tea and newly baked shortbread.

As they washed up together, they chatted as though they had always known each other.

'It's lovely to have someone from back home to entertain,' Annie confided. 'I know Drew loves me, and we have the children now, but sometimes I still feel a bit homesick for my ain folk. I know we shall not be living near but I hope we shall be able to meet sometimes when you get settled in, Emma.'

'I would like that. I'm sure I shall need a friend. I er . . . William said you know about us only getting married today, but he has told everybody else we're already married.'

'Yes, he thought it would be better this way. People don't need to know all your business.'

'But William has only married me because he feels it's his duty on account of — of me having Jamie.' Emma flushed with embarrassment. 'It was a shock. I didn't realize until he started kicking and Maggie said it was a baby.

Mrs Sinclair threw me out of the house as soon as she knew. I didn't have a chance to tell William, even if I'd wanted to. We didn't even have time to say goodbye.'

'I can imagine Mary and her so-called morals,' Annie said, her soft mouth tightening.

'It will be strange being married. We saw each other every day at Bonnybrae but we never got to know each other properly so we couldn't fall in love,' Emma said wistfully.

'But — but you must have liked each other, Emma? I — I mean to . . . to have a baby together and . . . '

'William has always been kind and he used to tease me and . . . well, we seemed to be friends. I — I didn't know it was so easy to make a baby. We only slept together once, because we were stranded on a misty hill.' She sighed, thinking of Aunt Vera and her sharp tongue and crude explanations about everything. 'I'm not so stupid now. I have learned a lot of things.'

'I'm sure you have, Emma. I didn't really know much about life either when Drew and I first got married, but I did know he loved me.'

'My father still loves my mother, even after all these years and all the troubles the four of us must have caused them. It will be a long time before William and I can be like that, if we ever do.'

'I don't think it will be as bad as you think,' Annie said slowly, but her eyes were troubled. 'Come and see what we have bought you for a wedding present,' she said, hoping to cheer Emma a little. They went through to the room where Drew and William were chatting in front of the fire, although the late summer evening was still warm. They each had a glass of whisky.

'Would you like a wee toddy to help you sleep, Emma?' Drew asked, rising to his feet.

'Oh no, no, thank you. I — I don't drink. Anyway, I shall not need anything to help me sleep tonight,' she said, struggling to stifle a yawn.

'Let me show you your wedding gift from Drew and me, and then we'll let you go to bed.' Annie led her over to a large cardboard box. 'The shop packed it all up so well I don't want to disturb it because it's breakable. I knew nobody back home would buy breakable wedding gifts when you would have to bring them on the train and you had so much to bring already. It's a china tea set with twelve of everything for when you have special friends to entertain.' She drew out a cup and saucer and plate in the finest Shelley china.

'Oh,' Emma gasped with pleasure, 'how pretty it is! And it's so fine I can almost see through it.' No one else had bought them a wedding gift, she thought. 'You're kind, so v-very kind,' Emma said huskily, blinking away her tears. She gave Annie a spontaneous hug and kissed her cheek.

'Hey, don't I get a kiss too?' Drew chuckled, getting to his feet and coming to give Emma a bear hug. He held his cheek for a kiss. Emma blushed shyly but she obliged. 'We wish you both a long and happy life together, and I can see you and Annie are friends already. I'm pleased about that, and glad to have a fellow Scotsman near at hand myself.'

'I think we must let Emma get to bed now and I'll make sure our two are sleeping. Do you feed wee Jamie last thing?'

'Yes, I do, and he sleeps through most nights now until about six o'clock. I don't need an alarm clock.'

'That's good,' William said. 'I'd like to make an early start. We shall have a lot to do tomorrow before we can go to bed again. I'll join you in a few minutes, Emmie, when I've finished this.' He held up his glass.

Drew was a great talker and he kept William later than he had intended. Eventually he got to his feet, determined to go to bed but Drew did the same.

'You know, old boy,' he said jovially, slapping William on the back, 'I was afraid you would have a shrew for a wife. I imagined your mother's maid had set out to trap you into marriage, but Emma didn't trap you at all. A man can see she's an innocent lassie still, even though she's borne a son.'

'Of course Emma didn't trap me,' William said indignantly. He guessed the whisky had made Drew talk more freely than usual. 'Such a thing would never have occurred to her. In fact, she didn't expect us to marry even when she'd had the bairn. She didn't tell her family I was the father.'

'I reckon ye're a lucky man, but be gentle with her.'

By the time William got upstairs, his baby son was asleep in a padded basket beside the bed and Emma lay with one arm flung above her head, her lips slightly parted. She had unpinned her hair and it lay in a long, shining plait over her chest, emphasizing the fullness of her breasts beneath the white embroidered nightgown. She looked young and vulnerable. William's heart filled with tenderness and he longed to take her in his arms. He spoke her name softly but she didn't stir. She was sleeping as soundly as the baby beside her and he knew it would be cruel to waken her after her hectic day and with an even busier day ahead of them tomorrow. He undressed and climbed in beside her but he lay awake for a long time, wondering what their future together would hold. How would she react when she saw the untidy, dirty house which was to be their home?

13

It had become a habit for Emma to listen for Jamie's first whimper in the mornings and prevent him disturbing the household. She put him to her breast and lay back against her pillows as he suckled contentedly. She had slept well and felt refreshed but she enjoyed this brief time before the real work of the day began. She thought William was asleep, with his long legs stretched almost to the bottom of the bed. She had forgotten how tall he was until she stood beside him at the altar yesterday. Could it be only yesterday? Jamie stopped sucking and looked up at her. She smiled down at him, knowing he wanted to move to her other side. She obliged, pleased to have her swelling breasts relieved but as she glanced down her eyes widened. William was lying with his head to one side, watching intently. Emma blushed, feeling exposed without her shawl.

'Don't be shy with me, Emmie,' he said softly. 'It suits you, being a mother. You look even prettier.' Emma eyed him warily. Did he really mean that? He reached out a hand and gently stroked Jamie's head. 'I wonder if this wee fellow knows how lucky he is snuggling in there.' His hand moved below the baby to lie on Emma's flat stomach. She drew in her breath, but she liked the warmth and strength of his fingers as they splayed out over her body, almost reaching from hip to hip. 'I'd forgotten how small you are, Emmie.'

'We — we barely knew each other really,' she said in a low voice. 'It will be strange being together every day without — without . . . '

'Without my mother's eagle eye on us?' William finished drily. 'I think we shall enjoy getting to know each other as man and wife. I will try to make you happy, Emma.'

'And I will try to b-be a good wife,' Emma stammered; his exploring hand was wakening all manner of feelings in her. Jamie stirred and struggled. 'I need to change this wet son of yours now. Sometimes I think he must sit in a pool he gets so wet.' She sat up and put her legs over the side of the bed. William sighed but he knew this was not the time or place to make love to his new wife, much as he longed to waken all the emotions they had shared the one night they had spent together on the hill.

'I suppose we must dress and prepare for a long hard day,' he said. His eyes were anxious. Emma smiled up at him as she fastened the safety pin in Jamie's nappy and laid him back in his basket.

'Both my father and yours are fond of saying a good day's work never killed anyone.'

'I know but I never saw a place like Moorend. Ed Dixon and his wife must have hoarded everything. Then there's the dirt inside and out.'

'Mother said we should look on the bright side and if I can wash and polish some of the furniture, it might save us buying so much. You did say there would be a bed, didn't you?'

'I didn't see upstairs but I'm expecting there is. Ed said he couldn't bring himself to throw away his wife's possessions.'

'The sooner we get there and find whether we shall have a place to sleep tonight the better,' Emma said briskly.

William was standing at the wash stand, stripped to the waist as he sponged himself in cold water from the ewer. She was not used to having anyone else in her room while she put on her clothes. William didn't seem at all embarrassed but he had always shared a room with his brothers.

'I get better as the day goes on,' Annie replied in answer to Emma's query about her health as they all gathered for breakfast.

Fran, the middle-aged maid, sniffed in disapproval as she set a small bowl of cream beside each plate of steaming porridge.

'These are Scottish people, Fran. Can you make sure the bacon is not burning, please? Now eat up, Emma. I've packed scones and cheese and a jar of new strawberry jam for you to take, but goodness knows when you'll get a proper meal again. Is there a grocer's shop in Silverbeck village, William? You will need to stock up on food.'

'I don't know. I was only at the blacksmith's,' he admitted. 'I was not thinking about that kind of thing. I shall need to get a pony and trap so Emma can drive herself to the village.'

'Can you manage a pony and trap, Emma?'

'Oh, yes. Maggie always let me drive home if we went to the village. I enjoyed it.'

Annie was almost in tears when they had to say good-bye.

'She's always emotional when she's pregnant,' Drew said, 'but I'm glad you'll be fairly near so we can all meet up occasionally.'

After the tidy farm yard at Bonnybrae, Emma could understand why William was shocked at the state of Moorend. When they arrived, she saw broken carts and bits of machinery poking through clumps of nettles and brambles.

'Emma might get a better impression if you took her in through the front door,' Drew suggested.

'It will be locked. Remember the struggle the old man had to open it?'

'Want to bet it's never been locked since the day we were here?'

'You could be right but I'm not a gambling man,' William said. Emma sensed his tension. Drew was right, the front door opened when William turned the knob. He turned and helped Emma down from the trap because she was holding Jamie in her arms, but he kept an arm around her shoulders, almost as though protecting her but she liked his strength and warmth. She saw a clutter of boxes and a pile of old coats but the hall itself was bigger than her bedroom at home. This was home now, she reminded herself. She must not look back. Drew opened a door on either side.

'I think one is a dining room, and the other a sitting room,' William said. 'They're both full of furniture,' he added apologetically. She turned in the circle of his arm and his clasp tightened.

'We'll manage so long as we have a bed to sleep in and a fire for cooking.'

'The kitchen is at the end if I remember correctly, though we only had a fleeting visit. I didn't think I would be making our home here.'

He opened the door into a very large

kitchen. Emma thought her parents' whole cottage would fit in it. Apart from the usual large table and about eight chairs, there was the biggest dresser Emma had ever seen, and it was festooned with cobwebs over the plate racks. A small chest of drawers stood along the back wall with a brass bedstead and a tangle of blankets. There was a horsehair sofa and an armchair as well as a wooden rocking chair.

'Ah, there y'are then,' a woman greeted them, coming through one of the doors. 'I thought I saw a pony and trap arriving.'

'This is Mrs Wright, the blacksmith's wife, Emma,' William introduced the cheery-looking woman. 'This is my wife.'

'Pleased to meet you, Mrs Sinclair. I brought my niece, your new maid. Come and say hello, Polly,' she said, drawing forward a young girl.

Emma saw how shy and nervous she looked and remembered her own first day at Bonnybrae. She smiled warmly as she took the girl's small hand.

'When you weren't here I thought we might as well be getting on with things,' Mrs Wright said to Emma. 'I've cleaned out all the flues and lit the fire. I don't think they've been cleaned since Doris Dixon died. I showed Polly what to do but you might need to show her again. She's a willing little soul but she has everything to learn.' She looked anxiously from William to Emma. Jamie whimpered and struggled in Emma's arms. He was ready for his feed. 'She's good with kiddies. She has seven younger than her at home.' Emma looked at Polly. The girl nodded eagerly.

'The first thing I must do is feed him then find a drawer or something to settle him to sleep while I decide what needs to be done first.'

'There's two wicker baskets in the wash-house,' Polly offered timidly. 'Well, one of 'em is falling to bits but the other is like new.'

'If you would bring it through here then, please, Polly? Set it on the kitchen table. I'll find a blanket when I unpack. He will be safe up there out of the way. I don't think Queenie would hurt him but she needs to get used to him.' The collie pricked her ears at the sound of her name and paused in sniffing out her new surroundings.

'I don't think she'll run away when she knows we're both here,' William said, 'but we'd better keep her inside for a few days until she gets familiar.'

'The railway dray has just arrived,' Drew said, coming into the kitchen with Emma's bags. 'It's delivering two wooden chests.'

'Oh dear.' Emma looked at William as

Jamie began to cry loudly. 'I really need to feed him before he'll settle. Would you take all our boxes and bags upstairs out of the way until I can unpack them? See if we have a bed to sleep in tonight, please?'

'Oh, there are beds in both front bedrooms,' Mrs Wright said. 'But there's an awful fusty smell everywhere so I opened all the windows and left the doors open. I hope that's all right. If I were you, Mr Sinclair, I'd bring down one of the mattresses while you have your friend to help you. A bit of fresh air and sunshine would help.'

'Shall we do that, Emma?'

'It depends on whether we can carry it back up ourselves.'

'Cliff will help you. I forgot to say your new man was waiting on the doorstep when we arrived. I told him to take his stuff up the back stairs. I expect that's where the lad will be sleeping?'

'Yes, that's right,' William said, disappearing into the hall with Drew, carrying one of the wooden chests.

Emma settled in the rocking chair and she shielded Jamie with her shawl. She was still shy about feeding him in public. Mrs Wright lowered her voice and said anxiously. 'Our Polly's frightened to sleep up the back stairs with only him up there.'

'I can understand that,' Emma said. 'I'm sure there must be a spare room we can find for you. Where do all these doors lead?' she asked, looking round the kitchen.

'That's the back door, leading down four steps into the wash-house and the dairy. That one over there is down into the cellar. Old Ed used to cure his pigs down there. Next one is into the hall. This door is into the pantry and that one seems to be a store room now. When Doris was alive, I think one of the maids slept in there.'

'See if it is big enough for a bed then, Polly. If it is, we'll clear it out and scrub the floor straight away, then we can move this single bed in. Perhaps this mattress would be better for a few hours in the sunshine too. The pillow can go to a bonfire when we make one. It's stained with grease.'

'I brought a sheet and a clean pair of blankets for her,' Mrs Wright said diffidently. 'I didn't know if there'd be any clean bedding. I don't think Ed's had a decent wash himself for the past year. I expect his sister will lick him into shape.'

'We brought some bedding with us. I didn't know what to expect.'

'Many a lass would have turned and run home at the sight of this place. Mr Sinclair is a lucky man.'

'I know that, Mrs Wright,' William said, coming through from the hall. He winked at Emma. 'Is that wee fellow feeding again? He never stops. Did I hear you want this mattress taken outside?'

'Yes, please. We'll put the bed in the room for Polly. I don't like having a bed in the middle of the kitchen, or that big black sofa.'

'This little room is full of wooden boxes,' Polly called. 'Some of them are empty but some are labelled drenches for cattle.'

'Mmm.' Emma considered. 'I think we'll store everything in the dining room until I can sort them. The empty boxes can go into a shed outside. They will probably make good sticks for lighting the fire. This rug is only fit for a bonfire too. It has so many greasy spills and burn holes in it. Don't throw anything outside, though, Polly, until Mr Dixon has left. I wouldn't like to hurt his feelings.'

Drew and William came back in together.

'We've done a day's work hefting all those boxes upstairs and putting mattresses out in the sun.' Drew grinned. 'By the way, I offered the old man a lift to the station but he said he couldn't leave until he'd met you, Emma, and introduced you to Strawberry and Petal.'

'Are they his cows?' Emma asked.

'Friends, he says. He wants to be sure you'll be kind to them.'

'He needna worry, Emma is kind to all animals. He was the same with his mare. I'm sure there were tears in his eyes when I agreed to buy her. He doesn't want any of them to go to a strange place. He says it would upset them. I've told him he can come and see them. That seemed to please him.'

'There,' Emma said, tucking Jamie into his basket. 'That should keep him quiet for a few hours while Polly and I get to work. I will make you a cup of tea and something to eat before you leave, Drew, but I'm afraid it is what Annie sent.'

'I'll do that if you like, Mrs Sinclair, while you go and deal with old Ed and his cows,' Mrs Wright offered. 'Then we can get on with sorting out some of this rubbish for the bonfire when he's gone.'

'I'm very grateful for your help, Mrs Wright, but — but I'm afraid I didn't expect you to work. I can't pay you . . . '

'Eh, lass, I'm not wanting your brass. I know you and your husband will have a lot of hard work to do before you've earned any. I'm happy that you're giving our Polly a place near us where she can earn her keep and a wee bit beside, and teach her how to keep a clean house and learn to cook. Oh, cooking! I forgot to say I brought a big pan of hash with us. I put it in the oven so it will be ready for your dinners. I left a dish of it in my own oven for Joe and me so I'll need to get home by then.'

'That's very thoughtful of you. Thank you. But what is hash?' Emma asked, surprised at the woman's kindness.

'Don't you have hash in Scotland then?'

'I don't think so. I've never heard of it.'

'We usually have hash on Mondays. Makes a quick dinner for wash day. We chop up the leftover meat from the Sunday dinner, add plenty of potatoes and whatever vegetables we've got — carrots, onions, and such like, then add well-seasoned gravy. I sometimes add a bit of that new Bovril you can buy to give it more flavour. Leave it to cook while you work.'

'We shall all be very glad of it until I can stock up with food. Now I must go upstairs and change into my working dress and find my pinafores, ready to get on with some cleaning,' Emma said, 'then I will meet Mr Dixon and his friends.'

She found the carpet bags where William had left them in a large, sunny bedroom. The house was far bigger than anything she had imagined, at least three times the size of her parents' cottage. She had always taken care of her clothes and she unpacked her wedding dress and her new green travelling outfit, intending to hang them in the wardrobe before they became too creased. She screamed in fright when a furry nose and two bright eyes looked out at her.

'What's wrong, lass?' Ivy Wright came panting up the stairs. 'Did you fall, Mrs Sinclair?'

'N-no,' Emma said, still holding a hand to her chest. 'I got a fright. There's some sort of animal in the wardrobe.'

'Animal? In the wardrobe? Can it be one of the cats?'

'Not a cat. It has a long nose and . . . ' Cautiously, Mrs Wright opened a long mirrored door.

'It reeks of mothballs. Ah, is this what you saw?' She began to laugh, clutching her sides in her merriment. 'It's Doris's fox fur. It's not alive. Real proud of it she was. She was a smart woman in her day. I remember she got it and a new brown winter coat, the year afore she died.'

'You mean she wore it round her neck?' Emma shuddered in horror. 'Will you take it down for the bonfire please, Mrs Wright? I can't bear the sight of those two beady eyes and its long nose.'

'Burn it! Oh, Mrs Sinclair, you can't mean that! It was Doris's pride and joy. I expect that's why it was in this room with so many mothballs.'

'There's a brown coat in here too. It looks almost new. It seems a pity to cut it up.'

'It would be a sin.'

'You're welcome to take the fur and the coat.'

'Oh my! I'd be proud to have 'em. I could never afford a fox fur.'

Emma wondered how Mrs Dixon had afforded one if they were so short of money they couldn't pay the rent, but she was relieved to get it out of her sight and Mrs Wright seemed pleased to have both the fur and the coat.

Emma hung up her dresses and William's suit, then found her oldest working dress, an apron and cap, and prepared to meet Ed Dixon and his cows before she set to work scrubbing out the kitchen. She must ask William if they ought to buy working dresses for Polly, as his parents had done for her. They had not had any opportunity to discuss how she should manage the household and pay for necessities. There were so many things they needed to talk about.

When Emma saw the old man and his two cows in the small paddock at the side of the cowshed, she got a surprise.

'What strange horns they have! They're curling round into their head instead of upwards.' She patted the dark roan cow.

'These be Shorthorn cows and you'll be used to Ayrshires, I suppose. My Strawberry is as good as any Ayrshire,' he told her proudly.

'I'm sure she is, Mr Dixon, and I promise you I shall look after her. What large teats she has. And Petal the same.' She moved to pat the light-coloured roan, who was more inclined to graze.

'This little 'un is Strawberry's calf. I called her Socks. D'ye see she has four white socks? She'll be nearly all red when she's grown, like Tindall's bull. Petal must have gone a-calling on him sometime.' He ran a hand over her belly. 'I'd say she'll give you another calf in October.'

'I see,' Emma said slowly.

She knew all the Bonnybrae cows had stopped milking for about six weeks when they were getting near to calving. Jim said they needed a rest to build up strength and produce plenty of milk when the calf was born. He had been meticulous at keeping dates about things like that. In the adjoining paddock, two Clydesdale mares were grazing and one of them ambled across to where they stood.

'This is Bell,' Ed Dixon said, leaning over the fence to pat her neck. 'I've already said good-bye to you, old girl.' His eyes were bright and watery and Emma was afraid tears might run down his lined cheeks. She changed the subject hastily.

'I see you still have some hens running around, Mr Dixon.'

'Aye, there's more than I thought. The fox got some of 'em last winter, but some of the old hens must've gone broody and reared their own chicks without telling me. Doris looked after the hens, see. She used to set broody hens on eggs and she knew when they would hatch.'

'Yes, I would like to rear some chicks myself.'

'You should wring the neck of yon old cockerel then and make him into broth. He's a Rhode Island Red but he's been busy enough when I see how many pullets there be that look like him. Mr Tindall has some nice black and white Wyandots so he'd likely sell you one.'

'I will ask my husband to speak to him,' Emma said.

'I've left a basket of eggs in the dairy. I'm taking some to my sister and a piece of bacon hanging in the pantry. I'm ready to go now. You have a kind face so I know you'll look after Strawberry and Petal. They like a few ground oats to eat while I'm milking 'em. You'll find them in the wooden chest in the stable and there's a bit of hay left.'

'Thank you, Mr Dixon, I promise to care well for them.'

'There's two hens nesting in the stable, and another one in the loft. You'll find a nest or two in the nettles. I found one yesterday by the old pony trap.'

Looking for hens' nesting places would be a good job for Polly, Emma thought. Most of them had laid in their nesting boxes at Bonnybrae but there were always one or two who liked to hide their eggs. She and Maggie had kept a sharp eye on them.

'The gypsies are back,' Ed Dixon said. 'They'll do you no harm if you're decent with them. Tell your husband they have a nice pony that would fit into my old trap. My Doris used to drive it. It needs a new wheel. Billy Little could fix it. He has a joiner's shed at the other end of village.'

'Thank you. I'll tell my — my husband. Would you like a cup of tea and scones and cheese before you leave?'

'No, thank you, lass. I've said good-bye to the old house. I don't want to go in again. I'll wait here till the other Scots gent takes me to the station.'

'Very well. I'll tell Mr Kerr.'

Drew and William were seated at the kitchen table, eating Annie's scones and jam for their mid-morning snack.

'I don't know how I shall make the scones,' Emma said. 'There's no swee on the range and we dinna have a girdle here.'

'We didn't have a swee when we came down here,' Drew recalled. 'I don't think they use them much in Yorkshire but Annie missed her girdle and I missed her soda scones, so I drew a pattern for the swee and asked the blacksmith to make one. He fixed us up in no time.'

'Well, then.' Ivy Wright came to the table, hands on hips. 'You draw whatever it is and my Joe will make it. If cousin Tom can do it, so can Joe.'

'I'd be glad if he would, Mrs Wright. I'm used to a girdle.'

'Aye, and I like scones,' William said.

'So I see,' Ivy said dryly. 'We make bread in Yorkshire.'

'Emma makes good bread too,' William said quickly, making Emma blink with surprise at his swift defence of her.

'We bake bread two or three times a week but we like some fresh soda scones for breakfast and girdle scones for tea,' Emma explained. 'I expect we shall get used to the different ways of doing things, but for now I would be happy if your husband can make a girdle and a swee for me.'

'He will. I'll tell him.'

'I need to buy some black-lead to polish the range. I think it's a long time since it has been cared for.'

'You'll be right there. Old Ed would never think of polishing anything. He didn't even clean the flues. George Milne sells polishes, and paraffin for the lamps, candles, buckets, scrubbing brushes and all that sort of thing. He and his brother have a hardware shop in Wakefield but he comes round with his horse and cart once a month. He was here last week so it'll be a while afore he's back. You can get it in Wakefield, though. It doesn't take long if you go on the train from Silverbeck Station.'

'I expect there will be other things we will need. Is there a grocer's in Silverbeck? We shall need a bag of flour and oatmeal, salt and sugar.'

'If you write a list I'll drop it in at Mr Nicholson's on the way home. He's an obliging man. I guarantee he'll make you a special delivery tomorrow. He might even come this afternoon. His brother has the cobbler's and Miss Nicholson, his sister, runs a little bakery and sweetshop. She sells newspapers to order as well.'

'Thank you. I will write a list now,' Emma said gratefully.

'We shall need to buy some bacon until I

can buy a pig to kill,' William said. 'I hadna considered household things but we need to eat.'

'Mr Dixon has left a side of bacon hanging in the pantry and I think there is a ham wrapped up in white cotton. He told me he had cut a piece off to take to his sister. It was almost as though he felt it already belonged to us,' Emma said sadly.

'Then I must pay him,' William said, rising from the table.

When the men had gone out, Emma made a long list for the grocer and gave it to Mrs Wright.

'I must get on while Jamie is sleeping. I want to scrub the kitchen floor so that it will be dry before dinner time. You can help me, Polly, if you have finished cleaning your bedroom, but I would like you to hang the nappies on the clothes line in the orchard first. I saw a bundle of pegs on the shelf beside the boiler. They looked new but you had better take a cloth and wipe the line in case it hasna been used for a while.'

'I'll hang the nappies now,' Polly said.

'We shall all feel the benefit when the kitchen is clean and fresh, and all the dishes have been washed and the cupboards cleaned. We must keep the boiler filled up in the dairy so we have plenty of hot water, and keep the fire going. Can I rely on you to see to that, Polly? I will help you put your bed up and bring in the mattress this afternoon, and I'll find a sheet, or some kind of material, to hang over the window until I can make some curtains.'

'I'm sure she'll be very happy here,' Mrs Wright said.

'Oh, I will. I never had a room of my own afore,' Polly said. 'I promise to work hard and try to learn everything, Mrs Sinclair.' Emma knew she was barely four years older than Polly but she felt more like twenty-four when she looked at the girl's earnest young face.

'I'm sure you'll do your best, Polly. I think we shall both be tired enough to sleep anywhere by evening. You will need to look after Jamie each afternoon while I milk the two cows. When we get more we shall all need to milk. I will teach you then.'

'M-milk a c-cow? M-me?' The girl stared in horror.

'They're very quiet. Don't worry. You'll soon get used to them.'

Emma remembered how frightened she had been when she had first been close to a cow, but William and Maggie had been very patient. She enjoyed milking now. She smiled encouragingly at Polly and Mrs Wright nodded her grey head with satisfaction, convinced that Mrs Sinclair might be strict about how things should be done but she would be a kind mistress to the lass.

Half an hour later, Ivy Wright gathered up her shawl and basket to return to her own home. The big kitchen floor was thick with dirt and greasy spills and mud from the farmyard. She watched Emma scrubbing energetically and shook her head.

'If you go on working as hard as that, lass, you'll have no milk to feed that baby of yours. Don't waste all your strength. There's another day coming, aye, and another after that. The little feller needs his feed and his mam.' Emma sat back on her heels for a moment and brushed the escaping curls from her brow with the back of her hand.

'I hate a dirty house, especially the kitchen. I intend to be the best wife I can be. Anyway, this will not be so bad next time — if I can get to the bottom of the dirt now.' She viewed the half of the flagged floor with satisfaction. 'It looks better and I'm sure it smells clean after so much hot water and soda.'

'Aye, I agree it looks grand, but I tell you, lass, you'll rue the day if you tire yourself out. Neither your husband nor your baby will think any more of you.' Emma smiled and thanked her once more for her generous gift of food and her help in clearing and cleaning

Polly's small room.

'You're welcome, but you take my advice and don't work too hard.'

Later, Mrs Wright reported to her husband. 'Mrs Sinclair is a pretty young woman, but when she smiles it lights up her little face, and she has lovely eyes. I'm sure she'll be kind to our Polly.'

'Let's hope so,' Joe Wright said, 'the poor lass needs a bit of luck.'

14

Emma saw Cliff Barnes for the first time when he ambled into the kitchen after William. She was amazed at the breadth of him, although he was not quite as tall as William. He peered at her from beneath the thatch of blond hair hanging over his eyes.

'Hello, missis,' he mumbled shyly when William introduced him.

'Cliff has earned a good dinner,' William said, eyeing the food Emma set on the table and they both sat down. 'I found two scythes but one has a broken handle. I managed to sharpen the other and Cliff has worked as hard as two men when I showed him how to use it.' William sounded pleased. 'We have cleared the nettles and brambles, and the rubbish round the dairy and the byre.'

'Found three lots of eggs.' Emma was to find Cliff always mumbled into his chest and rarely looked anyone in the eye.

'They must have been there a long time,' William said, eating his dinner with relish. 'I found a sickle with a broken handle too. I want to go down to the village to find the joiner and ask if he can repair them but I'll wait until Cliff has finished for the day. We found two cartwheels amongst the brambles. They're in fair condition if I can find a man to put a new rim on them.' He sighed. 'Back home I would have known where to take them.'

'Uncle Joe will know,' Polly said, then blushed shyly. 'Aunt Ivy says he knows everybody for miles around.'

'Aye, lassie, I'm sure he does. I'll call and ask him and I'll tell your aunt she brought us a tasty pot of — what did she call it?' Emma looked up and saw Cliff eyeing the remains. She guessed he was still hungry.

'I haven't made a pudding today,' she said looking at William. 'I should probably have gone to the village for some provisions instead of scrubbing the floor.'

'No, you've done well, Emmie. The place feels better already. It smells clean and fresh now. If we have bacon and eggs for tomorrow's breakfast, we'll manage with the bread and cheese Annie sent. I didn't think about things like food.' He grinned at her. 'Your mother would say 'men never do until they're hungry,' wouldn't she?'

'She would but Annie guessed how it would be and she's been very generous. I think Cliff wants to finish the remains of the hash, don't you, Cliff?'

He nodded vigorously. He didn't wait for her to spoon it onto his plate but reached for the pot and spooned every morsel into his mouth, as though he was afraid she would take it away. None of them knew he had spent many hungry days and weeks since he was a homeless thirteen-year-old, fleeing from the beatings of a drunken stepfather. Emma poured them all a glass of milk and gave them a piece of Annie's shortbread, keeping the rest in the tin. She guessed Cliff would finish off any food in sight.

'If I can get the other scythe repaired, we'll start scything the first of the fields now I've seen Cliff can work so well. The grass is too long for grazing, even if we had animals to eat it. It's too late to grow turnips so we shall need plenty of hay for the winter when I buy more cows.'

'We shall have milk to sell then, though,' Emma said with satisfaction.

'I'm glad you enjoy milking, Emmie. We need to sell plenty of milk to pay the bills. The blacksmith said he would try to fix Dixon's old mower. It will be a lot quicker than scything if he can.'

Later, he confided to Emmie that he dared not leave Cliff to work alone.

'He was going to scythe through the cartwheels instead of pulling them out first.

They were half-buried in nettles.'

'I suppose he has plenty of strength but not much intelligence,' Emma said, 'but we're lucky to have someone to help. You will remember to bring in the mattress for our bed before you go to the village, won't you?'

'We'll do that in a couple of hours.' He gave her the boyish smile which always made her heart give a little flip.

Jamie had slept well all morning but now he was demanding a feed.

'Polly, will you empty all the things from the top of this big dresser while I feed and change Jamie, please? I will wash the plates and dishes and throw out those that are badly cracked. You wash down the shelves ready to put them back. At least we shall know they're clean and ready to use. We'll clean out the bottom cupboards tomorrow.'

'Everywhere is filthy,' Polly said.

'It is, but at least Mr Dixon has left a lot of things which will be useful. That will save us having to buy everything. I haven't seen any flat irons yet. I'm making a list of the things I shall need to buy. I brought a supply of candles. I must remember and get them out before dark.'

'Aunt Ivy had a look in the cellar,' Polly said innocently. Emma hid a smile. The blacksmith's wife was a kindly woman but she had obviously been satisfying her curiosity. She enjoyed a gossip too and Emma was glad she didn't know they were so newly married. She must be wary. 'She said there were two pretty oil lamps on a shelf behind the cellar door, as well as some lamps for the cowshed.'

'They will be useful then,' Emma said, wondering when she would get round to discovering everything herself. William had told her the wardrobes and drawers in the other front bedroom were full of clothes. 'We shall be able to cut up some of the old clothes to make a hearth rug. Can you make rugs with rags and canvas, Polly?'

'My stepmother showed me but I'm not very quick.'

'You'll improve with practice. It's a job for winter evenings but I would like to make a rug to cheer up the kitchen as soon as I can.'

Emma was bringing in the two cows for milking when a man drove into the yard with a large pony and trap. He had a jovial manner and introduced himself as Ben Nicholson, the grocer.

'I've brought the things you ordered, Mrs Sinclair, and Bob Roberts the butcher has sent you some meat. We thought it must be difficult for you moving all the way from Scotland, especially with a youngster.'

'That's very good of you to make a special

delivery,' Emma said gratefully. 'Could you carry them into the kitchen for me, please, while I — '

'Don't worry about the money. Most of the farmers get their groceries on account and pay at the end of the month. I like my money prompt, though. I have my own bills to pay.'

'Of course, but if that suits you it will please my husband. That's the way it was in Scotland.'

'There we are then, I'll carry the bag of flour through to the pantry, and the oatmeal. You'll want it in there, I suppose?'

'Yes, please. We haven't got round to cleaning out the pantry yet but I washed and dried a stone crock for the salt. I shall be able to bake some bread tomorrow now you have brought everything. I'm very grateful.'

'My word, you've made a difference in here!' he exclaimed as he entered the kitchen. 'I haven't seen it look this clean since Doris Dixon was a young woman. She wasn't brought up to farming so she kept a couple of maids to do the work. She was a bit better than the rest of us — a nice woman, though. Her father owned a woollen mill and he re-furnished most of the house when she married Ed and he paid for her clothes. When he died, things went downhill. He left the mill to her two brothers. They were supposed to pay Doris an allowance, or so she said. The brothers quarrelled so the mill had to be sold.'

'I see,' Emma said slowly. The grocer obviously liked to gossip too. 'We have a lot more cleaning to do yet,' she said, stifling an unexpected yawn. 'We'll get around to everything eventually.'

'Of course you will. Ivy said that. How are you, young Polly?' Mr Nicholson asked, seeing Polly standing on a stool to reach the top shelf of the dresser. 'I heard you'd got a job here. It looks as though you'll get a thorough training before you go off to make some man a good wife, eh?' he teased. Polly blushed shyly.

'And you're on your way to milk the cows, are you, Mrs Sinclair?'

'I am. They'll know I'm strange. They may not milk well at first.'

'If you get any fresh eggs to sell, or any butter, you let me know. I can usually sell 'em so long as there's isn't a glut, as there usually is about Easter.' He went off whistling a merry tune, leaving Emma looking forward to sitting on her milking stool and resting her head against a cow.

True to his word William, with Cliff's help, had carried the large mattress back upstairs and laid it on the brass and iron bedstead, but as soon as he had eaten his evening meal he went to catch Peggy, his own Clydesdale mare. He had wrapped the scythe and sickle blades together in an old sack and bound them well with string so that he could carry them once he had mounted. Cliff, who was already an ever-willing helper, was there to pass them up to him.

William called at the forge and thanked Ivy Wright for her tasty pot of hash and returned her pan.

'I'm on my way to the joiner's. I believe you said he's at the far end of the village?'

'Aye, that's right,' Joe said. 'I expect you'll give him plenty of trade by the time you get the carts and tackle repaired.'

'Very likely. Can you recommend a good man to put two new rims on some cartwheels?'

'Judd Grimshaw'll be the man for that. He lives a couple of miles further on. You can't miss him. There's half a dozen cottages and his shed. He makes barrels for the brewery, but he mends all the wheels round here. Makes a good job, but you'll need to bargain him down. Start as you mean to go on, lad, that's my advice. If he'll not do it, there's a man on the road to Wakefield who makes carts and he's good.'

Billy Little, the joiner, was a cheery

middle-aged man with several children running around his premises and another one on the way.

'Joe Wright said you'd likely be needing some repairs so I'm pleased to meet you, Mr Sinclair. I can use all the trade I can get with my family to keep.' William showed him the scythe and sickle. 'The scythe will be no problem. I have a new handle in stock. I'd take a bit longer to make one for the sickle. When do you need them?'

'As soon as possible for the scythe,' William said hopefully. He was delighted when the man offered to do it right away if he cared to wait.

'That's splendid. I need to see a man called Grimshaw. I believe he lives further along this road?'

'That's right, he does. If you go to see him now, I'll have this scythe ready when you return.'

It was further than William had anticipated. He was glad of Joe Wright's advice, though. Grimshaw was a talkative man and it was later than he had expected by the time they had struck a deal. Although the summer evenings were long, the light was beginning to fade by the time William returned and Billy Little had gone inside for the night but he came out when he heard the horse's hooves.

He passed up the scythe, now beautifully repaired and William thanked him warmly.

'If you're along by Moorend, I'd be pleased if you'd call in and tell me which of the things you can repair and quote me a fair price. There's a couple of farm carts and a trap which were half-buried in nettles, and a wheelbarrow and what looks like a turnip barrow.'

'I believe you.' Billy sighed regretfully. 'Ed Dixon was a nice old man but I had to stop doing work for him. He could never pay me. A man can't work for nothing when he has a family to keep.'

'No, I know that. I promise ye'll not have the same problem with me.'

The two men shook hands and parted company. Joe Wright was leaning against the wall of his forge, smoking a pipe as William reached that end of the village. He guessed the blacksmith intended to waylay him, though for nothing more than curiosity. He sighed. He was tired and ready for bed. It had been a long day. Besides, he was looking forward to having Emma to himself, and holding her in his arms, in nothing more than her nightgown, and maybe not even that. He guessed she would still be the shy lassie he remembered. Reluctantly, he drew the mare to a halt. Bonnybrae had been some distance from the nearest village so he was not used to people being interested in his affairs, but he knew the blacksmith was not a man to offend, especially when they were employing his niece. He stayed to talk a while.

Emma was deadly tired by the time she had fed Jamie and made him ready for bed. Polly had helped her carry a large wardrobe drawer from one of the other bedrooms. They set it on two chairs beside her bed.

'The clothes basket will do for him during the day but he will have more room in this at night and I can reach him from the bed,' Emma explained.

'Mr Dixon told Aunt Ivy there's a cot in the attic. It used to be his. I expect she forgot to tell you.'

'Mmm . . . something else needing a good scrub, I suppose. It may be falling to pieces but we'll have a look up there when we get other things sorted out. You can go to bed if you like, Polly. Help yourself to a glass of milk if you want one.'

Emma went to get the blankets from one of the wooden chests they had brought, and wondered why her mother had bothered to put a padlock on the bedding when the other, containing all her personal things as well as some household goods and table linen, was only fixed with leather straps.

Wearily, she spread a clean sheet over the wide mattress and reached for the blankets, but when she pulled the first one out she saw there were several neatly-wrapped parcels snuggled amongst the folds of the one below. Curious, she tossed the blanket on the bed and opened the first parcel. She gasped when she discovered a silver cake basket. There was a neatly-written card attached which read *My love and best wishes to you both, from Maggie*. On a piece of paper she had written:

Dearest Emma,

I remember how much you enjoyed polishing Mother's silver when we spring-cleaned the cabinet and when we used things for the New Year festivities. I hope you will take pleasure in these wedding gifts. Be happy.

The next parcel was much bigger and wrapped in muslin and tied with string.

'Oh my!' Emma said aloud and clasped a hand to her mouth.

She wished William was home to help her unpack and share the surprise. The parcel contained a silver tea and a coffee pot, with a matching cream jug and sugar bowl. It was from James Sinclair. There was a matching silver tray from Bessie.

Emma barely knew William's other siblings. Annie, the youngest sister, who had sent a beautifully embroidered tablecloth with a matching tray cloth and six napkins, or Robin and Jack who had sent more table and bed linen. Emma set them out on top of a chest of drawers to show to William when he came home. She was sure he would be touched and pleased, and she hoped he would not be too hurt that his mother had maintained her unforgiving silence.

She spread the blanket over the bed, enjoying the scent of dried lavender which her mother always used when storing her bedding, then she lifted out the second blanket and the handmade quilt which she had seen her mother making, although she had not known it was for her and William. At the bottom of the chest there were two boxes wrapped in brown paper. Emma opened the larger one. It was a canteen of silver cutlery from Jim.

'It's so lovely,' Emma breathed, feeling tears spring to her eyes.

She wondered if Mrs Sinclair knew how kind and generous her family had been. How had they arranged everything without her knowing?

The smaller box was wrapped in a pillow case and a large towel, and when Emma saw the beautifully inlaid top she knew at once it was a writing box from Davy, who had never once blamed her or said she had brought disgrace to the family. It had a small key taped to the bottom and when she inserted it into the lock, she saw that it was well-stocked with writing paper and envelopes. Tears sprang to her eyes as she remembered how desperate she had been for just one sheet of paper when she was at Aunt Vera's. There was a small drawer containing two pens and spare nibs, a new pencil, and two sticks of sealing wax. Each neatly fitted into their compartments, were two sparkling glass ink bottles with silver tops. Beneath a small flap she found six postage stamps — everything she needed to write letters to her family, and the box itself was beautiful. She would treasure it always. There was a card in Davy's neat handwriting, saying the gift was from him and Julie, sending their blessings and good wishes for a long and happy marriage. There was also a thick-sealed package addressed to her and William.

Emma recognized her mother's writing and sank onto the bed as she read the letter from her parents. They had enclosed twenty-five guineas from them, Richard and Joe. Emma knew how long it took to save a sum like that out of their meagre wages. Tears streamed down her cheeks at their generosity.

> *We had planned to buy you a new outfit but we had not expected James Sinclair's generosity or Maggie's kindness and help. We have included the money we would have spent on your wedding day. I know there will be many things you will need to set up a home, but I pray you will set aside enough to buy train tickets back to Scotland if the farm does not work out. There will always be a roof and a bed for all of you here.*

Her mother went on to wish them happiness and good fortune. Her father and brothers had each added a short note too. Emma knew none of them found writing letters easy but she knew their words were sincere.

Eventually, she finished making the bed and closed the lid of the trunk. She arranged everything on top of the tall chest of drawers for William to see. Weary now, she washed her face and undressed, ready for bed. It was getting dark so she lit the candle she had brought up with her in case Jamie wakened in the night. It was early for his last feed but

Emma was tired. She wrapped her shawl around her and crept downstairs to leave a candle on the kitchen table for William. This was their first night together in their new home. She wished he had not needed to go out, or that he had not taken so long. Perhaps he already had friends in the village? He had said he needed her, but what he really wanted was a housekeeper, not a wife. She had been foolish to dream.

She lifted Jamie, climbed into bed and put him to her breast. As usual, he was ready for his feed. Emma had every intention of staying awake to show William their wedding gifts, and share his surprise and pleasure but her eyelids closed.

William was a lot later than he had intended but he was disappointed to find Emma had gone to bed without him. Her candle was still burning and Jamie slept contentedly in his improvised cot beside her. He knew she had worked hard all day and he knew he should have been home earlier, even though he had concluded some satisfactory business, yet he longed to demonstrate the passion he felt. He barely glanced at the wedding gifts as he undressed and climbed in beside Emmie.

Jamie wakened earlier than usual and Emmie crept out of bed so that she would not disturb William. He looked younger and more vulnerable when he was sleeping. She wrapped herself in her shawl and went down to the kitchen. Polly came through shortly afterwards.

'It's only half past five,' Emma said, glancing at the wig-wag clock on the wall. 'Jamie wakened early. I didn't intend to waken you yet, Polly.'

'I heard the stairs creak. Anyway, it will take me longer to clean the flues and light the fire than you or Aunt Ivy so I may as well get on with it.'

'Good girl. We shall need a hot oven today. I must bake some bread. The grocer brought rice and we have more milk than we can use so we will make a big rice pudding. The butcher sent us some beef and sausages. As soon as we have had breakfast, peel plenty of potatoes, carrots and onions. Cliff seems to have a bigger appetite than most people. Once the dinner is organized, we can concentrate on the rest of the work.'

'Cliff is a big fellow,' William said, coming into the kitchen, pulling on his braces and shrugging into his tweed waistcoat.

He had slept well and he felt a bit more cheerful when he saw Emma feeding the baby. He had wondered if she was avoiding him.

'I'll bring in the cows and start milking until breakfast is ready. I want to make an early start at scything that old grass in the middle field. It will be tough going when it's been left to grow wild for the past couple of years. Cliff is no use at sharpening the blades but he's very strong and gets through a lot of work. I suppose he needs more food.'

'We have more milk than we can use but we don't have enough to sell. Mr Dixon thinks Petal will have a calf around October so I suppose she will stop milking soon.'

'Did he say that? He didn't tell me. We shall only have Strawberry milking then. Will you make butter to use the extra milk?'

'I'd love to make butter, but we don't have a churn.'

'I never thought of that.' He sighed. 'I took a lot for granted back at Bonnybrae. There's nowhere in the village I could buy one. I'd take the train to town but we need to make the most of the fine weather to get some hay.'

'Aunt Ivy said Mrs Dixon used to make butter,' Polly said.

'Ed Dixon probably chopped up the churn for firewood. We shall scrub out the pantry today and scald the creaming pans, then I shall be ready when we do get a churn,' Emma said.

'Perhaps Mr Dixon put it in the attic, or in the cellar?'

'It's not in the cellar. I had a look. Even if it was a small one, I'm sure he wouldn't carry a churn up two flights of stairs.'

Later in the day, Emma led the way to the attic. As she expected, there was no butter churn but she did find the cot. It was coated in dust but she could see it was sturdy and made of solid oak with nicely turned spindles.

'I think this will come up beautifully if we wash it in vinegar and water. The base is made of pine laths like the one we had at home but it will need a good scrub. We'll take it down. I'll ask William to carry the cot.'

'Oh look, Mrs Sinclair!' Polly screwed up her face in distaste.

'Is that supposed to be the mattress?' Emma stared at the pad which was green with mould and growing white whiskers. 'That's another thing for the bonfire. We'll take it down now and fling it out. I shall make a new mattress. I think that is a bundle of baby blankets. They must have been there for years. It looks as though mice have been at them. We'll put them on the bonfire too.'

Polly stepped back, cringing. She hated mice.

'I'll take this lot if you take the mattress,' Emma said.

Cliff and William came in, ate their meals and went out to work again while there was still daylight. Again, Emma was sound asleep by the time William joined her but he was too tired to do anything except sleep. This became their routine while the fine weather lasted.

Although Emma was working hard, it was Jamie who exhausted her. He was fractious and unsettled all the time. Her mother and Annie had warned her that even young babies sensed when they were in a strange place, but surely he must be getting used to the different sounds and smells now. Queenie slept by his basket if she was not out with William and she whined softly when he cried. The only time Jamie seemed content was when she cuddled him and put him to her breast. Polly was patient and gentle with him but even she grew weary of rocking him in her arms and singing to him.

The young maid mentioned Jamie's crying when she visited her aunt and uncle at the smiddy on her half day.

'I expect the little fellow is hungry if Mrs Sinclair is still scrubbing and washing like she did that first day. She should buy him a teat and give him some boiled cow's milk in a bottle. It would top him up.'

'She has to work hard, Auntie. There is a

lot to do, baking and cooking and washing every day. All the rooms have cobwebs and dust.'

'Aye, the place was more neglected than I would have believed if I hadn't seen it with my own eyes. A baby makes a lot of nappies to wash and there's four of you to feed.'

'I never thought a man could eat so much, or so fast,' Polly remarked.

'I suppose he works hard. Are you happy enough there, lass?'

'Oh yes, Mrs Sinclair is ever so kind and she talks to me and explains things and I'm learning to cook. She doesn't just give orders. I love little Jamie. Mr Sinclair and Cliff eat porridge and cream every morning, as well as bacon and eggs and lots of bread. Then they eat as much at dinner time as Dad and Mam and the rest of us ate in a whole day. They're still ready for more by night time.'

'A man needs his food if he's working hard,' Uncle Joe said. 'And I hear Sinclair's making a difference up there already. I shall have his mower repaired and ready to go by tomorrow. Ask him if he has any knives needing repaired. I can do them for him. I've sharpened the one that's in the mower.'

'Is that the long thing that looks like big metal teeth?' Polly asked.

'It is, lass. Each of them triangles has to be

sharpened regularly on both sides or they drag the grass instead of cutting it clean, especially when there's a lot of dead grass in the bottom. It's hard on the horses if the knives are blunt. He'll need a couple of spare knives to keep him going for a day. I expect he'll need to sharpen them at night ready for the next day but it will be a lot quicker and easier than scything.'

'Are you going to make Mrs Sinclair a girdle to bake her scones?'

'I've made it. I just need time to come up there and fix it for her.'

William was pleased when Polly told him he could collect the mower the next day. Judd Grimshaw had already made an excellent job of the two cartwheels. He had even given them a coat of paint in spite of his haggling. Billy Little had repaired one of the carts and fixed on the extra rails, ready for bringing in the hay. He had promised to come one evening and finish repairing the other one.

The following morning William sent Cliff to clean out the hayloft above the cowshed, where the hay would be stored.

'I'm taking the horses and collecting the mower from the smithy,' he said. 'You take your time and clean the loft well. I don't want any rubbish or nails amongst the hay. Sweep it thoroughly. We'll clean the loft above the stable another day.' He took Emma aside. 'Will you keep an eye on him until I come back? Make sure he's getting all the rubbish nearest the trap door above the cowshed. He's willing but he doesn't use his brain. In fact, I wonder sometimes if he has one,' he added with a wry smile.

'He's very willing. Except for his extra-big appetite he's no trouble,' Emma said. 'He brings his washing down every Monday morning. He even makes his own bed which is more than the men in the bothy did.'

As soon as Emma had hung out a line of nappies and baby clothes, she climbed up the ladder to the loft, taking a small can of milk and a scone. Cliff gave her his shy smile when her head appeared through the hole in the floor of the loft.

'You're stirring some dust up here,' she remarked, beginning to cough as it caught her throat. 'I've brought you a drink and a scone.'

Cliff's eyes lit up as they always did at the sight of food. The loft was twice as long as Emma had expected but Cliff was only clearing the half nearest the trap door. She knew there was a loft over the cowshed but it stretched much further. She realized it ran over the adjoining shed where Mr Dixon had once reared his young cattle. She had not ventured in there yet although she suspected one of the hens had a nest there. The shed was filled with manure two to three feet deep. She had been surprised to find William was so pleased about that until he explained it would make the land more fertile when he got around to spreading it over the fields.

'Cliff will soon load the carts and we shall grow a grand crop of turnips next year. New tenants usually pay to take it over but Ed Dixon told Mr Rowbottom whoever took on the farm was welcome to it because he was too old for mucking out sheds.'

Emma thought there was probably a trap door at both ends of the loft for feeding the animals below. William had been adamant that everything must be cleared so she went for a closer look.

'You will need to move these things to that trap door, Cliff,' she called. 'Mr Sinclair said he wanted the whole loft cleaned. He hopes to make a lot of hay to fill the lofts.' She didn't really like telling other people what to do. She peered more closely at the bulky objects at the dark end of the loft. There was a stack of wooden sheep troughs, and a sturdy wooden chest for holding oats, a wheelbarrow without a wheel.

'Goodness me, this looks like a churn!' Emma moved closer, wiping a finger along the curved wood. 'It is a butter churn!' she exclaimed in excitement. 'Cliff, you must be careful how you move this. Don't break it and don't bring it down from the loft until Mr Sinclair returns. He will help you with it.'

Cliff grinned vacantly.

'I dun't need 'elp.' He proceeded to lift the butter churn, complete with stand and carry it towards the trap door above the ladder. He would have dropped it down to the cowshed floor below if Emma had not shouted at him to stop.

'Leave it there, Cliff!' she said as sternly as she could. 'Bring all the other things to this end of the loft, then sweep the rest of the floor but don't throw anything down below.' She stared at him earnestly. 'Do you understand?' He nodded his head and looked forlorn.

'Nothing through hole,' he repeated.

'That's right,' Emma said more gently. 'Things would break and I want to use the butter churn. You like butter, don't you?'

He said yes and went off to the back of the loft again, reminding her of Queenie when the little collie had done something wrong and hid below the table with her tail between her legs. She heard William returning with the two horses drawing the metal-wheeled mower. She ran to tell him she had discovered a butter churn.

'I couldn't see whether it is in good condition or not. I had to shout at Cliff to stop him dropping it through the hole onto the floor below. Will you help him get it down?'

'We'll get it this evening. I'd like to get started with the mowing.' He saw the disappointment on her face. She had never grumbled about chaos in the home he had provided. His face softened and he smiled. 'Hold the horses for a minute then and I'll go up and get Cliff. I need him anyway, to shake out yesterday's swathes of grass so they dry.'

At Bonnybrae everyone, including herself and Maggie, had helped with the hay and harvest. She wondered whether William expected her and Polly to help. The horses began to move restlessly. Then she saw William and Cliff coming towards her.

'We've set the churn in the dairy. It will take a lot of cleaning and it needs some oil but it seems sound.' He grinned at her. 'It's a good job you went up there. If it's any good it will save me buying one and there are a few other useful things we need.'

'William, are you expecting Polly and me to help turn the hay?'

'Extra hands are always welcome but you have too much to do already. Anyway, we haven't got much ready for turning yet. I hope we'll get on faster now I have the mower. Mrs Wright says you're working too hard anyway. She thinks Jamie is not getting enough milk.'

'Polly told me what she said.' Emma's eyes filled with tears.

'Emmie, lassie, dinna cry. He's thriving. I'm not blaming you.' He drew a gentle finger down her cheek, wiping away a tear.

'It upsets and tires me when he keeps crying. He was so good before we came here. I think he's missing my mother nursing him. I want to be a good wife, William, and make you a clean home like you had at Bonnybrae. I don't want you to regret having to marry me.'

'You are doing fine, Emmie. I'm proud of you. We must get off to the field now, though.' He hesitated. 'I'll tell you what would help me: send Polly out with food for Cliff and me. We wouldn't need to come back in with the horses until evening.'

'I can easily do that.'

'Things will get better, Emmie. That letter which arrived this morning was from Drew. He wants me to go with him to see some in-calf Ayrshire heifers. They don't calve until October and November. I shall be free to help with the milking by then. When we have milk to sell, it will bring in some money. I don't think Cliff will ever learn to milk, though, so it would depend on you and me, and young Polly, if you can teach her. We'll hire another man later on.'

'Mrs Sinclair, can you come?' Polly called. Her voice trembled and she sounded near to tears. She was rocking Jamie in her arms. 'I can't stop him crying and he's getting all hot and bothered.'

Emma looked at William helplessly then her humour surfaced. 'He has a temper when he doesn't get what he wants — like his daddy,' she whispered with a glint in her eye. It was good to see a spark of the old Emmie and he grinned, his spirits lightening.

15

William and Cliff finished eating their dinner in the field. The mowing was going well and Cliff was turning yesterday's swathes to the sun to dry. William led the horses to the burn at the far side of the field so they could drink. He was waiting patiently when he saw a young man coming towards him from the direction of the Common. He remembered the gypsies were camped there. Since Lord Hanley had renewed the boundary fences, the gypsies could no longer leave their animals to graze on Moorend land. William braced himself, expecting the man to complain and utter abuse. He was surprised when he asked if he could help Cliff to shake out the hay.

'You want work?' William asked.

'Want hay to feed my horses and three goats,' he said. 'I work for you and help make good hay. You give me enough hay to keep my animals in winter. Bargain? Yes?'

William eyed the young man warily. Mr Rowbottom and Joe Wright had said the gypsies would do no harm if he treated them fairly. Even Ed Dixon had said much the same to Emma.

'You would work to help with all the hay first?'

'Yes, but I need — I want promise you will leave enough hay in last field for me?'

'All right. We'll see how you work this afternoon,' William said.

'We have wooden rakes. You will buy two? To rake the rows into heaps. Is that right?'

'Why yes, that is how we do it once it is nearly dry. Have you made hay in this country before? Did you help Mr Dixon?'

'My father helped Mr Dixon. I was boy then. Mr Dixon did not make hay in fields near Common since my father die. I did not help. Good horses.' He grinned when the two mares lifted their heads from the burn after taking long drinks.

'Yes, they're working well together,' William said. 'Now I must get back to mowing.' He watched the man sprint away towards the gypsy camp and vault effortlessly over the boundary fence. In a short time he returned, carrying the usual two-pronged fork for turning the hay, as well as two long-handled wooden rakes with firmly fixed wooden teeth. He brought them for William's inspection.

'You will buy these?'

'How much?' William grinned, expecting to barter. 'I don't have much money yet.'

'One day you have lots of money.' The

young man grinned in response, showing a fine set of strong white teeth in his deeply tanned face. He was a good-looking fellow with his sparkling dark eyes and mop of black hair. 'My grandmother says you work hard and earn good fortune.'

'I hope she's right, but I need to get on with mowing right now.'

'You buy rakes for a dozen chicken eggs for two weeks? And fresh milk for our bambinos to drink.'

'Don't they drink goat's milk?'

'Goats have no milk. Expecting kids.'

'How much fresh milk?'

'What you can spare until next new moon.'

'That's a month then. All right, it's a bargain. I will tell Em . . . tell my wife. She deals with the milk and eggs. What's your name?'

'I am Garridan. You call me Dan.'

'All right, Dan. Will you take one of these rakes to Cliff over there? Tell him when he gets to the end of the row, he must go back to the far side of the field again and start raking into heaps from that end. Haycocks we call them. You understand?' The man nodded. 'You can show Cliff?'

Although he concentrated on his horses and the mower and keeping a straight swathe, William kept an eye on the two men until he was satisfied that the young gypsy knew what he was doing. If the weather held and he got half the fields mown, made into hay and gathered into the lofts, he would be pleased. Even if the weather broke, he intended to cut and gather up the rest of the long grass in the distant fields so that fresh grass would grow in the spring. Things were going better than he had dared to hope except for one thing — he and Emma were still no more than friends although they slept in the same bed. When he first came to Yorkshire, he had longed for company. When she had agreed to marry him he had looked forward to holding her in his arms again, seeing her smile, teaching her about making love, rousing her as he had the night they had spent together on the moors.

Annie had warned him to be patient. He knew Emma had been reluctant to marry him so he knew she didn't love him — whatever love is, he thought bitterly. His mother had never shown much love as far as he was concerned and now she had cast him aside like a leper. He was not the first man to get a girl pregnant out of wedlock. The trouble was his mother was a snob and she couldn't forgive him for consorting with her maid. His thoughts went round in circles as he went up and down the field and back again.

He wondered whether the gypsies were reliable. Would Dan turn up the following day? He need not have worried. In the morning, the young man was there waiting for them when he and Cliff got to the field. He had brought his cousin too.

'This is Manfred. We call him Fred.' He was much younger but he said he wanted to work in return for hay to feed his goat and two kids.

'Our uncle will sharpen knives. He is lame but he says he do them if we take them to the fence.' He grinned. 'Wife shout at him when he do nothing.'

'And how much does he expect me to pay him?' William asked wryly.

He had been half-asleep last night by the time he had finished sharpening all three knives ready for a fresh start today. He had been too tired to do anything but fall into bed. Emma was already sleeping anyway and she was up before he wakened again this morning. He sighed. It was not much of a start to married life.

'Uncle is happy to do the knives because you give us hay.'

'All right,' William agreed. 'You can take it in turns to take a knife to him, leave it, and bring back the sharpened one each time.'

He had told Emma about the gypsy

helping them so she sent out a generous basket of food at dinner time but when they stopped to eat, a young gypsy girl was already halfway across the field with food for the two boys. William had thought they would expect free food. They worked well and seemed happy. Sometimes they sang as they worked. It pleased him that they talked to Cliff. They seemed to understand he was slow-witted and needed help to do things but they were patient and didn't make fun. In the distance, their uncle looked bent and old as he leaned on the fence, but he made an excellent job of sharpening the pointed teeth of the knives and William was grateful for that. He was anxious to keep going for as long as the weather held. Back home in Scotland he was used to having only a week at a time, or two at most, to snatch in the hay crop.

'We've been lucky to get a dry spell of weather,' he remarked, scanning the skies as he settled on a heap of hay to eat his dinner.

'Not a spell. Mother Yakira knows about weather,' Dan said. 'She looks at the moon and watches clouds. She says it was wet and upset for first half of month. Now we can have real summer but thunderstorms at end of August. We finish hay by then?'

'If she's right we shall be fortunate indeed. We could even mow all the fields and cart the hay into the lofts. Where do you store your hay to keep it dry?'

'We have a shelter to cover top. Not so good. We take hay on small cart when we move. But we leave hay here for return in spring. Grass grows late on common. Sometimes hay is wet and black when we come again.'

'When do you move on?'

'End September.' Dan shrugged and pulled a face. 'October maybe. Elders decide. We follow.'

'Do you know how to build a stack to protect the hay from rain?'

'Protect without shelter? How you do that?'

'If we have time, and we get all the grass cut and made into hay, I will give you enough to build a small round hay rick or stack. Then you must thatch it. Make a round, pointed peak so that the rain runs off. It will be as good as the day we made it when you return in spring.'

Dan frowned. 'You swear? I have seen pointed stacks in Ireland with no shelter to keep out rain. I thought it would be . . . ' He shrugged. ' . . . rotten.'

'Not if you thatch it properly. Ask your friends to collect some strong canes and sharpen one end. They could collect some dry bracken as well perhaps. Straw would be better but I don't have any. Maybe next year I shall plough a field and sow oats to feed my animals. And turnips too.'

'I know turnips,' the younger man said with a wide grin. 'Lots of turnips in Ireland. I cut with knife and eat.'

'Aye, they're very tasty for man and beast,' William agreed. He was beginning to enjoy the company of the young gypsies. He had always been used to working with Jim and the rest of the men at home. He pushed away a wave of homesickness.

The old gypsy was right in her forecast. William worked hard, never quite believing there would be another fine day. The more time he and Cliff spent in the fields, the more work Emma and Polly did, milking and cleaning up after the two cows and calf, feeding hens and collecting eggs, searching for hidden nests, as well as trying to get the house clean and keep up with cooking for the four of them. Emma found herself baking bread four times a week as well as girdle scones in between. It was a great help having a weekly delivery from the grocer and the butcher with their horse-drawn covered carts, but there were several items they didn't stock.

Jamie seemed to be constantly hungry and unsettled, and he tired her out. There were days when he barely seemed to sleep at all and it made both her and Polly weary. She knew it was no use complaining, especially when William was working so hard in the fields. She resolved she would try Mrs Wright's advice and give him extra milk.

It was a Sunday evening and for the first time since their arrival at Moorend, William went to bed at the same time as Emma. Her cheeks flushed when she became aware of William lying on his side watching Jamie suckling, his tiny fists kneading her breasts. When he had finished she laid him down to sleep. William curled one arm around her, drawing her closer.

'Life will get easier and better, Emmie, I promise you,' he said softly. His other hand moved to her stomach. It was strong and warm and his fingers spread over her. She drew in her breath. There were days when she had longed to go back home, but most of all she had longed for him to take her in his arms and love her as he had out on the mountain.

'Emmie?' he said her name softly, questioning, then more sharply, he asked, 'What's this?' as his hand moved lower and discovered her extra layer of clothing. She groaned silently and sighed.

'It — it's almost finished b-but I've started b-bleeding again,' she said. It wasn't a subject she had discussed with anyone so she hoped William understood about such things. She longed for him to love her, but not when she was like this.

'I see,' he said flatly and withdrew his hand.

He lay staring at the ceiling for a few moments then withdrew his arm and turned away, ready to sleep. Emma turned over too, unwilling to let him see the tears trickling down her cheeks onto her pillow. If he had married her for love he would have kissed her, sympathized, comforted her. Had Aunt Vera's bitter words been true when she said men were like animals and only wanted one thing?

William had sisters and in spite of their efforts to be discreet, he had occasionally seen bloodied cloths soaking in the wash-house at Bonnybrae, but he understood little about that side of a woman's bodily functions, the rhythms and moods and timing. Once he had heard men discussing the subject at the thrashing mill. One had been convinced his wife used it as an excuse when she didn't want him. Would Emma do that? Maybe she didn't want him in that way now she knew what it was like to be a woman. She had matured in so many ways since she left Bonnybrae. The stay with her aunt and uncle, and the birth of her baby had changed her. He had been surprised and grateful at the calm and competent way she had tackled the cleaning and organizing of her work in the house and dairy, and the way their young maid worked so willingly for her. Mrs Wright had told him he was a lucky man to get a wife like Emma who was both pretty and hardworking. He enjoyed good food and a clean home, but he wanted more than a housekeeper — he yearned for the responsive, passionate girl he had discovered by chance on top of a mist-covered moorland.

Neither William nor Emma slept well that night and Jamie wakened even earlier than usual so Emma was downstairs when William opened his eyes.

'Will you want food brought out to the field again today?' Emma asked at breakfast time.

'Yes, but this should be the last day if we can finish carting in the hay, then we shall be glad to have a hot dinner again,' William said with feeling. 'Mother Yakira, the old gypsy, is prophesying there will be rain before tonight.'

'It doesn't look like rain,' Emma said, glancing out of the window at the blue sky.

'Dan swears Yakira knows about such things. He insisted I should show him and Fred how to thatch their stack of hay on Saturday evening. They had a lot of eager helpers and they don't bother about the Sabbath so I think they will have finished it.'

Emma set aside a can of fresh milk for the gypsies to collect according to William's agreement.

'I'll set the rest in the creaming pans in the pantry,' she said, 'and tomorrow I should have enough cream to churn into butter.'

She washed and scalded the milking buckets while Polly hung the first load of washing on the line in the orchard.

'I miss not having a rubbing board for these dirty collars and the soiled nappies,' she muttered, struggling to remove the stains. 'I don't think I can wait until Mr Milne comes round with his hardware. I need a flat iron.'

'I tried hard to scrub off the rust from the one you found in the cellar, Mrs Sinclair,' Polly said unhappily.

'I know you did, Polly,' Emma said, her lips tightening, remembering the rusty streak the old iron had left on her white pinafore. She couldn't blame the young maid. 'I think it has been used as a hammer. The sole is so rough and pitted.'

'I could ask Aunt Ivy if we could borrow hers. She has two big ones and a small one.'

'Thank you, Polly. I don't like to borrow things. I think I must go to Wakefield today and buy the things I need. This is the last day when Mr Sinclair and Cliff will be in the fields all day. You and I can eat early. If I feed Jamie a bit early too, I could catch the train from Silverbeck station. I shall be back in plenty of time to milk the cows and give Jamie his next feed. I shall take your aunt's advice and buy a teat so that I can try giving Jamie some boiled cow's milk from a bottle. We can't go on with him waking and crying most of the day.'

'Oh yes,' Polly said fervently. 'Auntie Ivy is sure he'll sleep better.'

'All right. You collect the eggs and see if you can find where that hen is laying in the orchard. Bring in the washing and put it on the clothes horse in front of the fire if there is any sign of rain.'

Emma washed herself, pleased to be able to dispense with the monthly cloths. She donned her best brown skirt and the high-necked cream blouse she had made before her wedding. The day was warm and sultry but, bearing in mind the gypsy's warning, she folded her shawl and put it in her basket then hurried the two and a half miles to Silverbeck station, remembering she had to turn off at the fork in the road because the station was a good half mile from the village.

Her stomach was churning with nerves but

she didn't want Polly to know she had never ventured beyond Locheagle on her own before. Her father had accompanied her to Aunt Vera's and home again and William had been with her on the journey to Yorkshire. She had caught an unnerving sight of people bustling everywhere when they had arrived at the station in Wakefield, but Drew Kerr had been waiting for them and he had taken her bag, held her elbow and ushered her and Jamie to the pony and trap. She'd had a glimpse of tall buildings and more people than she had ever before seen in her life. She had never imagined buildings so high they could have three storeys and there was at least one church spire reaching to the sky. Drew had told them Wakefield was a city now.

She clutched the handle of her basket until her knuckles shone white. She had brought one of the precious guineas her parents had sent since William had not mentioned how they should pay for their household bills. Apart from their train journey together, there had barely been opportunity for serious conversation on their own since they arrived at Moorend Farm. She understood how important it was to make all the grass into hay while the fine weather lasted but she would be heartily glad when they could get into a normal routine. She bought her ticket and put the change carefully in her purse, and hid the purse beneath her shawl in her basket. She had heard there were pickpockets and thieves in all big towns.

Outside the station she looked around in bewilderment, wondering which direction to take. A plump, middle-aged woman walked by.

'Excuse me,' Emma said nervously. 'Could you tell me where I can find a chemist's shop please, and a hardware shop?'

'We-ell, let me see. I usually go to Milne's. There's nearly every kind of shop you could want down that way. I'm going in that direction. If you walk with me I'll direct you before we part company. I'm not shopping today. I'm going to visit my sister. She's been ill but she's getting better now.'

The woman chattered on as they walked.

'I can tell you're not from these parts, lass, the way you talk. Where you from?' Emma did not always notice when they turned right or left as she answered the woman's questions. 'And there's Walter Moorhouse, the chemist along there. I'd forgotten about that. I usually go to Lambert's,' the woman said as she directed her when they parted.

Emma found the chemist first. She went in and asked for a teat but she ended up buying a banana-shaped bottle with a sort of teat on both ends which was supposed to let the air out when the baby sucked and prevented wind. She hoped she had not wasted her money.

Further along she discovered a haberdashery shop. She needed wool to knit William some new stockings and she wanted to put new feet in two pairs which he had almost worn away. He'd had nobody to darn his socks since he came to Yorkshire. She had found one pair which he had tried to darn himself. The sight of it tugged her heart strings. She visualized him struggling to mend his own socks after all the loving care he had received from Maggie at Bonnybrae. The darns were large and rough around the edges and she knew they must have been uncomfortable for walking. She wondered if William had been as miserable away from his home and family as she had been at Aunt Vera's.

He had also lost some of the buttons from his shirts. She bought some more and blue wool to knit Jamie a bigger jacket, as well as some strong, closely-woven calico to make a new mattress for the cot. She renewed her sewing threads and bought a packet of needles, a thimble and two of the hooks for making rugs. She intended to teach Polly how to make rugs during the winter. She thanked the woman for wrapping her purchases and made her way to the ironmongers across the street as the seamstress had directed. She had noticed a man lounging against a doorway earlier. He was still there so she assumed he must be meeting somebody.

George Milne, the ironmonger, came to serve her himself when he heard her Scottish accent, ushering his young assistant to another job.

'Are you the wife of the new tenant at Moorend Farm then?' he asked. 'We heard it was a Scotsman that had taken it. He's a brave man to tackle a place as run-down as that.'

'We don't mind hard work so long as we can make a living,' Emma said firmly. The man nodded.

'Aye, we've all to make a living. What can I get for you today? We travel round the villages with the horse and dray, you know. My brother carries most things. He'll fill up your paraffin can for the lamps.'

'We just missed his last round and I need two flat irons now.'

'They'll be heavy to carry,' he said, eying Emma's slight figure.

'I'll manage. I shall need new wick, enough for two house lamps and three byre lanterns.'

'Byre lanterns, eh?' he smiled.

'Lamps for the cowshed,' Emma amended, flushing. She had forgotten they didn't talk about byres in Yorkshire. 'I also need a rubbing board and black lead polish for the range. We need a tin bath, a large one. Do I need to order that?'

'We have some in stock through the back. I could pack everything in the bath and send it by train for your husband to collect at Silverbeck Station in a day or two?'

'That would be kind of you but I need to take my irons and the black-lead with me today.'

'All right. It's a good order and we shall value your custom in future so I'll give you a small iron for your frills and things. You could take that and one big one with you, and the polish. Do you want some steel wool for hinges on the oven? I'll make a parcel and send the rest. How about that?'

'Thank you. That would be a great help.' Emma beamed at him and he grinned.

'Milne brothers are always pleased to oblige, Mrs Sinclair, and there's not much we can't get for you even if we don't stock it.'

Emma paid and put the parcel carefully in her basket, pleased with her purchases but Mr Milne was right, her basket was full and heavy. She put the change in her purse and tucked it under the basket's cover.

She was shocked to see how the sky had darkened when she got outside. A big black cloud glowered overhead. It seemed the gypsy Yakira was right about the weather. She saw the man again, on this side of the street now but still lounging against a wall. She frowned, feeling uneasy. More importantly, she had to catch the train home and she had forgotten which way to go. She walked quickly away, aware of the man eying her up and down.

She slowed her pace when she came to a clothes shop but she didn't stop. Her own green dress and jacket were much smarter than anything in the window. She realized she had not passed the shop before. Was she walking in the wrong direction? She had crossed the street from the chemists of course. She crossed back again and kept on walking but none of the shops seemed familiar. When she looked around she was surprised to see the same man in a brown jacket nearby. He stopped when she stopped. Was he following her? Was he a pickpocket? She felt in her basket and clutched her purse in her hand, feeling reassured. Two women came towards her and she asked directions to the railway station.

'You're going in the wrong direction, lass,'

one woman answered and began to give directions.

'Come on, Bertha,' the other interrupted. 'It's coming on rain.' The first woman grimaced. 'Anybody'd think we'd melt,' she muttered, and continued with her directions before hurrying after her friend. She turned and called over her shoulder. 'You could take a shortcut if you turn second left, then third right.'

Emma mentally repeated the directions. People were scurrying for shelter or going home now. A plump woman with a child bumped into Emma, almost making her drop her basket. She half-turned. That man was close behind her. She walked faster. The quicker she walked the louder and faster his footsteps seemed to get, although Emma knew it could be other footsteps with so many people about. A steady drizzle had begun to fall. She stopped at a shop window and propped her basket on the ledge while she pulled her shawl more firmly over her shoulders and tucked the ends into the waistband of her skirt. The soft wool would not turn much rain. She glanced over her shoulder. The man was closer now, pulling up the collar of his brown jacket, near enough for her to see the whites of his eyes and his hard grey stare assessing her as though she was an animal for sale. She clutched her basket and purse and hurried on, almost running now.

She had passed two turnings. Perhaps if she took the next one she would lose the man. Could the woman have meant this narrow entry? The buildings towered above her, shutting out the light but doing nothing to stop the rain. She glanced over her shoulder. Her heart thumped. The man had followed her. There were fewer people around now. She took another turning, hoping it would take her back to the main street. It didn't. Still the man followed, closer now. Emma realized she was hopelessly lost. Her basket seemed to be getting heavier. Her heart was pounding, her breath coming in little gasps. She hurried on. Some of the buildings looked derelict. She could smell stale tobacco. She fumbled in her purse and took out her return ticket for the train. At least she could get home if he snatched her purse. Why didn't he just grab it? There was nobody to see him now. Emma knew it had been a mistake to leave the shops and people behind but she didn't know how to get back so she could ask for help and proper directions. She turned down another street but it was no wider than the first one. She was almost sobbing now and there was a stitch in her side. All she wanted was to get home. She cannoned into a figure. She stifled a scream. The man seemed to have stepped out of nowhere. She was trapped between them.

16

At Moorend, William had just finished carting the hay home before the rain came in earnest. The two young gypsies had worked with him to the end. He had thought they wouldn't come back now they had their own stack of hay, but Garridan had come and even brought his own gelding to pull one of the carts in place of William's little mare.

'It will be good for him to work between the shafts again,' Dan grinned. 'Soon he will need to pull the caravan many miles every day.'

'Where will you go?' William asked curiously. He had grown to like the two young men. They knew even more than he did about the countryside and nature. He gathered they also knew a lot about poaching and he wondered what Mr Rowbottom would say if he heard them.

'We go to Ireland for the winter.'

'I see,' William said. 'And when you come back, do you have a hay knife for cutting the hay from your stack?'

'Hay knife?' Dan asked and shook his head, then he grinned. 'We never had stack of hay.

Uncle says you're good man although not Romany.'

William knew he would not have got all the hay made and gathered in without their help. It would have gone to waste.

'I am glad of your help. You earned the hay but you will need a special knife to cut it neatly into trusses.'

'Trusses? What are they?'

'Squares of hay cut neatly from the stack. You must keep the face of the stack straight so the hay does not spoil.'

'What is this knife?'

'I could ask the blacksmith to make you one.'

'No, no. We have cousin make metal tools.'

'All right.' William took a stick and began to draw in the damp earth. 'It is shaped like a very big arrowhead but it is flat and smooth and the two sides from the point are very sharp to cut into the hay. You need a long handle from the third side and you press down with your feet, like a spade.'

'You will tell this to our uncle before we leave?'

'All right.' William grinned and waved them on their way as they both jumped easily onto the gelding's back and set off towards the common.

He was surprised to see Strawberry at the

gate of the field, mooing restlessly, clearly wanting to be relieved of her milk. Petal stood nearby, chewing her cud. He wondered why Emma had not milked them. She had a strict routine for the cows, just as they'd had at Bonnybrae. He walked towards the house and met Polly coming out. She seemed distraught and near to tears. She was holding Jamie in her arms, trying desperately to quieten him but his little cheeks were hot and red, and he was throwing his tiny fists around like a boxer.

'What's the matter with him?' William asked bluntly.

'Sir, he's hungry and Mrs Sinclair has not come home. She said she would be back in time to milk the cows because Jamie had an early feed this afternoon.'

'Wait! What do you mean, Mrs Sinclair has not come home? Has she gone to the village?'

'No, sir, she . . . '

'Don't keep calling me sir,' William snapped, feeling his tension rising. 'Sir makes me feel like a schoolmaster. Where has my wife gone?'

'She's gone on the train to Wakefield, s — s — s, Mr Sinclair. She said she would be home . . . I don't know what to do with Jamie.'

'Have you learned to milk the cows yet?'

'Milk the . . . ? Oh no, I — '

'All right, all right! But you'll have to learn soon.'

He hurried past Polly and into the house, running up the stairs without removing his boots. He had barely looked at the wedding presents still set out on the tallboy but he knew that none of them bore his mother's name, while Emma's parents had been generous and forgiving. They must have sacrificed half their lifesavings. He opened the writing box and saw that Emma must have taken out some of the money. His heart beat faster. Had Emma run away?

He had counted himself fortunate to have such a long spell of dry weather. He had spent every minute making hay. What a fool he was to bring Emma to a strange place, to live in a cheerless home amongst people she didn't know. He had neglected her shamefully. He thought she understood how important it was to make the pastures suitable for grazing so he could take sheep to graze and earn some money, but Emmie was so young. Could he blame her if she was sickened by the demands of a baby, cooking, washing and cleaning? Annie had been well-loved but she had still been homesick. His heart sank. Had Emma seen the train north and gone to her parents?

He sank down onto the side of the bed and put his head in his hands. What would be the point of all his work if Emma had left him? The cries of his son pierced his consciousness. Surely Emma would not leave her baby behind. So where could she be? The crying irritated his frayed nerves. Maybe it had become too much for Emma if she hadn't enough milk to satisfy him. He remembered how the tears had sprung to her eyes when he had passed on Mrs Wright's advice. She had felt she was a failure. Slowly he got to his feet and went downstairs.

Jamie was sucking noisily on Polly's little finger but that did not soothe him for more than a few seconds.

'Can't you give him something?' he asked, forgetting Polly was barely more than a child herself.

'My stepma sometimes gave the little 'uns boiled cow's milk.'

'Then you can give him some. I can't stand a noise like that. I'll bring the cows in from the field now. You scald one of the enamel mugs and bring it to the byre.'

'B-but he can't d-drink, not from a m-mug, not yet.'

'Well, spoon it into him then,' William snapped. He went out, leaving Polly to bite her lips and wipe away tears. She wished she could run away to Auntie Ivy's. She hated the master. She wouldn't blame Mrs Sinclair if she never came back, she decided crossly.

She watched William carefully wash and dry the cow's udder, then wash his hands in a bucket of clean water. He dried them before he sat on the little stool and started milking. He made it look so easy. The milk streamed into the pail with a steady thrum. He asked her to pass the mug then squirted milk from one teat until it was half-full of warm frothy milk. Polly carried it and Jamie back to the kitchen, and found a towel to put under his little chin. She had seen her stepmother feeding the babies often enough to know they always spilled as much as they ate at first. Jamie was impatient and kept knocking the spoon with his fists then crying because he didn't get any milk but Polly persevered. She told Cliff to get his own meal from the pan of stew in the oven and to leave enough for everybody else.

Eventually Jamie grew calmer and began to understand he had to suck the milk from the spoon even if he didn't like the feel of the cold metal. Polly knew a bone spoon would be better but they didn't have one.

William finished milking the two cows and turned them back into the field. It was raining steadily now and they seemed reluctant to leave the shelter of the buildings. He cleaned the two stalls and made sure everything was washed and in order in the dairy. He couldn't settle to go indoors and eat his supper, even if young Polly had made any. He paced the farm yard and went into the byre, then back out. He looked in the stable but Cliff had turned the two horses out to the field. Most of the hens had gone into their hut to escape from the rain. He chased in the few which were lingering near the door and shut them in until morning. Emma did all these things every day. She didn't moan or grumble. What would he do if she didn't come home? It wouldn't be home if Emma was not here. It came to him like a flash of lightning. Wasn't that what Drew had been trying to tell him?

He stood still in the pouring rain. He had said he didn't know what love was because his mother had brought them up not to show their emotions and she had always seemed stern and aloof.

'Loving a wife is different,' Drew declared. 'I'd do anything to make Annie happy. I'd even go back and work for my brother. You'll know when you find the woman you can't live without.'

Well, he did know now. No one had forced him to marry Emma. He could have sent her money to look after the baby, but he wanted Emma beside him. He had longed for her company ever since they had been parted and he came to Yorkshire. Now she was his wife and he knew he needed more than her company. He remembered she had been reluctant to say she would marry him. His heart was heavy. If she was so homesick, if she had gone home to her parents then he would follow. He wouldn't stay here without her. There would be work somewhere. He would work for other farmers if he had to, as long as Emmie was with him. What a blind fool he was.

He collected his tweed jacket from the peg behind the door, pulled his cap on and set off for the station. He would wait until the last train had come and gone. He would pray that Emma was coming back to him and not on her way back to Scotland and her family.

* * *

Two strong hands gripped Emma's shoulders.

'Steady lass, steady now,' a deep voice rumbled above her head.

Emma glanced fearfully over her shoulder, expecting the other man to grab her, or snatch her purse, but the narrow passage was empty. She raised her eyes and saw a silver button next to her nose, and another further up. Her eyes widened. She stared upwards. The man seemed like a giant with his domed policeman's helmet on his head and the black cape around his broad shoulders.

'Th-there was a m-man,' she gasped, unable to resist looking back again. 'H-he was f-following me, I ken he was . . . '

PC Brownlee could feel Emma's slight body trembling beneath his hands. She was distraught. He noticed her fresh young face, her wide frightened eyes, the quality of her shawl and high-necked blouse.

'I believe you, lass.' Over her head he had seen the man in the brown coat slink into an entry which ran between the backs of rows of houses. 'You're not from these parts, are you?' he asked, noting her Scottish accent. It was more pronounced in her agitation.

'N-no. I must get to the railway station. P-please, can you direct me?'

'You're heading the wrong way.'

He took her elbow and turned her around the way she had come. She shuddered, afraid she would run into her pursuer. They walked a few yards and the policeman slowed, and looked down the entry where the man had disappeared. He thought he saw a figure flattening himself against a brick wall. He raised his voice.

'I can do better than give you directions, miss. I'll escort you there myself and make sure you're safe.'

Emma wondered if he thought she was deaf. The narrow rutted lane was full of puddles and she was struggling to keep pace with his long strides.

'Can I carry your basket for you, miss?' He noticed the wedding ring on her finger as she gave him the basket. 'This is heavy. What have you been buying today?'

'It's the irons, smoothing irons. For ironing clothes,' she said, seeing his puzzled expression. 'This is the first time I've been to a town. I — I'm sorry to trouble you,' she added when they came to a busier road with people around. It was not the one she had seen before. 'I — I could find my way from here.'

'It's no trouble, Miss . . . er, Mrs . . . I'd like to be sure you're safe.'

'Y-you do believe there was a man? He was following me, I'm sure.'

'Aye, I caught a glimpse of him myself. Greasy fair hair sprouting from under his cap and a brown coat. Is that the one?'

'Yes! If he'd asked for money to buy a cup of tea I would have given it to him, but he didn't look like a tramp. He didn't speak.' She shivered. 'His eyes were like grey glass staring through me.'

It didn't seem too long before they reached the station but the police constable went in with her. There was a train already in and Emma went to get on it.

'Just a minute, miss! Which train do you want? Where do you live?'

'Silverbeck. I need to get to Silverbeck station,' Emma said urgently, afraid the train would leave without her. The constable stopped a porter and asked if it was the right train.

'Silverbeck? No, it left a good ten minutes since. There'll be another in about an hour.'

'An hour!' Emma gasped.

'Don't worry, miss. I know the stationmaster here. His daughter is a friend of my younger sister.' He took her elbow again and steered her to the stationmaster's office. He explained that Emma had had a fright and that she wanted the train to Silverbeck. The two men went outside the door, speaking quietly.

'I reckon he was after more than her purse,' PC Brownlee said grimly. 'We've had four cases of women being attacked in the last eighteen months, all from other parts of the country. The sergeant thinks there could be more but the women don't report it in case their husbands blame them.'

The two men came back in. PC Brownlee said, 'I need to get back to my beat now, miss, but I'm leaving you in safe hands. Mr Hanson is the stationmaster and he'll see you onto the right train for Silverbeck.'

'Thank you, I — I canna thank ye enough, Constable,' Emma said.

'That sounds like a Scots tongue to me,' the stationmaster said. 'We had some boxes to deliver to Moorend Farm at Silverbeck for a Scotsman about three weeks ago. Would that be a relation of yours, miss?'

'My husband arranged for two chests to be delivered. His name is William Sinclair.'

The stationmaster nodded. 'That's the name. Generous he was, even though they say Scotsmen are tight with their brass. She'll be all right with me, Constable.'

'She's still shaking. She had a nasty shock,' PC Brownlee said as they went outside together. 'She'd never been in a town before. She was completely lost, poor lass.'

'I'll give her a cup of tea and see she gets the right train.'

When the stationmaster returned, he rinsed a pint pot in a bowl of scummy water and dried it on a grey-looking cloth. He lifted an enamel teapot from the rib in front of a small fire and poured the black liquid.

'There, miss, I'll stir in plenty of sugar. Sweet tea's good for shock and it'll warm you. Let me shake some of the rain off your shawl. I hope you don't get a chill by the time you get home tonight. You drink up while I see to this train that's coming in.'

Emma's teeth chattered against the thick pot. The stewed tea tasted horrible but she drank it. Thank goodness William would not have missed her yet. He and Cliff had worked until dark every night since they arrived at Moorend. The cows would be waiting for her to milk them though, and Jamie would be starving. Poor Polly, she hoped the girl was managing.

True to his word, the stationmaster saw her onto the train to Silverbeck in a carriage with two other women. He seemed to know one of them.

'This young woman is a stranger to these parts. Will you tell her when the train is approaching Silverbeck station, Mrs Armstrong?'

The woman promised she would but Emma clutched her basket and sat on the edge of her seat and offered a silent prayer of thanks when at last she stood on the Silverbeck platform again. It was raining hard now but she clutched her shawl tighter and set off as fast as she could along the deserted lane towards the main road between Silver-beck and Moorend Farm. She had almost reached the road when she saw a man heading up the lane towards the station. She slowed nervously but common sense told her few men would notice her, even less follow her. Still her insides churned with nerves as she hurried on, her eyes fixed on the ground.

'Emmie! Emmie . . . ' The man was running towards her now. 'Oh, thank God you're back.' He pulled her into his arms.

'William? Oh, William, it is you,' she almost sobbed with relief.

'Of course it's me, my love. Who else could it be? Thank God you've come back,' he said fervently and hugged her tighter to his chest. 'You're soaking, Emmie,' he added with tender concern. 'I must get you home and into some dry clothes before you catch a chill.'

He took her cold face in his hands and kissed her lips. His mouth was warm and soft and lingered. Emma was surprised. She knew he never showed emotion in public, even though there was nobody to see them.

'You're shivering, my wee Emmie.' He peeled off his jacket and insisted she put it on in place of her shawl. 'I'll carry your basket.'

'But I'm wet already, William, and you will be soaked to the skin before we get home.'

'Home,' he echoed softly. 'Dearest Emmie, I thought you'd left me and gone back to your family.'

Emma stopped and stared up at him.

'I'd never leave you, William! You are my family now, you and Jamie.'

'Are we, Emmie? I couldn't blame you if you had gone. All you've had is hard work, but I do love you, Emmie. I know now no place would be home unless we were in it together.'

'Oh William, that's the nicest thing anyone has ever said to me.'

His arm tightened around her shoulders and they hurried through the rain together. 'There's a lot more things I want to say to you, Emmie, as soon as you're warm and dry again.'

'I shall have to change before I milk the cows.'

'I've milked the cows and put them back in their field. Polly gave Jamie some warm milk with a spoon. I er . . . I'm afraid I upset her. I was worried when you weren't at home, Emmie, and I bit her head off. I didn't mean to upset her. She thinks the world of you and Jamie.'

'I'm sure she'll forgive you,' Emma said. 'I

promised to be home to feed Jamie and milk the cows.'

As they walked, she told him what had happened and how frightened she had been. He stopped and held her tightly in his arms again.

'Thank God the policeman came along when he did.'

'I heard him tell the stationmaster he thought the man wanted more than my purse, but I had nothing else, no jewellery or anything.'

William looked tenderly down at her. She was still his innocent, modest Emma.

'Dearest Emmie. I'm glad you're my wife. You're a very pretty woman, even though you don't seem to realize that. I can't blame any man for wanting you but I'd like to kill the man who frightened you so badly.'

Polly greeted them with relief as soon as they entered the kitchen.

'Oh, Mrs Sinclair, I'm glad you're back. I knew you'd be soaked walking from the station. I brought one of the stone pigs from the cellar. I've washed the dust off. The kettle's boiling. Shall I fill it to warm your clothes? I don't know how we'll manage if you've caught a chill.'

'Thank you, Polly. You're very thoughtful.'

'You go on up and change, Emmie, I'll

bring the hot water bottle up.'

'But you're wet too because I had your jacket.'

'Don't worry about me. I'll be changed in no time.'

Even as he spoke, he unbuttoned his shirt and peeled it over his head. Polly gasped at the sight of her master stripped to the waist. He realized she didn't know he and Cliff did the same every evening and washed under the pump outside when they had been hot and dusty. He grinned and reached for the kitchen towel, rubbing his hair until it sprang into dark curls and then drying his neck and shoulders. He went to the kitchen door and stood at the top of the steps to aim his shirt and the towel expertly towards the wash tub.

'Thanks, Polly, I'll take this up to your mistress.'

He was about to lift the stone hot water bottle but Polly yelled, 'No! No, 'tis hot. I'll wrap it in a towel or else it'll burn you.' She crossed to the dresser and brought out a clean towel and wrapped it round the bottle. William took it from her.

'You're a good lassie, Polly. I'm sorry I was impatient earlier.' He smiled at her, unaware how charming that smile could be now that he was happy again.

Emma stepped out of her best woollen skirt

and carefully hung it to dry, hoping she would be able to brush off the mud later. Everything else would go to the washtub. Shivering, she peeled off her blouse. She hadn't heard William enter the bedroom in his stockings. He rolled the hot water bottle into the bed and wrapped her nightgown round it, then wrapped the warm towel around her, gently rubbing her back and shoulders.

'Oh, that's lovely and warm,' she said.

He leaned forward and kissed her cheek. He pushed aside her petticoat and pantaloons. Emma gasped and blushed.

'Step out of them, Emmie,' William said softly against her ear but without waiting he swept her up in his arms and carried her to the big bed. He set aside the hot bottle and her nightgown and laid her on the warm mattress.

'That's wonderfully warm,' Emma said but her cheeks burned as William smiled down at her, taking in her nakedness. His blue eyes sparkled as he stepped out of his own damp trousers and jumped in beside her, moving the hot bottle and nightdress to the floor.

'I will warm you better than any hot bottle, Emmie,' he whispered, wrapping his arms around her and holding her close so that every part of their bodies were skin to naked skin. 'I love you, Emmie, and you're even more desirable than you were the night we spent together on the hill. I knew then you were as innocent and pure as the first rose of summer.'

'I didn't know I loved you, William, but I do.'

'Then nothing can separate us. We shall spend the rest of our lives together. I shall make you happy, Emmie.'

He talked softly but his hands were doing magical things, moving over her body, warming and thrilling every part of her, arousing a greater joy than she had ever dreamed of. She turned into his embrace, her mouth seeking his as they found again the passionate rapture of their first loving — and so much more.

Other titles published by Ulverscroft:

BEYOND REASON

Gwen Kirkwood

Young Janet Scott loves books and learning, and is happy living at the schoolhouse where her grandfather is the dominie. Her world is shattered when he dies and the new schoolmaster's petty cruelty becomes intolerable. Sent to work for farmer Wull Foster, Janet becomes the target of his dangerous lechery, and escapes. Taken in by the kind philanthropist Josiah Saunders, an old friend of her grandfather's, she is pitched into a dilemma when he offers her the security of an amiable but passionless marriage. For her heart belongs to another: her childhood friend, the penniless lawyer's clerk Fingal McLauchlan . . .

DARKEST BEFORE THE DAWN

Gwen Kirkwood

Billy Caraford has lost his best friend in a car accident and is badly injured himself, yet he is still determined to be a farmer. He summons his courage to go to university, but privately he regards himself as a cripple, convinced no woman could love him. Kimberley moves to Scotland with her aunt when her father dies, but is nervous about changing schools, until Billy helps her to find new friends. Both Kim and her aunt become involved in the affairs of the Caraford family and, as Kim grows into a lovely young woman, she must find the strength to fight for the life and the love she craves . . .

ANOTHER HOME, ANOTHER LOVE

Gwen Kirkwood

Rosemary Palmer-Farr loves farming and animals — her childhood was spent mostly at Bengairney Farm with her dear friends the Carafords. Now a young woman, she wants to prove her worth in running the gardens of her father's dwindling estate. However, her mother Catherine only wants her to secure a good marriage and believes that tenant farmers like the Carafords are inferior. So when her daughter's childhood friendship deepens into love, Catherine takes action to keep the young couple apart. She throws her daughter into the company of eligible young gentlemen whom Rosemary despises, yearning only for Sam's love . . .